Hometown Sweethearts

SERENITY CROSSING: THE HARTWELL'S BOOK #1

TARA BAISDEN

STERLING RIDGE PRESS LLC

Printed in the United States of America

First Edition: February 2026

For permissions, contact: tara@tarabaisden.com or visit www.tarabaisden.comHometown Sweethearts © 2026 by Tara Baisden

This is a work of fiction. Names, characters, places, and incidents either are the product of the author's imagination or are used fictitiously. Any resemblance to actual persons, living or dead, events, or locales is entirely coincidental.

All Scripture quotations, unless otherwise indicated, are taken from the Holy Bible, New International Version®, NIV®. Copyright ©1973, 1978, 1984, 2011 by Biblica, Inc.™ Used by permission of Zondervan. All rights reserved worldwide. The "NIV" and "New International Version" are trademarks registered in the United States Patent and Trademark Office by Biblica, Inc.™

Cover designed by Sterling Ridge Press LLC

Published by: Sterling Ridge Press, LLC www.sterlingridgepress.com

ISBN: 978-1-966093-48-0

Dedication

Dear reader,

Before you step into this love story, I want you to know you're about to read more than a romance.

You're about to meet a dog named Boone.

Boone is the kind of companion who doesn't simply live alongside the people he loves—he belongs to them in a way that feels almost sacred. He has his own brand of mischief, his own uncanny timing, and that almost-human way of knowing when someone needs comfort more than conversation. If you find yourself smiling at his antics or pausing because a single moment with him hits a little deeper than you expected, you're not imagining it.

This story is a work of fiction, but woven through these pages are real pieces of my life—real emotions, real days, real heartaches, and real hope. Some things about Boone were born from memory rather than imagination, because I've lived the kind of love that doesn't require words... the kind that shows up on four paws and stays.

Writing Boone into this novel became its own kind of balm. It helped me grieve the loss of my Dalilah—my sweet, steadfast, four-legged fur baby—who was my constant companion through so many chapters of my life. She was mine, and I was her whole world.

So as you read, I hope you'll enjoy Boone—his loyalty, his humor, his heart—and I hope, in the quiet places between the romance and the laughter, you'll feel what I felt while writing him: that love like that is real, and once you've been chosen by it, you're never quite the same.

Dedication

For Dalilah—my Lilah girl.

You were the kind of miracle I got to witness with my own eyes. I watched you enter this world in my home on December 31, 2012, and from your first breath, you were a steady heartbeat in my life.

You grew up alongside my children—quietly present as they learned and laughed and, one by one, grew wings and stepped into adulthood. You allowed yourself to be my constant through seasons in my life that tried to break me: the unraveling of a marriage, the ache of leaving what was familiar, and the brave, trembling step of buying my first home on my own. You stayed close through the kind of vehicle accident that almost took me from this earth, and you stayed even closer through the long aftermath—years of learning how to live inside limitations I never asked for.

You sat with me through hard goodbyes—sending a child off to college, burying people I loved, enduring an ice storm that made the world feel small and dangerous and sharp and cold. I could fill a thousand pages with all the things you were a part of in my life and the many ways that you helped me, protected me and simply loved me.

And through it all, you were by my side. You never demanded anything from me, you just were. You never needed me to be anything but your human.

You weren't "just a dog." You were comfort with fur and warmth and steady eyes. You knew when I needed a hug before I admitted it to myself. You knew when I was thinking too hard, fretting too long, carrying what I should've laid down. You had your own way of "talking," your own opinions, your own sweet persistence—especially when chicken jerky was involved.

I believe, with my whole heart, that God placed you in my life on purpose—because He knew the road ahead of me and He knew I would need a companion who loved without conditions and stayed without wavering.

In the last week of your life, I tried to give you everything I thought you needed, because I knew your time was coming. But what you wanted most was simple: you wanted me. You wanted my lap. You wanted to snuggle by my side, and you wanted my presence.

And that final morning—October 8, 2025—your face peaceful, your eyes soft, your mouth curved into a smile—I understood. When you took your last breath, it was as if you were telling me, *Thanks for a good life, Momma. You're going to be all right.*

I'll see you again someday, and you and I will hop on a four-wheeler once more. We'll go climb a mountain or two together, you sitting right next to me, ears flapping in the wind, enjoying life.

I know you are running those streets of gold with the speed you had in your youth—chasing squirrels and racing deer, free of every ache.

Fly high, Lilah girl.
Momma loves you.

Contents

Chapter 1

Grace Bennett eased her SUV into the paved parking area beside the Mountain Laurel Inn, the U-Haul trailer rattling behind her, and put the vehicle in park. For a long moment she simply sat there, hands still wrapped around the steering wheel, staring through the windshield at the three-story Craftsman that was now her home.

White paint. Barn red shutters. The wraparound porch with its stone columns that she used to think looked like something from a storybook. The mature rhododendrons flanking the front steps had grown wild in the past year, their branches reaching toward the windows as if they were trying to get inside. A few of the porch boards looked weathered, and one of the shutters on the second floor hung at a slight angle, but it was still beautiful.

Grace released the steering wheel and rolled her shoulders, wincing at the stiffness that had settled deep into her muscles. Five hours of driving this morning after a restless night. Five hours of gripping the wheel like it was the only thing keeping her anchored to the earth. Her neck ached. Her lower back protested when she shifted in her seat.

And somewhere deep within her, in that hollow space she had been trying to ignore for months, exhaustion lived like a permanent tenant.

She had driven away from Atlanta early this morning with the windows down, hoping the March wind would carry away the staleness of the past few years. It hadn't worked. Two years of marriage to Lee Bennett had left a residue that no amount of fresh air could sweep clean. But she was here now. She'd made it. And whatever came next, at least it would be of her choosing.

The driver's side door groaned softly when she pushed it open, and Grace stepped out of her vehicle, her legs unsteady after so many hours behind the wheel. The mountain air hit her immediately, cool and clean and carrying the faint scent of early spring. So different from Atlanta, where the air always tasted of exhaust and ambition. Here, the breeze came down from the Smokies with nothing to prove, and Grace pulled it into her lungs like medicine.

She turned in a slow circle, taking in the view she had almost forgotten. Cedar Street stretched in both directions, its tree-lined sidewalks flanked by brick storefronts on either side of the inn and across the way. This part of downtown Serenity Crossing had always felt like a postcard, the kind of place tourists photographed and came back to often. Behind the inn was a back porch and a grassy area where guests could relax outdoors, with a larger shared parking lot beyond that serving the neighboring businesses. And beyond all of it, the mountains ringed the valley like protective arms. The sky above was that particular shade of blue that existed only in places where the air was thin and the larger cities were far away.

She'd been away for fourteen years. She'd been eighteen when she left for Virginia Tech, her head full of architectural drawings and big-city dreams. She had come back to visit, of course, every Christmas and most Thanksgivings, but visiting wasn't the same as belonging.

Visiting meant sleeping in her childhood bedroom at her parents' farmhouse and leaving before the small-town rhythms could pull her back in. Visiting meant keeping one foot out the door.

Now both feet were planted firmly on Serenity Crossing soil for good, and Grace wasn't entirely sure how she felt about that.

She walked around to the back of the U-Haul and checked the lock on the trailer door. Everything she owned was packed inside that metal box. Fourteen years of life condensed into cardboard boxes and plastic bins. Clothes. Books. The kitchen items she couldn't bear to leave behind, including her grandmother's cast-iron skillet and the ceramic mixing bowls her mother had given her when she got married. The divorce settlement had been generous enough, and selling the condo fully furnished had simplified things considerably, but standing here now with her entire existence contained in a rental trailer, Grace felt untethered in a way that was both terrifying and oddly liberating.

She had sold the sleek, modern furniture along with the condo without a second thought. The minimalist artwork Lee had chosen for the walls. The king-sized bed where she had spent too many nights wondering why her husband always seemed to be somewhere else, even when he was lying right beside her. Good riddance to all of it. Good riddance to the woman she had become in that marriage, the one who'd stopped trusting her own instincts and started believing that maybe Lee was right, maybe she was too demanding, too suspicious, and too much.

Grace fished the key to the inn from her jacket pocket as she walked toward the inn's front entrance. The wraparound porch creaked beneath her feet in the familiar way she remembered from childhood summers spent helping Ellie Hartwell, her grandmother, change linens and arrange fresh flowers in the guest rooms. The white paint on the porch railing was peeling in places, and the wooden boards beneath her feet were dingy with weathering in spots where the finish had worn away. Cosmetic issues. Nothing that couldn't be fixed with time and effort and a healthy portion of sandpaper.

She crossed to the main entrance, where the original oak doors with their beveled glass panels waited for her, and hesitated.

This was real. This was actually happening.

For the past month, since the divorce had been finalized and she'd signed the papers that officially ended her marriage to Lee Bennett, Grace had been operating on autopilot. Pack. Sort. Donate. Sell. Cancel utilities. Forward mail. Call the cleaning service in Serenity Crossing and arrange for them to prepare the inn for her arrival. One task after another, each one a small brick in the wall she was building between her old life and whatever came next.

But standing here now, with the key in her hand and the weight of the moment pressing down on her shoulders, Grace realized that all those tasks had been building to this moment. The enormity of how quickly her life had changed hit her hard. The terrifying freedom of starting over at thirty-two with nothing but an inn in need of renovating and a desperate desire to become someone other than Lee Bennett's ex-wife.

She turned the key in the lock and pushed the door open.

The foyer smelled like lemon furniture polish and cleaning products, and Grace smiled in relief. The cleaning service had done its job well. The hardwood floors gleamed in the soft light filtering through the windows, and the built-in coat closets on either side of the entrance stood ready to receive guests who would not be arriving anytime soon. The staircase rose toward the upper floors, its oak newel posts and Mission-style spindles exactly as she remembered them, though the finish on the banister had dulled over time.

Grace stepped further inside and let the door fall closed behind her. The sound echoed through the empty building, and for a moment she simply stood there, breathing in the quiet. The inn had been closed for over a year now, ever since Ellie's passing, and the silence had a quality to it that felt almost sacred.

She moved through the foyer and into the main parlor, her footsteps muffled by the worn oriental rug that covered the center of the hardwood floor. The stone fireplace dominated the far wall, its oak mantel dusty despite the cleaning service's efforts, and the built-in bookcases on either side still held Ellie's collection of leather-bound classics and local history volumes. The tall windows let in the late morning light, illuminating the space in a way that revealed both its charm and its neglect.

The furniture was dated. That was the kindest word for it. The sofas and armchairs had been stylish years ago, but now their floral upholstery looked tired, and their wooden frames showed the wear of decades. The coffee table bore rings from countless cups of coffee or tea, and the lamps on the side tables were the sort of brass and crystal combination that had fallen out of fashion a decade ago.

Her architectural training kicked in automatically, cataloging what she saw with the clinical precision that had served her well in her career. Structural versus cosmetic. Urgent versus eventual. The bones of the room were excellent. The original crown molding was intact; the hardwood floors beneath the rug were solid, and the fireplace surround showed the kind of craftsmanship that simply did not exist anymore. But the cosmetic updates needed were substantial. New furniture. Fresh paint. Refinished floors. Updated lighting. The list was already forming in her mind, organized and prioritized, because that was how Grace dealt with overwhelming situations. She broke them down into manageable pieces and tackled them one by one.

She crossed the parlor and pushed through the French doors into the sunroom, where the 1940s addition extended from the main building like a glassed-in afterthought. The terrazzo floors were scuffed but serviceable, and the walls of windows on three sides flooded the space with natural light. Ceiling fans hung motionless overhead, their blades coated with a thin layer of dust the cleaning service had missed. The wicker furniture in here was actually in better shape than the furniture in the parlor.

Back through the parlor and into the dining room, where Ellie had served breakfast to guests every morning for forty years. The built-in china cabinets with their leaded glass doors still held Ellie's collection of mismatched vintage dishes, the ones she claimed had more character than any matching set could offer. The oak wainscoting was scratched in places, and the wallpaper above it had started to peel at the seams, but the bay window with its built-in window seat remained the most charming feature of the room. Grace could remember sitting in that window seat as a child, watching the birds in the rhododendrons while Ellie bustled around the dining table, setting out pitchers of fresh orange juice and platters of her famous blueberry pancakes.

Grace moved through the doorway at the far end of the dining room and stepped into the kitchen. What she saw stopped her in her tracks.

Ellie had always said the kitchen was the heart of any home, but this heart was showing its age. The cabinets, painted cream at some point in the distant past, were chipped and worn, with hardware that belonged in a museum of mid-century design. The appliances were old enough to qualify as antiques. The refrigerator hummed with the labored determination of machinery that had exceeded its expected lifespan by at least a decade, and the stove wore a patina of age and hard use. The countertops were some kind of laminate that had been popular years ago, and the overhead lighting consisted of a single fluorescent fixture that buzzed and flickered when Grace flipped the switch.

This room would need to be completely gutted and modernized if she had any hope of passing the health department inspection required to serve food to guests. Grace added it to her mental list under the heading of urgent and expensive, then forced herself to move on before the scope of the project could overwhelm her.

The library was a small gem tucked into the corner of the first floor, its walls lined with built-in bookcases featuring glass-fronted doors that protected the volumes inside from dust and time. A window seat beneath the single window looked out at the side garden, and the warm wood tones of the shelving created an atmosphere of cozy intimacy that felt like a hug from the house itself. This room needed only minor attention. Fresh cushions for the window seat. Perhaps a comfortable reading chair or two to replace the worn leather one that currently occupied the corner. But the bones were perfect, and Grace could already imagine guests curling up here with books from Ellie's collection on rainy mountain afternoons.

Finally, she made her way to the innkeeper's quarters at the back of the first floor, the private suite where Ellie had lived for four decades and where Grace would now make her home.

The living room was small but functional, with windows that looked out at the backyard and furniture that, while dated, looked comfortable enough for the time being. Floral wallpaper covered the walls in a pattern that had been fashionable ages ago, and the carpet was a shade of mauve that made Grace's designer sensibilities cringe. But the space was clean and warm and private, separated from the guest areas of the inn by a door that could be closed for privacy.

The bedroom was larger than she remembered, with a brass bed frame that held a mattress she would need to test before committing to sleeping on it. More wallpaper, in a delicate blue and cream stripe that was less offensive than the florals in the living room. A dresser and side table set that matched the bed frame. Curtains that had seen better days.

The bathroom was a pleasant surprise. The fixtures were not exactly modern; they were functional and reasonably attractive. A claw-foot tub sat beneath a window, and a pedestal sink occupied the corner.

The kitchenette was the final space to inspect, and Grace found it cramped but workable. Upper and lower cabinets for storage, a small sink, and a small counter with room for a table and chairs. The refrigerator, she noted with dismay, was not currently running. A problem for later. For now, she could use the main kitchen's aging refrigerator until she figured out a more permanent solution.

Grace completed her circuit of the innkeeper's quarters and found herself standing in the center of the small living room, surrounded by floral wallpaper and furniture that belonged to another era.

This was home now. This collection of outdated rooms in a building that needed more cosmetic work than she had allowed herself to imagine. This was what she had chosen instead of the sleek Atlanta condo with its granite countertops and stainless-steel appliances and a husband who had been lying to her since before they said their vows.

She would take the floral wallpaper. She would take every outdated inch of this place.

Her shoulders ached. Her back protested. And the exhaustion that seemed to be a constant these days had spread through her entire body until she felt like she was moving through water. But there was too much to do to stop now. If she stopped, she might have to feel the weight of what this day meant. She might have to acknowledge that she was thirty-two years old, divorced, and starting over in her childhood hometown with nothing but a rundown inn and a determination to prove that she was capable of building something on her own.

She rolled her shoulders to release a little tension and headed toward the office. There would be paperwork there, records of the inn's operations, and information she would need as she began the process of restoration and eventually, God willing, reopening. The office was a small room off the main foyer, tucked away near the staircase in a space that had probably been a closet in the building's original design.

The office door stuck when she pushed on it, the wood swollen with humidity, but it gave way with a complaint of hinges that required oiling. Inside, a wooden desk sat beneath a small window, its surface covered with neatly stacked papers that the cleaning service had wisely left undisturbed. A filing cabinet occupied one corner, and the walls were covered with framed photographs of the inn through the decades, images of guests smiling on the front porch, of Christmas trees in the parlor, and of Ellie herself standing proudly in front of the Mountain Laurel Inn sign that still hung beside the front door.

Grace lowered herself into the desk chair, which groaned beneath her weight, and began sorting through the papers. Utility bills. Tax documents. Correspondence with guests from years past. A calendar from the year Ellie died, still turned to September.

The top drawer of the desk yielded pens, paper clips, a roll of stamps, and a small flashlight with dead batteries. The middle drawer held more paperwork, receipts, and invoices, organized with Ellie's characteristic precision. But the bottom drawer, when Grace pulled it open, contained something that made her breath catch.

A leather-bound journal, worn at the edges from years of handling, its cover embossed with a simple floral pattern.

Grace lifted it carefully, as if it might crumble at her touch, and opened it to a random page. Ellie's handwriting greeted her, the familiar loops and curves that Grace had seen on birthday cards and Christmas letters her entire life.

"Unless the Lord builds the house, they labor in vain who build it." Psalm 127:1.

I wrote that down this morning after the coffee burned—again—and the radiator on the third floor started knocking like it wanted to argue with me before breakfast. I've owned this place long enough to know that a house can stand straight and still be unfinished. Paint peels. Hinges loosen. People arrive tired in ways no mattress can fix. I've learned that my job was never to have all the answers, only to keep the doors open, the lights warm, and the table steady. If there's any good that comes from these walls, it isn't because I planned it cleverly or kept things perfect. It's because I showed up, day after day, and trusted that faithfulness—plain, unremarkable faithfulness—counts for more than grand ideas ever could. Some days, that's all a woman can manage. And most days, it's enough.

Grace closed the journal and pressed it against her chest, feeling the worn leather beneath her fingers. The words hadn't promised rescue or transformation. They hadn't offered comfort wrapped in sentiment. They had simply named a truth Grace recognized in her bones—that a life could be built one ordinary day at a time, without certainty, without applause, and still matter deeply.

She set Ellie's journal on the desk and pushed herself to her feet. The U-Haul was waiting. Her boxes were waiting. Her new life, such as it was, was waiting for her to unpack it and arrange it into some kind of order.

Dinner with her family wasn't until six o'clock this evening. She had hours yet. Hours to carry boxes into the innkeeper's quarters and begin transforming this dated little suite into something that felt like hers. Hours to keep her hands busy and her mind occupied, to stay one step ahead of the emotions that kept threatening to catch up with her.

Grace squared her shoulders, ignored the protests from her aching muscles, and headed for the front door.

She paused on the threshold, one hand on the frame, and looked back at the foyer with its gleaming floors and its waiting staircase, and its air of patient expectation.

"Okay, Grandma," she said aloud. "It's you and me and this run-down inn. Let's see what I can make of it."

Chapter 2

The McKenna farmhouse glowed against the evening sky like a lighthouse calling Grace home.

She turned her SUV onto the long gravel drive that wound through the flower farm, passing rows of early spring blooms that would explode into color in another month or two. The fields stretched out on either side of her, familiar and unchanged, the mountains rising in the distance behind the sprawling white farmhouse with its wrap-around porches and multiple wings. Her parents had built this place to hold a big family, and it had done exactly that for more than thirty years.

She counted the vehicles as she approached. Her father's truck. Her mother's sedan. A police cruiser that had to be Cain's. A small pickup she recognized as Josie's. Several other cars and trucks lined up along the circular drive in front of the house, telling her that most of her siblings had made it tonight. They'd all come to welcome her home.

Grace parked at the end of the line of vehicles and turned off the engine, taking a moment to collect herself before she stepped out. She'd spent the past few hours unpacking boxes and hauling her belongings into the innkeeper's quarters, and her muscles ached from the effort. But it was the emotional exhaustion that weighed on her most heavily. She'd been running on determination and caffeine for weeks now, and being here, being home, made her want to stop running and just collapse into the arms of the people who loved her.

She couldn't do that. Not yet. Maybe not ever. She needed to prove she could stand on her own two feet, that the past year hadn't broken her completely.

The front door of the farmhouse burst open before Grace could even reach for her door handle, and suddenly they were all pouring out onto the porch, a wave of McKennas descending the steps and crossing the lawn toward her. Her mother was in the lead, wiping her hands on a dish towel she'd apparently forgotten to put down, her face bright with tears she wasn't even trying to hide. Her father followed close behind, tall and silver-haired and still the most handsome man Grace had ever known; his smile was so wide it transformed his entire face.

And behind them came her siblings, all eight of them, a chorus of voices calling her name as they surrounded her vehicle.

Grace barely had the door open before her mother pulled her into an embrace so fierce it squeezed the breath from her lungs.

"My girl," Jean McKenna said, her voice thick with emotion. "My sweet girl, you're finally home."

"Hi, Mama." Grace wrapped her arms around her mother and held on, breathing in the familiar scent of her perfume mixed with something savory from the kitchen. "I'm home."

"Let me look at you." Jean pulled back and cupped Grace's face in her hands, studying her with the sharp eyes of a mother who missed nothing. "You look thin."

Grace laughed because some things never changed, and her mother's concern had always manifested as commentary on her weight. "I'm fine, Mama. I promise."

"You're too thin. We'll fix that tonight." Jean kissed her forehead and then stepped aside so Bruce could take his turn.

Her father didn't say anything at first. He just wrapped his arms around her and held her close. Bruce McKenna had always been a man of few words, preferring to show his love through presence rather than speeches, and right now his presence was exactly what she needed.

"Welcome home, sweetheart," he said quietly, his voice rough with emotion. "We've missed you."

"I've missed you too, Daddy."

Then her siblings descended, and Grace found herself passed from embrace to embrace like a beloved package being handed around a circle. Faith reached her first, pulling her into a hug that lasted longer than the others. Her dark hair brushed against Grace's cheek as she held on tight. Faith understood what Grace was going through in a way the others couldn't. She'd walked this divorce road herself eighteen months ago when her own marriage had ended, and that shared understanding passed between them without a single word being spoken.

"I'm so glad you're here," Faith said softly.

"Me too."

Cain was next, her brother the police officer, all broad shoulders and protective energy as he lifted her off her feet in a bear hug that made her laugh despite herself. "About time you came back where you belong," he said, setting her down with a grin that softened his usually serious face.

Miranda practically bounced into her arms, all warmth and enthusiasm. "I have so many books set aside for you," she said, her eyes bright with excitement. "Comfort reads. You're going to need them while you're working on the inn, and I have the perfect recommendations."

"I'm sure you do." Grace hugged her tightly, marveling at how her youngest sister had grown into such a vibrant, confident woman since opening a bookstore.

Logan hung back slightly, waiting his turn with the careful patience that had always defined him. He was the only biological child among them, the son Bruce and Jean had conceived after years of trying, but he'd never treated his adopted siblings as anything less than fully his. When he finally stepped forward to hug her, his embrace was brief but sincere.

"Good to have you back," he said, his voice quiet and measured.

Graham appeared at her elbow, quiet and steady as always. His handshake turning into a one-armed hug that felt exactly right for his reserved nature.

Josie punched her shoulder lightly before pulling her into a quick, fierce hug. "You look like you could use some fresh air and hard work," she said with a grin. "Lucky for you, we've got plenty of both around here."

"I'm counting on it."

Chad swept her up in an embrace that lifted her feet off the ground, his search-and-rescue training evident in the easy strength of his arms. "The prodigal sister returns," he teased, but his eyes were warm and his smile was genuine.

Mandy was last, her honey-blonde hair catching the evening light as she wrapped Grace in the kind of hug that felt like coming home all by itself. Of all her siblings, Mandy was the one Grace had always felt closest to, perhaps because they shared a love of hospitality and creating welcoming spaces for others.

"I'm so happy you're here," Mandy said. "And I want to hear everything about your plans for the inn. Professional curiosity, you know."

Grace laughed. Mandy managed the Serenity Crossing Inn just down the street from her own inn, so her interest in Grace's restoration project was more than just sisterly support. "I'll tell you everything I know, which isn't much yet."

"That's what planning is for." Mandy squeezed her hand. "And you're going to be amazing at it."

They walked toward the house together, the whole group of them moving as one unit toward the warmth and light spilling from the windows. Grace found herself in the center of them, surrounded by the people who had known her longest and loved her best, and she had to blink back the sting of tears that threatened to fall.

She'd forgotten what this felt like. Being known. Being loved not for what she could accomplish or how she looked on paper, but simply for who she was.

In Atlanta, she'd had colleagues and acquaintances and the kind of friendships that existed primarily through text messages and occasional brunches. Here, she had people who remembered her first lost tooth, who'd seen her through awkward adolescence and teenage heartbreak and the terrifying excitement of leaving for college. Here she had family.

The farmhouse kitchen wrapped around her like a warm blanket the moment she stepped inside. The scent of roasted chicken and fresh bread and something sweet baking in the oven filled the air, and Grace's stomach growled loudly enough to make Miranda giggle.

"Someone's hungry," her mother said with satisfaction, steering Grace toward the long farmhouse table that dominated the center of the dining area. "Sit down, sweetheart. Everything's ready."

The table was set for eleven, with mismatched plates and vintage silverware that had been in the family for generations. Platters and bowls covered nearly every inch of available surface: roasted chicken with herbs, mashed potatoes, green beans from last year's garden that Jean had canned herself, fresh rolls that were still steaming, a salad with early spring greens, and what looked like three different casseroles contributed by various siblings.

"Mama, this is too much," Grace protested, even as her mouth watered at the sight of it all.

"Nonsense. You need to eat. And your brother and sisters wanted to contribute." Jean gestured around the table at the dishes. "Faith made the rolls. Mandy brought that sweet potato casserole. Miranda made a salad because she's convinced we all need more vegetables."

"We do," Miranda said primly.

"And I made dessert," Josie added, jerking her thumb toward the oven. "Apple pie. Don't get too excited; it's from a new recipe I'm testing out."

"Josie's being modest," Graham said quietly. "Her pies are better than anything you'd find at Sweet Surrender Bakery."

"Now that's just not true," Josie protested, but Grace could see the pleased flush on her cheeks.

They settled into their seats around the table, the familiar chaos of a large family dinner unfolding exactly as Grace remembered. Bruce took his place at the head of the table, with Jean at his right hand and Grace in the spot they'd saved for her at Jean's other side. The siblings filled in around them, their voices overlapping as they continued conversations that had apparently been going on before Grace arrived.

Bruce cleared his throat, and the table fell silent with the ease of long practice.

"Let's say grace," he said, extending his hands to Jean and to Chad, who sat at his left.

Everyone joined hands around the table, and Grace felt Faith's fingers squeeze hers gently as Bruce bowed his head.

"Lord, we thank You for this food and for the hands that prepared it. We thank You for bringing our Grace home safely to us. We ask Your blessing on her and on her new beginning. Watch over this family, Lord, and keep us always in Your care. Amen."

"Amen," they said in unison.

Nothing had changed. After everything that had happened, after all the ways her life had fallen apart and had turned into something she barely recognized, this remained constant. Her family gathered around this table, giving thanks before they shared a meal together. It was such a simple thing, and yet it meant more to her in this moment than she could possibly express.

The meal began in earnest, platters passing from hand to hand as everyone served themselves. Grace filled her plate with more food than she'd eaten in a single sitting for months, and her mother watched with obvious approval.

"So tell us about the inn," Mandy said, leaning forward with genuine interest. "What's the situation?"

Grace swallowed a bite of chicken and considered her answer. "It needs work. A lot of work. The bones are good, but everything is dated. The furniture, the wallpaper, the kitchen especially."

"That wallpaper," Faith said with a groan. "I remember it. It's floral-like in the parlor, right?"

"Yep, still there. And somehow even more offensive than I remembered."

"Ellie loved that wallpaper," Jean said with a fond smile.

"Mom had questionable taste in wall coverings," Bruce countered, and the table erupted in laughter.

"The kitchen is the biggest issue," Grace continued once the laughter died down. "The appliances are ancient, the cabinets are falling apart, and the layout could be improved. It's going to need a complete overhaul."

"That sounds expensive," Logan said.

"It will be," Grace replied. "But I have some money set aside, and I'm planning to do as much of the work myself as I can."

"You know we'll all help," Cain said. "Whatever you need."

"I appreciate that, but you all have your own lives and jobs. I'll figure it out."

"Grace." Jean's voice carried the gentle warning of a mother who knew her daughter too well. "There's no shame in accepting help from people who love you."

"I know, Mama. I just... I really need to do this on my own."

A brief silence fell over the table, and Grace saw several of her siblings exchange glances. They understood what she wasn't saying. That her marriage had made her feel small and incapable. That Lee had spent two years undermining her confidence until she'd started to believe his criticisms were true. That coming home and rebuilding the inn wasn't just about creating a business. It was about creating a new version of herself.

Faith caught her eye and gave her a small nod of understanding.

"Well," Bruce said, breaking the silence with his calm, steady voice, "if you want to do the work yourself, I respect that. But the offer stands. We're here when you need us."

"Thank you, Daddy."

The conversation shifted to other topics as they continued eating. Miranda told a story about a customer at her bookstore who'd tried to return a book because they didn't like the ending. Cain mentioned a minor fender bender he'd responded to that afternoon involving a tourist who'd been too busy taking photos of the mountains to watch the road. Chad described a training exercise his search and rescue team had completed last week, and Josie reported on the progress of this year's flower crop.

Grace listened and laughed and contributed where she could, feeling herself relax into the familiar rhythm of family dinner. These were her people. This was her home. Whatever else had gone wrong in her life, this remained true and unchangeable.

"So," Logan said during a lull in the conversation. "The divorce is... it's all finalized now, right?"

The table went quiet.

Grace felt everyone's eyes on her, felt the weight of their concern and their uncertainty about how much they could ask. She appreciated that they'd been dancing around the subject all evening, giving her space, but she also knew that avoiding it entirely would only make things more awkward in the long run.

"It's final," she said, keeping her voice steady. "The papers were signed a month ago. Lee got what he wanted, I got what I wanted, money has been transferred, and now it's done."

"And you're... okay?" Logan asked, clearly unsure whether he should have started this conversation at all.

"I'm getting there." Grace smiled at him, hoping to ease his obvious discomfort. "Having sold the condo in Atlanta and coming home helps more than I thought it would. That door is closed, and it feels right. Having the inn as a project helps; it gives me something else to focus on and look forward to. And having all of you helps most of all."

"Lee's an idiot," Josie said flatly. "Anyone who'd let you go isn't worth the space he takes up."

"Josie," Jean said in a warning tone.

"What? It's true."

"It's also not helpful," Faith said quietly. She turned to Grace, her eyes soft with understanding. "You don't have to talk about it if you don't want to. We all know how exhausting it is to rehash the details. Been there, done that."

Grace reached over and squeezed her sister's hand, grateful for the solidarity. Faith had walked this road. Faith knew.

"I'm fine, really. Or I will be. The important thing is that I'm here now, and I'm ready to start the next chapter. The past is in the past, and I'm ready to move forward."

She deliberately changed the subject, steering the conversation toward safer waters. "Mama, tell me about the Heritage Festival. Is the town still doing the full weekend celebration?"

Jean's face lit up at the change of topic. "Oh, honey, it's bigger than ever. The last weekend in June, just like always. Historical tours, heritage demonstrations, and river activities on Saturday. And the big concert is still Friday night downtown."

"Mom always hosted some of the key people during the festival," Bruce added. "The entertainment, the special guests who came in from out of town. She sponsored one of the events too, the heritage craft demonstrations, I believe."

"The inn was always fully booked for the festival weekend," Jean said. "People reserved rooms a year in advance."

Something clicked into place in Grace's mind. A deadline. A goal. Something concrete to work toward instead of just the vague notion of "someday" that had been floating around in her head since she'd decided to move back.

"The last weekend in June, you say?"

"Last weekend in June," Jean repeated. "The twenty-sixth through the twenty-eighth. We'll be supplying flowers for it just like in the past."

Grace did the mental math. That gave her almost exactly three months. Twelve weeks to transform a dated, neglected inn into something worthy of hosting guests. Twelve weeks to gut a kitchen, replace furniture, strip wallpaper, and pass inspections. It was ambitious. Maybe too ambitious.

But it was also exactly what she needed.

"I'm going to have the inn open by then," she said. "For the Heritage Festival. That's my deadline."

The table erupted in reactions. Josie whistled low. Mandy's eyes widened with what looked like professional concern. Logan frowned slightly, probably running calculations in his head. But it was her parents' response that Grace focused on: the pride in her father's eyes and the fierce, unwavering belief in her mother's smile.

"If anyone can do it, you can," Jean said firmly.

"It's going to be a lot of work," Bruce added, his tone measured but supportive. "But Mom would be proud to see you carry on her legacy."

Grace felt the weight of that statement settle over her shoulders like a mantle. Ellie's legacy. The inn that had been in their family for decades, that had welcomed guests and created memories, and that had served as a cornerstone of the community. She was taking on more than just a renovation project. She was taking on a responsibility.

But for the first time since her marriage had fallen apart, she felt something other than exhaustion and shame. She felt purpose.

The rest of the dinner passed in a warm blur of conversation and laughter, second helpings, and promises to save room for Josie's apple pie. By the time the plates were cleared and the pie was served, Grace's cheeks hurt from smiling, and her heart felt full.

As her father cut generous slices and passed them around the table, Grace let her gaze travel from face to face, taking in each of her siblings and her parents in turn. Logan, careful and kind. Faith, who understood her pain without needing explanations. Josie, fierce and loyal. Mandy, warm and welcoming. Graham, quiet but steadfast. Cain, protective to his core. Chad, brave and passionate. Miranda, bright and optimistic. And her parents, Bruce and Jean, who had built this family through love and faith and stubborn determination.

She'd spent fourteen years chasing a career and a life that looked impressive on paper. A couple of those years were spent trying to build a marriage, then trying to hold it together. And in the end, none of it had made her feel the way she felt right now, sitting at this dinner table with these imperfect, wonderful people.

"You okay?" Faith asked softly, noticing the emotion on Grace's face.

Grace blinked back the tears that had gathered in her eyes and smiled at her sister.

"Yeah," she said, and for the first time in a long time, she meant it. "I think I'm finally going to be okay."

Jean reached over and squeezed her hand, her eyes bright with the same tears Grace was fighting. "You will be just fine, sweetheart. Now eat your pie... you need the calories."

Grace laughed and picked up her fork, the sound blending with the voices of her family as they continued their conversations around her. The kitchen was warm; the pie was sweet, and somewhere in the back of her mind, a clock had started ticking.

Twelve weeks until the Heritage Festival.

She had a lot of work to do.

Chapter 3

G race stood in the center of the parlor with a pen tucked behind her ear and a fresh legal pad already half-filled with notes, and for the first time in months, she felt like herself. Not Lee's wife. Not Lee's ex-wife. Not the woman who'd been too blind to see what was happening in her own marriage. Just Grace Bennett, architect, doing what she'd been trained to do.

Evaluating a building. Making a plan. Turning chaos into order.

She'd divided her legal pad into three columns: Contractor Required, DIY With YouTube, and Cosmetic Only. The first column was already longer than she would have liked, but that was the reality of a building that hadn't been properly maintained in over a decade. Ellie had kept the inn clean and welcoming, but she'd also been in her seventies, living on a fixed income, and more concerned with her guests' comfort than with updating infrastructure that still technically functioned.

Grace walked slowly around the parlor, letting her eyes move from floor to ceiling the way her professors had taught her years ago. Start at the foundation and work your way up. Look for water damage, settling, and cracks that indicate structural movement. Check the windows for drafts, the floors for levelness, and the walls for signs of moisture intrusion.

The good news was that the bones of this building were solid. The original Craftsman construction had been done right, with quality materials and careful attention to detail. The stone foundation showed no signs of cracking or shifting. The load-bearing walls were plumb and true. The roof, from what she could see when she stood outside, appeared to be in reasonable condition.

The bad news was everything else.

She added "refinish hardwood floors" to the Contractor Required column. The floors throughout the first floor were original to the building, beautiful quarter-sawn oak that would be stunning once they were properly restored, but refinishing hardwood was not a job for amateurs with YouTube tutorials. She'd seen too many DIY disasters in her career to attempt it herself.

The electrical system was another concern. The main panel in the basement was outdated, probably original to when the building was wired for electricity sometime in the 1940s. It would need to be upgraded to meet current code before she could pass inspection, and electrical work was definitely not something she was willing to tackle on her own. She wrote "electrical panel upgrade" in the Contractor Required column and underlined it twice.

The plumbing was a question mark. Everything seemed to function, but the pipes were old, and she'd noticed some discoloration on the ceiling of the first-floor bathroom that suggested there might be issues in the walls she couldn't see. She added "plumbing inspection" to her list and made a mental note to ask around town for recommendations on a reliable plumber.

But the kitchen. The kitchen was going to be the biggest challenge.

Grace stood in the doorway and surveyed the space with a critical eye. The layout was inefficient, designed for a time when inn kitchens served different purposes than they do today. The appliances were ancient and would need to be replaced entirely. The cabinets were falling apart; the countertops were scarred and dated, and the single fluorescent light fixture overhead cast everything in an unflattering greenish glow.

A complete kitchen renovation would eat up a significant portion of her budget, but there was no way around it. She couldn't serve breakfast to guests with equipment that belonged in a museum, and she certainly couldn't pass a health department inspection with a kitchen in this condition.

She wrote "KITCHEN" in capital letters at the top of the Contractor Required column and drew a box around it.

The dining room was less dire. The built-in china cabinets were beautiful and only needed cleaning and perhaps new hardware. The wainscoting had some scratches and dings, but those could be touched up with wood filler and stain. The wallpaper above the wainscoting was peeling at the seams and would need to come down, but wallpaper removal was something she could handle herself.

She moved into the sunroom and felt some of the tension in her shoulders ease. This room needed only minor attention. A good cleaning, some fresh paint on the trim, new cushions for the wicker furniture. She wrote "sunroom refresh" in the Cosmetic Only column and felt a small surge of satisfaction at finally having something in that category.

The library was similarly manageable. The built-in bookcases were in excellent condition, protected by their glass-fronted doors. The window seat cushion was faded and worn, but that was an easy fix. She made a note to measure for new fabric and added it to her DIY list.

Back through the parlor and into the foyer, where she paused at the foot of the staircase. The banister was loose in two places, something she'd noticed yesterday. But tightening banister spindles was something she could manage with the right tools and a decent YouTube tutorial.

She wrote "banister repair" in the DIY With YouTube column and smiled to herself. Her father had always said that anything could be learned if you were willing to put in the time. She was about to test that theory extensively over the next twelve weeks.

The innkeeper's quarters were last on her inspection list, but she already knew what she'd find there. Dated but functional. Livable. The wallpaper would have to go eventually, and the mauve carpet was an offense against good taste, but those were cosmetic issues that could wait until the guest areas were finished. For now, she had a roof over her head and a bed to sleep in, and that was enough.

Grace completed her circuit of the first floor and returned to the parlor, where she settled into one of the tired floral armchairs and reviewed her lists. The Contractor Required column was intimidatingly long. The DIY With YouTube column was optimistic but manageable. The Cosmetic Only column was shorter than she would have liked, but represented real progress once she got to it.

Twelve weeks suddenly felt very short.

She let out a long breath and let her head fall back against the chair. The ceiling above her was pressed tin, original to the building, with an intricate pattern of flowers and geometric shapes that caught the light from the windows. It was beautiful. It was also probably a nightmare to clean and would need to be carefully preserved during any painting or renovation work.

Details. So many details. Every room held a thousand decisions waiting to be made, a thousand problems waiting to be solved. And she was doing this alone, with a self-imposed deadline that was probably unrealistic and a budget that was definitely going to be tested.

But she was also doing this for herself. For the first time in years, she was working on something that was hers, using skills that were hers, and making choices that no one else could overrule or undermine. Lee had always had opinions about her work, suggestions that were really criticisms, and ideas that were really demands. Here, in the inn with its dated furniture and peeling wallpaper, she answered to no one but herself.

The thought was terrifying. It was also exhilarating.

Grace pushed herself up from the chair and decided she'd earned a break. She'd been at this for three hours, walking and measuring and cataloging every square inch of the inn, and her brain was starting to feel fuzzy around the edges. What she needed was a cup of coffee and a change of scenery, even if the change was just moving from one room of the inn to another.

She made her way to the innkeeper's quarters, where several boxes still sat unpacked in the corner of the small living room. She'd unpacked the essentials yesterday—clothes, toiletries and the kitchen items she'd need immediately, but the rest of her belongings were still waiting to be sorted and put away.

One box in particular caught her attention. It was smaller than the others, and she recognized it immediately.

Her memory box.

Grace settled onto the floor beside it and lifted the flaps. Inside were photo albums from her childhood, yearbooks from high school, ticket stubs, and programs from events she'd attended with friends and family. A pressed flower from her senior prom corsage. A ribbon she'd won at a 4-H competition when she was twelve. The kinds of things that had no practical value but were impossible to throw away.

She pulled out her senior yearbook and flipped through the pages, smiling at the faces of classmates she hadn't thought about in a while. There was Missy Clark, who'd been her lab partner in chemistry. And Miles Davenport, who'd asked her to homecoming sophomore year and then spent the whole dance talking about his car. And Jenny Miller, one of her close friends until Jenny's family moved to Nashville midway through senior year.

And there, tucked between the pages like a bookmark someone had forgotten to remove, was a photograph. It was a prom photo; the kind taken by a professional photographer against a backdrop of fake stars and silver streamers. Her seventeen-year-old self grinned at the camera in a deep green dress that matched her eyes, her hair swept up in an elaborate style that had taken her mother two hours to perfect.

And beside her, with his arm around her waist and a smile that lit up his entire face, was Jim Hartwell.

She'd forgotten how young, happy, and in love they'd been. How completely certain they'd been that the world was full of nothing but possibility and promise.

Grace studied the photo more closely. Jim had been so handsome in his rented tuxedo, his dark hair neatly combed for probably the only time in his life. They'd dated for two years in high school, her junior and senior year, and he'd been her first love in the way that only first loves could be. Intense and consuming and absolutely certain that what they felt would last forever.

It hadn't, of course. She'd gone off to Virginia Tech, and he'd stayed in Serenity Crossing, and the distance had done what distance always did to young love. They'd agreed to end things amicably, promising to stay friends, and then had slowly lost touch the way everyone did when life pulled them in different directions.

She wondered how he was doing these days. Her mom had mentioned him occasionally over the years, updates delivered in the casual way Jean shared all the town gossip. Jim had taken over the hardware store when his grandfather retired. He'd gotten married a few years back to a woman from out of town. And then he'd gotten divorced.

Just like her.

Funny how life has a way of throwing in twists and turns you never expected.

Grace tucked the photo back between the pages of the yearbook and closed the cover. That was a lifetime ago. A different Grace, a different Jim, a different world entirely. Whatever they'd been to each other back then had no bearing on who they were now.

Still, she knew she'd run into him, eventually. It was inevitable in a town this size, and especially inevitable given that he owned the hardware store. She was going to need supplies. A lot of supplies. And Hartwell's Hardware was the only game in town.

She set the yearbook aside and reached for another photo album, this one filled with pictures from her childhood. Her parents' flower farm in full bloom. Family celebrations around the big table in the farmhouse kitchen. She and her siblings playing in the fields, covered in dirt and grinning at the camera.

A simpler time. A good time before she'd headed off into the world to learn how to be an adult.

Grace spent another twenty minutes flipping through memories before she finally closed the album and pushed herself to her feet. Break time was over. She had wallpaper to remove, a contractor to find, and approximately a thousand other tasks waiting for her attention.

But as she carried her clipboard back toward the parlor, she found herself thinking about the hardware store. About the supplies she'd need. About the inevitable encounter that was waiting for her somewhere in the near future.

She wondered if Jim Hartwell had changed much in fourteen years. She wondered if he'd even remember her.

Chapter 4

J im Hartwell stood in the plumbing aisle of Hartwell Hardware with a compression fitting in one hand, and Harvey Dalton's full attention was focused on him.

"See this ring here?" Jim turned the fitting so Harvey could see the internal mechanism. "That's what creates the seal. You slide it onto the pipe, tighten the nut, and the ring compresses against the copper. No soldering required."

Harvey nodded slowly, his weathered face creased with concentration. He'd been coming to Hartwell's Hardware for years, first when Jim's grandfather ran the place and now that Jim stood behind the counter. Some things in Serenity Crossing didn't change, and Harvey Dalton's tendency to tackle plumbing repairs himself was one of them.

"And you're sure this'll hold?" Harvey asked, eyeing the fitting with the skepticism of a man who'd been burned by shortcuts before.

"I've used these in my own home. Three years now, not a single leak." Jim straightened and handed Harvey the fitting along with two more from the shelf. "You'll want extras. Trust me on that. Nothing worse than being under the sink and realizing you're one fitting short."

"That's the truth." Harvey tucked the fittings into his basket alongside the pipe cutter and Teflon tape Jim had already recommended. "Martha's been after me about that leak for two weeks now. Says she can hear it dripping at night."

"How is Martha? Her knee still giving her trouble?"

"She's better since the surgery. She's already talking about getting back to her gardening, which means I'd better fix this sink before she decides to do it herself."

Jim laughed. He'd known Harvey and Martha Dalton his entire life. They'd been at his christening, his high school graduation, and his wedding. They'd witnessed his horrible divorce too, though they'd had the grace not to mention it. "Tell her I said hello. And if you run into any trouble with the installation, give me a call. I can walk you through it."

"Appreciate that, Jim. Your granddaddy would be proud of how you've kept this place running."

The compliment settled into Jim's chest with a warmth that never got old. His grandfather had built Hartwell's Hardware from nothing and had made it a cornerstone of the community through sixty years of honest advice and fair prices. Carrying on that legacy meant more to Jim than he usually let himself acknowledge.

Boone, who had been lying patiently in the aisle during this entire exchange, lifted his head and thumped his tail against the floor. The Bluetick Coonhound had appointed himself the store's unofficial greeter four years ago when Jim had adopted him as a pup, and he took his responsibilities seriously. He followed Jim everywhere, from the front counter to the back office to the loading dock, and customers had come to expect his calm presence as much as they expected Jim's expertise.

"Come on, boy," Jim said as he gave Boone's ears a scratch. "Let's get Harvey here checked out."

They walked together toward the front of the store, where Tuck Brennan was restocking a display of flashlights near the register. Tuck had been his best friend since they were kids building forts in the woods behind the home where Jim had grown up on the outskirts of town, and he'd been the store's manager for going on six years now. He knew the inventory as well as Jim did, and the customers even better.

"Harvey," Tuck nodded in greeting as they approached. "Martha finally getting you to fix that sink?"

"You know how she is. I've learned it's easier to just do what she says."

"Smart man." Tuck rang up the purchase with ease while Jim lingered nearby, mentally reviewing the afternoon's tasks. He needed to check on a shipment that had just been delivered, and there was paperwork in his office that had been waiting for his attention since Monday.

Harvey collected his bag and headed for the door with a wave. Jim watched him go, then turned to head toward the back of the store.

"I'm going to check on that lumber delivery," he told Tuck. "Holler if you need me."

He made it halfway down an aisle before stopping dead in his tracks, causing Boone to bump into the back of his legs.

There, standing in front of the paint display with a handful of color swatches fanned out in her fingers, was Grace McKenna.

No. Grace Bennett now. She'd gotten married. He remembered hearing about it a few years ago.

She hadn't seen him yet. She was studying the swatches with the focused attention of someone making an important decision, her brow slightly furrowed, her lips pressed together in concentration. Her hair was different than he remembered, longer and wavier, falling past her shoulders in a way that made his fingers itch with the memory of how soft it used to feel.

Fourteen years.

Fourteen years since she'd left for college and taken something with her he'd never quite gotten back. Fourteen years of building a life that was good, that was full, that was everything he'd told himself he wanted. And all it took was one glimpse of her in his store to make all of that feel like a house of cards.

She was beautiful. More beautiful than she'd been at eighteen, which shouldn't have been possible.

His heart was doing something it hadn't done in quite some time. He told himself it was just the surprise and shock of seeing her. It wasn't.

Boone nudged his leg, and Jim realized he'd been standing frozen in the middle of the aisle like a love-struck teenager. He forced his feet to move, forced his face into something that hopefully resembled casual friendliness, and walked toward her.

She looked up when she heard his footsteps. Her eyes met his, and for a moment neither of them moved. Then she smiled, and Jim felt the last fourteen years collapse into nothing.

"Jim."

"Grace." He was surprised his voice worked. "I didn't know you were in town."

"Just got here Monday." She said as she turned to face him fully. "I'm staying at my grandma's place. The Mountain Laurel Inn."

"I heard about Ellie." Jim's voice softened. He'd always liked Grace's grandmother, a sharp-minded woman who'd run that inn with warmth and efficiency for as long as he could remember. "I'm sorry. She was a good woman."

"She was." Grace's smile turned bittersweet. "I inherited the inn. I'm planning to fix it up and reopen it."

"The inn? That's a big project."

"Tell me about it. I spent yesterday walking through with a clipboard and making lists. The lists have lists."

Jim laughed, and some of the tension in his shoulders eased. This was Grace. He knew Grace. Or he had known her once upon a time. "Sounds about right for a renovation project. I remember hearing how Ellie kept the inn running smoothly, but she wasn't much for updates."

"That's a kind way of putting it." Grace glanced down at the paint swatches in her hand. "The wallpaper alone is going to take me a week to remove. Maybe longer."

"Are you doing the work yourself?"

"Some of it. The parts I can handle." She met his eyes again, and something flickered there that he couldn't quite read. "I need to stay busy, and I want to be a part of all the work that needs to be done to make the inn come alive again."

"How long are you in town for?" he asked, genuinely curious.

"Permanently. I moved back."

He felt his heartbeat pick up speed, and he tried to ignore it. "That's... great. Your folks must be happy to have you close again."

"They are. Mom's already trying to feed me every chance she gets. She thinks I'm too thin."

"Moms," Jim shook his head with a grin. "Mine's the same way. I see her twice a week for dinner, and she still acts like I'm wasting away and sends me home with leftovers."

Grace laughed, and the sound of it hit him somewhere deep. He'd forgotten that laugh. Or maybe he'd just forced himself to stop remembering it.

"So you're still close with your family," she said. "Are all of them still in town?"

"Every last one. Dave's a CPA and has his own business here in town. Sarah started her own construction company. Rebecca's got the beauty shop on Main Street. All six of us are still here, still in each other's business." He paused. "How about your family? I see your mom and dad now and then."

"They're all good. My brothers and sisters are all doing well. It's been good being back with everyone." She hesitated, then added, "It feels like home in a way Atlanta never did."

Atlanta. Right. That's where she'd been living. With her husband.

The thought prompted him. "Listen, we should catch up properly sometime. Maybe grab dinner, you and me and your husband. I'd love to hear about what you've been up to all these years."

Grace went very still.

Jim's eyes dropped to her left hand.

No ring. No ring at all.

His gaze snapped back up to her face, but not fast enough. She'd seen him look.

"I'm divorced," Grace said quietly. "Recently, actually. And that's about all I'm going to say about that."

Divorced. The word settled into him like a key turning in a lock.

"Grace, I'm sorry. I didn't know." The apology sounded hollow and inadequate for the awkwardness he'd just created.

"It's fine." She squared her shoulders, and he watched her visibly pull herself back together. "Anyway. I actually came in for a reason. I needed some wallpaper removal supplies, and I'm trying to pick out paint colors. And I was hoping you might be able to recommend a good contractor. I can handle the cosmetic stuff at the inn, but the kitchen needs a complete overhaul, and there's some other work that's definitely beyond my skill set."

Jim's brain kicked into gear, grateful for something he knew how to do. "Sarah. My sister. She's the best contractor in the county." He paused. "Don't tell her I said that, though. Her ego's big enough already."

Grace's lips curved into a smile, and some of the tension in her posture eased. "I'll keep that between us."

"Tom Reeves is good too, for general contracting. He's been around forever. He'll give you a straight answer even if you don't want to hear it."

"That's undoubtedly what I need." Grace pulled out her phone. "Do you have their numbers?"

Jim rattled off both numbers from memory, watching as Grace typed them into her contacts.

Boone, who had been sitting quietly beside Jim during this entire conversation, chose this moment to rise from the floor, stretch elaborately, and pad directly over to Grace. He sat down at her feet, tail wagging, and gazed up at her with the soulful expression that had charmed countless customers over the years. Then he lifted one paw and held it out to her.

Grace looked down at him with surprise that melted into delight. "Well, hello there." She crouched down and took his paw, shaking it gently. "Aren't you a handsome boy?"

Boone's tail wagged harder. He leaned into her touch when she released his paw and scratched behind his ears, his eyes half-closing with pleasure.

Jim stared. Boone was friendly with everyone, but this was different. He didn't offer his paw to strangers. He didn't press himself against their legs like he was trying to become part of them. He was acting as if he'd known Grace his whole life, like he'd been waiting for her to walk through that door.

"Your dog, I assume?" Grace asked, still scratching Boone's ears.

"Got him about four years ago. His name's Boone. He runs the place mostly. I just work here."

Grace laughed and gave Boone one final pat before straightening. "He's beautiful. And clearly a good judge of character."

"He thinks so, anyway."

They stood there for a moment, the silence between them filled with everything they weren't saying. Jim wanted to ask her more. Wanted to know what had happened with her marriage, why she'd come back, and whether she was okay. But those weren't questions you asked someone you hadn't seen in fourteen years, no matter how much history you shared.

"I should let you get back to work," Grace said finally. "And I need to head home and figure out what shade of paint I want for the parlor. Apparently there are about four hundred options."

"Classic problem. My advice? Pick one and don't second-guess yourself. They all look different on the wall than they do on those little cards, anyway."

"Voice of experience?"

"I've painted more walls than I can count. Trust me on this one."

Grace gathered the basket she'd filled with supplies that was sitting on the floor near her feet. Jim walked her toward the front of the store, keeping the conversation light.

Tuck was still at the register, and his eyes flicked between Jim and Grace with an expression that Jim was absolutely going to call him out on later. But Tuck, to his credit, didn't make any comments and rang up Grace's purchases with his usual efficiency.

"Welcome home, Grace," Tuck said as he handed over her bag. "Let us know if you need anything else."

"I'm sure I will. This is probably the first of many trips." Grace smiled at both of them, then headed for the door with Boone trailing after her like a lovesick teenager.

Jim whistled softly, and Boone reluctantly returned to his side. Together, they watched through the front windows as Grace walked to an SUV parked at the curb, climbed in, and pulled away.

The store felt different after she left. Quieter. Emptier. Like something had shifted, and he couldn't quite put it back the way it was.

Boone sat down heavily beside him and let out a long sigh.

"Yeah," Jim murmured. "Me too, buddy."

Tuck appeared at his elbow, arms crossed, expression carefully neutral. "So. Grace McKenna's back in town."

Jim didn't take his eyes off the window, even though her SUV had long since disappeared.

"Yeah," he said. "She is."

Tuck waited. Jim could feel him waiting, could practically hear the questions his best friend was choosing not to ask.

"She's divorced," Jim added.

"Huh." Tuck was quiet for a moment. "And how do you feel about that?"

Jim finally turned away from the window. Boone was still sitting at his feet, looking up at him with those knowing eyes.

"No comment, Tuck. Don't even go there."

Chapter 5

Grace stood in the parlor with a spray bottle in one hand and a scraper in the other, glaring at the stubborn strip of floral pattern that refused to separate from the wall. She'd been at this for three hours already, and the pile of garbage bags near the front door was growing.

The chemical smell of the removal solution hung heavy in the air despite the front door being propped open to catch the morning breeze. Her arms ached. Her shoulders burned. And a headache was building that had nothing to do with the fumes and everything to do with the fact that she'd barely slept last night.

She attacked another section of wallpaper with more force than necessary, peeling away a satisfying strip that left the wall underneath looking wounded and raw.

Good. At least something was cooperating.

The sleepless night hadn't been about the inn or the renovation or even the impossible timeline she'd set for herself. It had been about Lee, and she'd wondered for the thousandth time how she'd missed all the signs. He'd been charming. Attentive. Everything she thought she wanted. And she'd walked right into a marriage with a man who'd been lying to her from the beginning, too blinded by what she thought was love to see what was actually happening right in front of her face.

She was an architect. She was trained to notice details, to see what others missed, to find the flaws hiding beneath the surface. And yet she'd spent two years married to a man whose flaws were so obvious in hindsight that she felt like a fool for not seeing them sooner.

Grace scraped another strip of wallpaper with unnecessary aggression. The past was the past. She couldn't change it. She could only move forward and try to rebuild something better from the wreckage.

Starting with these walls.

"Looks like you're making progress."

Grace spun around, scraper raised like a weapon, and found Sarah Hartwell standing in the open doorway with an amused expression on her face.

"Sorry," Sarah held up both hands in mock surrender. "Didn't mean to startle you. The door was open."

"Sarah," Grace said. "I wasn't expecting you for another twenty minutes."

"I finished my last job early. Figured I'd come by a little early and see what we're working with." Sarah stepped into the foyer and looked around, taking in the garbage bags full of stripped wallpaper and the walls in various stages of demolition. "Wow. You've been busy."

"The wallpaper and I have been having a disagreement." Grace set down the scraper and wiped her hands on her jeans. "I'm winning, but only by a narrow margin."

Sarah laughed, and the sound of it triggered something familiar in Grace's memory. The tilt of her head, the way her eyes crinkled at the corners. The Hartwells all had that same quality, that steady confidence that made you feel like everything was going to be okay.

"It's so good to see you," Grace said as she crossed the room and pulled Sarah into a hug. "It's been too long."

"Way too long." Sarah hugged her back with genuine warmth. "When Jim told me you were back in town and needed some work done, I couldn't believe it. Grace McKenna, back in Serenity Crossing. I never thought I'd see the day."

"Bennett, actually. Or McKenna again, I suppose. I haven't quite decided what to do about that yet." Grace stepped back and managed a smile. "It's a long story."

"You don't have to explain." Sarah's eyes softened with understanding. "I'm just glad you're here. And I'm glad you called. This place has been sitting empty too long."

"That's what I'm hoping to change." Grace gestured around the parlor. "As you can see, I've got my work cut out for me."

"Speaking of which." Sarah pulled out her phone and checked the time. "Tom should be here any minute. I ran into him at the coffee shop this morning, and we figured we'd coordinate. Makes more sense to do one walk-through together than two separate ones."

"That works for me."

As if on cue, the sound of a truck pulling into the parking area drifted through the open door. A moment later, Tom Reeves appeared on the threshold, a weathered man in his fifties with the kind of face that looked like it had seen everything and wasn't impressed by much.

"Mornin', ladies." He stepped inside and shook Grace's hand with a firm grip. "Nice to meet you, Grace."

"You as well. Thank you for coming on such short notice."

Tom's eyes were already scanning the room, cataloging details. "Twelve weeks to open is your goal, right? That's pretty aggressive for such a large building, and I don't recall Ellie having any updates done to this place for quite some time before she passed."

"I know. But the Heritage Festival is the perfect opportunity to relaunch, and I don't want to miss it."

Tom nodded slowly. "Let's take a look-see at what we're dealing with, then."

They started in the kitchen, which Grace already knew would be the biggest challenge. Tom moved through the space with methodical attention, opening cabinet doors, checking under the sink, running water in the faucets, and listening to the way it moved through the pipes.

"The plumbing's old," he said, frowning. "Probably original. We won't know how bad it is until we open up the walls, but I'd budget for the worst and hope for the best."

Grace made a note on the clipboard she'd grabbed from the counter. She was used to being the architect on projects, not the client, and the role reversal felt strange. But she appreciated Tom's honesty. He wasn't sugarcoating anything, and that was exactly what she needed.

"The kitchen itself needs a complete overhaul, just like you mentioned to me on the phone," Tom continued. "New appliances, new cabinets, new countertops. The layout's not bad, actually, just dated. We can modernize it without changing the footprint too much."

"Sounds good. I've got some ideas about how to open up the space while keeping the original character."

Tom raised an eyebrow. "You're an architect, right? Jim mentioned that."

"I am. Was. I mean, I still am. I just—" Grace stopped herself. "Yes. I'm an architect."

"Good. Then you know what you're looking at. That'll make this easier."

They moved through the rest of the first floor, with Tom noting the bathrooms that would need updating and the various plumbing concerns throughout the building. Sarah trailed behind them, occasionally adding observations of her own about structural elements that fell under her expertise.

When they reached the back porch, Sarah took the lead. She stepped out onto the weathered boards and immediately shook her head.

"This has to go. Half of these boards are rotted through. It's a liability waiting to happen." She crouched down and pressed her thumb against one of the planks, which gave way with alarming ease. "See? The whole structure's compromised."

Grace had noticed the porch's condition during her own assessment, but hearing it confirmed by a professional made it feel more real. "I was hoping to add a gazebo out here too. More outdoor seating for guests."

"That we can definitely do." Sarah straightened and looked out at the grassy area behind the inn. "Actually, that's a great idea. A nice big gazebo, maybe with a few flat stone walking paths added back here... string lights, even a few benches placed strategically, would look great. Think about possibly doing some heavy landscaping back here, and you can avoid having to mow the grass. It would be perfect for events."

"I like it. I can envision it."

One of Sarah's employees, a young man named Derek who had arrived with her, appeared around the corner of the building. "I checked the roof like you asked, Sarah. The shingles are shot, and there's some damage to the underlayment. It needs to be replaced, not patched."

Sarah nodded as if she'd expected as much. "We'll add it to the list."

They continued upstairs, where Tom assessed the bathrooms and made notes about updating the plumbing and fixtures throughout. The guest rooms themselves were in decent shape, needing mostly cosmetic work that she could handle herself.

By the time they returned to the first floor, Grace's clipboard was filled with notes, and her mind was spinning with numbers and time-lines.

"Alright." Tom leaned against the parlor doorframe and crossed his arms. "Here's the bottom line. The kitchen is the biggest job. I can have my crew in here by Monday, and if everything goes smoothly, we're looking at four to five weeks to get it done. The bathrooms are another two weeks, maybe three if we run into surprises in the walls."

"And the structural stuff?" Grace turned to Sarah.

"The back porch and gazebo, we can start on right away. I've got a crew finishing up a job tomorrow, and they can be here Saturday. Figure two weeks for the porch and another week or so for the gazebo. The windows are going to take longer, maybe three weeks total. And the roof..." Sarah glanced at Derek. "Two weeks if the weather coop-erates. Could be more if we get rain."

Grace did the math in her head. It was tight. Really tight. But if everything overlapped correctly, and if she busted her tail on the cosmetic work in between...

"You'll need the kitchen certified by the health department before you can serve food," Tom reminded her. "And a fire inspection before you can have guests overnight."

"I know. I've already started looking into what's required here in Tennessee."

"Twelve weeks." Sarah shook her head slowly. "It's aggressive. But I've seen tighter."

"So have I," Tom agreed. "It's doable. But you're going to have to be willing to work alongside us. The more of the cosmetic stuff you can handle yourself, the more time we can focus on the big projects."

"That's exactly what I'm planning to do." Grace gestured at the half-stripped walls around them. "I've already started, obviously."

Sarah and Tom exchanged a look that Grace couldn't quite read. Then Sarah smiled, and again Grace was struck by how much she resembled her brother. That same steady confidence. That same way of making you feel like everything was going to work out.

"Alright," Sarah said. "We're in. Let's make this happen."

They spent another twenty minutes going over details and logistics. By the time Sarah and Tom headed for the door, Grace had a clear picture of the weeks ahead: a whirlwind of construction and renovation that would push her limits and test her patience, and demand everything she had to give.

She walked them out and stood on the front porch, watching as their trucks pulled away. The morning sun was climbing higher now, warming the air and burning off the last of the early chill. The mountains rose in the distance, steady and unchanging, the same view she'd grown up with.

Twelve weeks. Aggressive, but possible.

She'd take possible.

Grace went back inside and closed the door behind her. The parlor looked worse than it had before; somehow, the stripped sections of wall highlighted just how much work remained.

She walked to the center of the room and sat down heavily in one of the old floral armchairs. For just a moment, she let herself feel the weight of what she'd committed to. The money she was about to spend. The timeline she was about to chase. The risk she was taking on a building that had been empty for a year and a dream that had been forming for less than a month.

She put her head in her hands and took a deep breath.

This was huge. This was terrifying. This was possibly the craziest thing she'd ever done in her life.

And it was hers. All of it. Every decision, every risk, every possible failure, and every possible triumph. No one else's opinion to consider. No one else's approval to seek. Just Grace and the inn, and the life she was choosing to create.

She lifted her head and looked around the room with fresh eyes. The walls were a mess, but they were her mess. The work ahead was enormous, but it was her work. And for the first time in longer than she could remember, she felt something that had been missing from her life for months.

Excitement.

Grace pushed herself up from the chair, grabbed her scraper, and attacked the wallpaper with renewed energy.

She had an inn to open.

Chapter 6

The stained-glass windows of Serenity Crossing Community Church cast colored light across the sanctuary, painting the wooden pews in soft shades of gold and blue, and rose as the congregation settled into their seats for the Easter morning service. Grace sat between her mother and Faith in the McKenna pew, third row from the front on the right side, the same spot her family had occupied for as long as she could remember. The familiar scent of old hymnals and lemon wood polish wrapped around her, reminding her of her childhood.

She smoothed her hands over the skirt of her pale blue dress and tried to quiet the restlessness that had been building in her chest since she'd walked through those double doors twenty minutes ago. Easter Sunday. The church was fuller than it would be on an ordinary week, with families crowded into pews and folding chairs set up along the back wall to accommodate the overflow. Children squirmed in their Sunday best. Women wore spring colors and floral prints. Men tugged at ties they probably only wore a handful of times a year.

Grace had dressed carefully this morning, choosing the blue dress because it was pretty without being attention-seeking, because it was appropriate for church without looking like she was trying too hard. She had spent more time than she wanted to admit deciding what to wear, and she still wasn't sure she'd made the right choice.

When had church become something she had to prepare herself for?

She knew the answer, even if she didn't want to examine it too closely. College had started the drift. Sunday mornings became study sessions, then brunch with friends, then simply sleeping in after late Saturday nights. By the time she'd moved to Atlanta, church attendance had dwindled to Christmas Eve services and the occasional Easter, more out of tradition than conviction. Then, after she had married, Lee had never been interested in faith, and she had let his disinterest become her excuse.

Pastor Warren Davis stepped up to the pulpit, and Grace felt the weight of all those absent Sundays pressing down on her shoulders.

Her mother reached over and patted her hand, a gesture so familiar and so achingly maternal that Grace had to swallow against the sudden tightness in her throat. Jean McKenna had never asked why Grace had stopped attending church regularly. She had simply welcomed her back every time she came home, saved her a seat in the family pew, and acted as though no time had passed at all.

That grace, Grace thought, might be harder to accept than any sermon.

Pastor Warren Davis was a man in his late fifties with kind eyes and a voice that carried without ever seeming to shout. He had baptized Grace when she was twelve years old. She wondered if he knew she was divorced now. In a town this size, he probably did.

"This morning," Pastor Davis began, his hands resting on either side of the pulpit, "I want us to think about the beginning of Easter. Not the triumph. Not the celebration. Not the hallelujah moment when everything became clear. I want us to think about the quiet beginning, before anyone understood what had happened."

Grace opened her Bible to John 20, the passage printed in the bulletin, and followed along as Pastor Davis read.

"Early on the first day of the week, while it was still dark, Mary Magdalene went to the tomb and saw that the stone had been removed from the entrance. So she came running to Simon Peter and the other disciple, the one Jesus loved, and said, 'They have taken the Lord out of the tomb, and we don't know where they have put him!' So Peter and the other disciple started for the tomb. Both were running, but the other disciple outran Peter and reached the tomb first. He bent over and looked in at the strips of linen lying there but did not go in. Then Simon Peter came along behind him and went straight into the tomb. He saw the strips of linen lying there, as well as the cloth that had been wrapped around Jesus' head. The cloth was still lying in its place, separate from the linen. Finally, the other disciple, who had reached the tomb first, also went inside. He saw and believed. They still did not understand from Scripture that Jesus had to rise from the dead."

Pastor Davis looked up from his Bible and let his gaze travel across the congregation. "Mary didn't go to that tomb expecting a miracle. She went expecting to find a body. She went to grieve, to perform the rituals of death, to do the faithful, ordinary thing that needed to be done. And when she got there, everything was different, and she didn't understand why."

Grace listened as Pastor Davis continued, his voice gentle and unhurried as he walked through the passage.

"God was already at work," Pastor Davis said. "The resurrection had already happened. The stone had already been rolled away. But the people who loved Jesus most didn't see it yet. They didn't understand it yet. They were still living in the 'before,' even though God had already moved them into the 'after.'"

Something in those words snagged at Grace's heart, catching on edges she hadn't known were exposed.

"Sometimes," Pastor Davis continued, "God moves in ways we don't recognize. Sometimes the miracle has already happened, and we're still looking at the empty tomb and asking where they've taken Him. Faith isn't always about the triumphant moment. Sometimes faith is just showing up, doing the next faithful thing, and trusting that God is working even when we can't see it."

Grace stared at the words in her Bible without really reading them. She thought about the inn, about the overwhelming list of repairs and renovations, about the impossible deadline she had set for herself. She thought about the divorce papers she had signed a month ago and the marriage she had failed to see clearly until it was too late. She thought about all the Sunday mornings she had let slip away, all the prayers she had stopped praying, all the distance she had put between herself and the faith she had grown up with.

Had God been working in those years, even when she wasn't paying attention?

She didn't know. She wasn't sure she was ready to ask.

Later, the congregation stood for the closing hymn, and Grace rose with them, reaching for the hymnal her mother held open between them. The first notes from the piano filled the sanctuary, and Grace recognized the melody immediately. "Christ the Lord Is Risen Today." Her grandma Ellie's favorite Easter hymn.

Grace opened her mouth to sing, but the words caught in her throat.

She could hear her grandma's voice in her memory, strong and clear and joyful, lifting this same hymn in this same sanctuary year after year. Ellie had loved Easter morning. She had loved the flowers, the celebration, the promise of new life that the season represented. She had believed with a certainty that Grace had always admired and never quite managed to replicate.

Grace forced herself to keep singing, her voice unsteady on the familiar words. Beside her, Faith glanced over and gave her a small, understanding smile. Faith had lost her marriage too. Faith understood what it was like to stand in a place that used to feel like home and wonder if you still belonged there.

The hymn ended, and Pastor Davis offered a final blessing. Then the sanctuary erupted into the controlled chaos of a congregation released from their pews, everyone standing and stretching and turning to greet their neighbors.

Grace followed her family into the center aisle, moving with the slow current of people flowing toward the back of the church. She smiled and nodded at faces she recognized, accepting welcomes and good-to-see-yous with as much warmth as she could muster. Mrs. Patterson, who had taught her Sunday school class when she was eight. Mr. and Mrs. Holloway, who owned the farm next to her parents' property. The Brennan family, including Molly, who caught her eye and mouthed "Call me!" with enthusiastic emphasis.

The congregation's reaction to her presence was subtle but present. A few curious glances. A whispered comment here and there. Nothing unkind, just the natural interest of a small town in one of its own who had gone away and come back under circumstances that would probably be discussed over Sunday dinners all across Serenity Crossing.

Grace kept moving, kept smiling, kept her shoulders straight and her expression pleasant. She had known this would happen. She had prepared herself for it. That didn't make it any easier.

They emerged from the church into the bright April morning, and Grace paused at the bottom of the steps to let her eyes adjust to the sunlight. The church grounds were beautiful today: the old cemetery peaceful under the shade of ancient oaks, and the fellowship building visible behind the main sanctuary where the fellowship hour would be held.

Her parents were already heading toward the fellowship hall, her father's hand resting on the small of her mother's back as they walked. Faith had stopped to talk to someone Grace didn't recognize. The rest of her siblings were scattered across the church lawn in various conversations.

Grace was just about to follow her parents when she heard her name.

"Grace."

She turned, and there was Jim, walking toward her across the grass in a charcoal suit that fit him well. His tie was a deep burgundy, and his dark hair was neatly combed, and he looked... different. Older. More solid. The boy she had known in high school had grown into someone substantial, someone who carried himself with a quiet confidence that drew her attention in a way she hadn't expected.

"Jim. Happy Easter."

"Happy Easter." He stopped a few steps in front of her, his hands in his pockets, and his expression warm but uncertain. "Any plans this afternoon?"

"Not really... why do you ask?"

"I was wondering... would you like to grab lunch? I thought maybe we could catch up. If you're not too busy."

The invitation caught her off guard.

"I was going to join my family for fellowship," Grace heard herself say, "but honestly, I'm starving, and it would be nice to catch up more. We didn't really get much of a chance at the hardware store."

Jim's smile widened. "Minnie's Diner? They're doing an Easter brunch special, but they'll have the regular menu too."

"Minnie's sounds perfect."

They walked together toward the parking lot, falling into step beside each other with an ease that surprised her.

"I'll meet you there," Jim said as they reached her vehicle. "Unless you'd rather ride together?"

"Separate cars is probably easier. That way neither of us is stuck if…"

She trailed off, not sure how to finish that sentence. If what? If lunch was awkward? If they ran out of things to say? If being alone with Jim turned out to be a mistake she wasn't ready to make?

"Makes sense," Jim agreed easily, not pressing her to explain.

He reached past her and opened her driver's side door, holding it wide so she could climb in.

Grace paused with her hand on the frame of the door. When was the last time someone had opened a car door for her? She searched her memory and came up empty. Lee had never been the door-opening type. He had always been too busy, too distracted, and too focused on wherever he was going next to pause for something as simple as a courtesy.

"Thank you," she said.

"Of course." Jim waited until she was settled behind the wheel before closing the door gently. Then he turned and walked toward his truck.

Grace watched him go.

He moved with an unhurried confidence, a man who knew exactly where he was going and felt no need to rush getting there. His shoulders were relaxed, his stride steady, and his entire bearing that of someone who was comfortable in his skin.

Lee had never walked like that. Lee had always been moving toward the next thing, the next deal, or the next person who could advance his interests. Even in their home, he had carried the restless energy of a man who was always performing for an audience only he could see.

Jim climbed in his truck, and a moment later she heard the engine turn over.

Grace put her key in the ignition and sat there for a moment, her hands resting on the steering wheel. She had just agreed to have lunch with her high school boyfriend on Easter Sunday, and Grace realized she didn't mind; it felt almost natural.

Chapter 7

Jim pulled open the door of Minnie's Diner and held it wide, letting Grace step through ahead of him into the warmth and noise of the Sunday lunch crowd. The familiar scents of coffee, fried chicken, and fresh-baked pie wrapped around him like a welcome home, and he watched Grace's face as she took in the scene before them.

The black-and-white checkered floor gleamed beneath the overhead lights, kept clean and shining the same way it had been for as long as Jim could remember. Red vinyl booths lined the windows, most of them occupied by families still dressed in their Easter Sunday best. Chrome-trimmed stools ran the length of the counter, where a handful of regulars had already claimed their usual spots. The walls were covered with framed photographs of Serenity Crossing through the decades, newspaper clippings celebrating local teams and milestones, and vintage advertisements that had been there since before Jim was born. In the corner, the jukebox played a Patsy Cline tune that blended with the hum of conversation and the clatter of dishes.

This place was as much a part of Serenity Crossing as the town square itself. Jim had been coming here since he was old enough to sit on one of those spinning stools without falling off, and he'd eaten more meals at these tables than he could count. The diner felt like an extension of home, and he hoped Grace still felt that way too.

"Well, well, well." The voice came from behind the counter, and Jim looked up to see Minnie Whitfield emerging from the kitchen with a coffeepot in one hand and a dish towel thrown over her shoulder. Her silver hair was pinned up in its usual twist, and her apron was already spotted with the evidence of a busy morning. Her eyes, bright and sharp as ever, locked onto Grace with the intensity of a woman who never forgot a face. "Grace McKenna, as I live and breathe. Get yourself over here and let me look at you."

Grace barely had time to react before Minnie set down the coffeepot and wrapped her in a hug that lifted her slightly off the ground. Jim watched Grace's surprised laugh, watched her arms come up to return the embrace, and something in his chest warmed at the sight.

"It's Bennett now, actually," Grace said when Minnie finally released her. "Or McKenna again. I haven't quite decided."

Minnie waved a hand as if that was the least important detail in the world. "You'll always be a McKenna to me, sweetheart. Your grandma Ellie was one of my dearest friends, God rest her soul." She held Grace at arm's length and studied her with the kind of thorough inspection that only women of a certain age could get away with. "You look good. Thin, but good. We'll fix that... need to put some meat on them bones. I heard you're planning to open up the Mountain Laurel again."

"Word travels fast."

"Honey, word travels at the speed of light in this town. I overheard your mama telling Louise Pinkerton at the beauty shop the other day that she's tickled pink to have her girl back home where she belongs."

Minnie finally seemed to notice Jim standing there and turned her knowing gaze on him. "And you brought our Jim along for lunch. Isn't that something?"

Jim felt the tips of his ears go warm. "Mornin' Minnie."

"Don't you 'Mornin' Minnie' me, James Hartwell. I've known you since you were stealing cookies off my counter when you thought I wasn't looking." She picked up two menus and tucked them under her arm, then grabbed the coffeepot again. "Come on, you two. I've got a booth by the window with your names on it."

She led them through the maze of tables to a booth near the front, one that offered a view of Main Street through the plate-glass window. Jim slid into one side, and Grace settled across from him, and Minnie flipped over the coffee cups that were already waiting on the table and filled them both without asking.

"You still take yours black?" she asked Jim.

"Yes, ma'am."

"And Grace, if I remember right, you like yours with cream and enough sugar to give a person diabetes."

Grace laughed, and the sound of it did something to Jim's pulse that he chose not to examine too closely. "My tastes have matured a little since high school. Just cream now."

"Growing up will do that to ya," Minnie said as she set down the coffeepot and pulled a few creamer pods from her apron pocket like a magician producing a rabbit from a hat. "I'll give you two a minute to look at the menus, but I already know Jim's getting the chicken fried steak because that's what he always gets on Sundays when he drops in, and I'm guessing you're going to want the chef's salad, easy on the cheese, because you've been living in the city too long and forgot what real food tastes like."

"Actually," Grace said, scanning the menu with a smile playing at the corners of her mouth, "I'll have the chicken-fried steak too."

Minnie's eyebrows rose toward her hairline. "Well now. Maybe there's hope for you yet." She scribbled on her pad, collected the menus, and headed back toward the kitchen with a final glance over her shoulder that Jim pretended not to notice.

"She hasn't changed a bit," Grace said, wrapping her hands around her coffee cup.

"Minnie? She'll outlive us all, and she'll still be running this place when she does." Jim took a sip of his coffee. "She was at the store last week complaining about her grandson, Danny. He's been late to work three times this month, and she found out about it."

"Danny works at the hardware store?"

"Started about six months ago. Good kid, just not great with mornings." Jim watched Grace add cream to her coffee and stir it with the small spoon. She looked different in the soft light coming through the window.

"So," Grace said, setting down her spoon and meeting his eyes. "Fourteen years. That's a lot of catching up to do."

"It is." He leaned back against the vinyl seat and made a conscious effort to keep his posture relaxed and casual. Like this was just two old friends having lunch. Like his heart wasn't doing something complicated every time she smiled. "Where do you want to start?"

"How about you? What have you been doing all this time? I mean, I know you took over the hardware store, but what else? What's your life like these days?"

Jim considered the question. His life. What was his life like? "I took over the store about eight years ago full-time. Granddad had already retired, and Dad had stepped in to make sure I knew the ropes and could handle everything. Then a couple of months later, I guess Dad decided I could handle it, and he admitted store life wasn't for him and he'd rather spend more of his time at the lumber mill. It was always going to be mine eventually, but I thought I'd have more time to prepare." He shrugged. "Turns out you're never really ready for something like that. You just figure it out as you go."

"Do you like it? Running the store?"

"I love it." The answer came easily because it was true. "I know it probably sounds boring to someone who lived in Atlanta, but there's something about helping people solve problems. Someone comes in with a leaky faucet or a broken cabinet hinge, and I can point them to exactly what they need. I know every product on those shelves. I know which brands are worth the money and which ones are a waste of time." He paused, aware that he was rambling. "Sorry. You probably didn't need that much detail."

"No, I like it. You sound happy."

"I am. Mostly." He took another sip of coffee to buy himself a moment. "What about you? I know you went to Virginia Tech for architecture and graduated... then it was off to Atlanta, right?"

"Yep. I worked for the same firm in Atlanta for years after I graduated. Designed office buildings, mostly. Some residential projects." She traced a pattern on the tabletop with her finger, her eyes following the movement. "It was good work. Challenging. I learned a lot."

"But?"

She looked up, and something flickered across her face. "But it wasn't what I thought it would be. I spent so much time chasing that career, trying to prove I could make it in a big city, and then one day I realized I wasn't sure what I was proving anymore. Or who I was proving it too. The money was great...but I wasn't happy. "

Jim understood that feeling better than he wanted to admit. After Amanda left, he'd spent months questioning everything about himself and everything he'd built, wondering if any of it had been worth the effort.

"So the inn," he said, steering the conversation toward safer ground. "That's what brought you back?"

"Partly." Grace wrapped her hands around her coffee cup again, and Jim noticed the way her shoulders had started to relax, the tension she'd been carrying beginning to ease. "When Grandma Ellie died, she left it to me. I wasn't sure what to do with it at first. Selling seemed like the practical choice. But then..." she trailed off, her gaze drifting toward the window. "I don't know. Something about the idea of letting it go felt wrong. That inn was her whole life. She poured everything into it for so many years. It felt like giving up on her legacy."

"So you're going to restore it instead."

"That's the plan." A small laugh escaped her. "Whether it's a good plan remains to be seen. The place needs more work than I realized. The kitchen alone is going to eat up a quarter of my budget."

"Sarah mentioned that. She said you're looking at a pretty aggressive timeline."

"The Heritage Festival. I want to be open by then. I'm thinking just a soft opening." Grace met his eyes, and Jim saw something there that he recognized. Not just determination. Hope. The kind of hope that came with risk, with putting yourself on the line for something that mattered. "It's probably crazy. Everyone keeps telling me it's too much, too fast. But I need something to work toward. Something that's mine. Something I can focus on and take my mind off... other things."

Jim nodded slowly. He understood that, too.

Minnie appeared with their plates, sliding the chicken fried steak in front of each of them with the efficiency of someone who'd done this a thousand times. "You two need anything else? More coffee? Ketchup? A chaperone?"

"We're fine, Minnie," Jim said, giving her a look that she cheerfully ignored.

"Alright, alright. Just holler if you need me." She patted Grace's shoulder as she passed. "It's good to have you home, sweetheart. I've missed you."

Grace watched her go, then turned back to Jim with amusement in her eyes. "We're gonna be the gossip of the diner for the rest of the day, aren't we?"

"By dinner, the whole town will know we were here. By tomorrow morning, they'll have invented details that didn't happen." He picked up his fork. "Welcome back to Serenity Crossing."

They ate in companionable quiet for a few minutes; the conversation flowing easily between bites.

"And you built a house, I heard?" Grace asked, reaching for her water glass. "My mom mentioned that once, I think. When I was home for Christmas a few years ago."

"Out on the family property, yeah. There's a spot on the southeast corner, near the treeline, where you can see the mountains in the morning when the light's right." He could picture it perfectly: the cabin he'd designed, the wraparound porch where he sat with Boone on summer evenings. "It took about two years to finish. Sarah and her crew built it, and I helped when I could."

"That's impressive."

"It kept me busy." He left it at that, not wanting to explain that he'd started the project during his marriage to Amanda and that the house had become a kind of therapy when everything in his life had fallen apart after she'd left.

"Speaking of keeping busy," Grace said, "tell me about Boone. He seemed like quite the character at the hardware store."

Jim grinned. "Boone is a menace. A lovable menace, but a menace nonetheless." He thought about his dog, probably lounging on his bed back at the cabin right now, and felt a familiar wave of affection. "I got him about four years ago. He showed up at the store one day, skinny and scared, and I fed him. After that, he just... stayed."

"He offered me his paw. At the store. Did you teach him that? Is that something he does with everyone?"

"No." Jim held her gaze for a moment longer than necessary. "That's not something he does with everyone, and yes, I did teach him that trick. He's usually pretty selective about who he approaches like that. I guess he likes you."

Grace looked away first, reaching for her coffee. "He's sweet."

"He's a troublemaker. Last month he got the zoomies in the storage room, and it took me an hour to clean up everything he knocked over. And he looked at me the whole time like it was my fault for not dog-proofing the shelves."

Grace laughed, and Jim cataloged the sound, the way it changed her whole face, the way it made her look lighter and more like the girl he remembered from high school.

"Do you remember," he said, the memory surfacing unexpectedly, "that time junior year when we tried to sneak into the Granville Theater after hours?"

Grace's eyes widened. "Oh, my gosh. I had completely forgotten about that."

"You were convinced there was a ghost in the projection room."

"There were noises, Jim. Unexplained noises."

"It was a raccoon. We found out later it was a raccoon that had been living in the ceiling for months."

"But we didn't know that at the time." She was laughing now, really laughing, and Jim felt something shift in his chest. "You were so brave, going up those stairs first. I was terrified."

"I was terrified too. I just didn't want you to know."

Their eyes met across the table, and for a moment the years fell away. They were seventeen again, sneaking around in the dark, holding hands because they were scared and because they wanted to, because back then everything had felt possible and permanent and safe.

Grace looked away first. "That was a long time ago."

"Yeah," Jim cleared his throat. "It was."

The moment passed, but something lingered in its wake. Something warm and complicated that Jim didn't have a name for yet.

They finished their meal, and Jim insisted on paying despite Grace's protests. He left Minnie a generous tip and waved off her knowing smile as they headed for the door.

Outside, the afternoon sun was warm on Jim's face, and Main Street stretched out before them in both directions, quiet and familiar. Grace's SUV was parked a few spaces down from his truck, and they walked toward it together, their footsteps falling into an easy rhythm on the sidewalk.

"This was nice," Grace said when they reached her car. "I'm glad you asked."

"Me too." Jim opened her door for her, the same way he had at the church, and watched her settle behind the wheel. "Listen, I meant what I said before. If you need help with the inn, anything at all, I'm around. I know you want to do it yourself, but sometimes an extra pair of hands makes things go faster."

Grace studied him for a moment, her expression thoughtful. "That's a lot to offer, Jim. You've got your own business to run."

"I've got time. And I know my way around a renovation project." He shrugged, keeping his tone light. "Besides, what are old friends for?"

She smiled at that, a real smile that reached her eyes. "Alright. I might take you up on that."

"I hope you do."

He closed her door and stepped back, watching as she started the engine and pulled away from the curb. She gave him a small wave through the window, and he raised his hand in return, holding it there until her SUV disappeared around the corner.

Jim walked to his truck and climbed inside, but he didn't start the engine right away. He sat there in the quiet cab, replaying the last two hours in his mind. The way she'd laughed. The way she'd relaxed. The way she'd looked at him when they talked about sneaking into that old theater.

She needed a friend right now. That's what he'd told himself when he'd asked her to lunch. That's what he kept telling himself.

He turned the key in the ignition and pulled out onto Main Street.

Just friends. That's all this was.

He almost believed it.

Chapter 8

The Hartwell dining table had been in the family for three generations, its oak surface worn smooth by countless meals. Jim sat in his usual spot near the window, Boone lying across his feet beneath the table, and watched his family move through the familiar chaos of Sunday dinner like a well-rehearsed dance.

His mother sat at the head of the table, passing a platter of roast beef to Dave. His father sat at the opposite end, quiet and watchful, his hands wrapped around a glass of sweet tea. Sarah was arguing good-naturedly with Rebecca and Anna about something that had happened at church that morning, their voices overlapping in the way of sisters who enjoyed lively banter. Mike sat two chairs down from Jim with his six-year-old daughter Lizzie in between them, cutting her meat into small pieces while she chattered about the Easter egg hunt she'd participated in after the children's service.

This was home. This table, this room, and these people. The farmhouse had been built by Jim's great-grandfather and expanded twice since then, but the bones of the place remained the same. Wide plank floors that creaked in familiar places. Windows that looked out over the generous yard stretching toward the mountains.

"Jim, you're quiet tonight." His mother's voice cut through his thoughts, and he looked up to find her watching him with that particular expression she got when she was paying closer attention than she wanted him to know. Olivia Hartwell was a small woman with silver-streaked hair and sharp eyes that missed nothing. She had raised six children on this farm, buried her own parents in the cemetery behind the church, and somehow managed to keep track of every detail of all their lives without ever seeming to pry.

"Just tired," Jim said, reaching for the basket of biscuits. His mother's biscuits were legendary: light, flaky, and buttered before they even hit the table. She always made extra on Sundays so each of her children could take some home.

"Tired from what?" Anna asked from her spot next to Rebecca. At twenty-six, she was the youngest of the Hartwell siblings, with their mother's dark hair and their father's dry sense of humor. "It's Sunday. What could possibly have worn you out?"

"Maybe he's coming down with something," Rebecca suggested, her eyes twinkling in a way that made Jim immediately suspicious. Rebecca owned the Fluff & Curl Beauty Shop on Main Street, which meant she heard every piece of gossip in Serenity Crossing approximately five minutes after it happened. "You do look a little flushed, Jimmy."

"Don't call me Jimmy. You know, Mom's the only person allowed to do that."

Rebecca smiled sweetly and took a bite of her green beans.

Beneath the table, Boone shifted. He glanced down to see Lizzie sneaking a piece of roast beef to the dog; her face a picture of innocence when she caught him looking.

"Lizzie," Mike said without looking up from his own plate. "What did I say about feeding Boone at the table?"

"That I shouldn't do it?"

"And what are you doing?"

"Giving him a tiny piece because he looked sad."

Mike sighed, but Jim caught the ghost of a smile on his brother's face. Mike had lost his wife, Jenny, three years ago in a car accident, and for a long time afterward, smiles had been rare. Lizzie had been the one to pull him back, her constant questions and boundless energy demanding his attention when grief threatened to swallow him whole. She was six now, with her mother's red hair and her father's quiet strength, and she had every adult in this family wrapped around her little finger.

"I noticed you weren't at fellowship this morning," Olivia said, and the casual tone of her voice fooled absolutely no one, and her eyes were fixed on Jim.

Jim felt several gazes shift in his direction. Dave, sitting to his left, had gone still in that particular way he did when he was analyzing something. Sarah had stopped arguing with Rebecca. Even his father had looked up from his plate.

"Just lunch plans, Mom," Jim said.

"Lunch plans." Olivia's eyebrows rose slightly. "On Easter Sunday."

"Yes, ma'am."

Everyone around the table waited. Jim could feel them waiting, the way you could feel a change in air pressure before a storm. His family didn't push, not directly, but they had ways of creating silences that demanded filling.

"I ran into Grace Bennett after church," he said finally. "Grace McKenna, I mean. I asked her out for lunch."

Sarah reached for her tea glass. "We started working on the inn's back porch yesterday. The whole thing was rotted through." She shook her head. "That place needs more work than she probably realizes, but she's got a good eye. Knows what she wants. I'm glad she's home. I missed her."

"You're working on Grace's inn?" Rebecca leaned forward, her earlier teasing forgotten in favor of new information. "Why didn't you tell me?"

"Because I didn't think you'd care."

"Well, I do... I absolutely do. I have to keep up on everything that goes on around this town, you know." Rebecca turned to Jim with renewed focus. "So you had lunch with Grace. That's interesting. Where did you go?"

"Minnie's."

"Minnie's." Rebecca exchanged a look with Anna that Jim chose to ignore. "How was that?"

"It was fine. We caught up."

"And?" Anna prompted.

"And nothing. We're old friends. She's been gone for fourteen years. There was a lot to talk about."

Bill Hartwell cleared his throat, and the table fell quiet. Jim's father was a man of few words, but when he spoke, people listened. He had the same broad shoulders and dark hair that Jim had inherited, though his was mostly gray now, and the same steady presence that made you feel like everything was going to be okay even when it wasn't.

"Grace is a good woman," Bill said simply. "Always was. Her grandmama thought the world of her."

"She did," Olivia agreed, her expression softening. "Ellie used to talk about Grace all the time. How smart she was, how driven. She was so proud when Grace got into that architecture program... where was it that she went to school? For the life of me, I can't remember any-how... dear sweet Ellie missed her something fierce and never stopped hoping Grace would move back home... she missed that girl something awful."

"Virginia Tech," Jim supplied. "She graduated top of her class."

Dave's eyebrows rose slightly at that, and Jim felt his twin's attention sharpen. Dave was the analytical one, the accountant who saw patterns and numbers where Jim saw people and problems. They had been born eight minutes apart and had spent their whole lives understanding each other in ways that didn't require words. Right now, Dave was seeing something in Jim's face that Jim probably should have been hiding better.

"Is she doing okay?" Olivia asked, and this time her voice was genuinely gentle. "I heard about the divorce. That's a hard thing to go through, especially when you're far from home."

Jim thought about Grace at lunch that afternoon. The way she'd talked about the inn like it was a problem to solve, when really it was something more. The way her shoulders had gradually relaxed as the meal went on. The way she'd laughed at his story about Boone.

"She's getting there," he said. "I think moving back was the right choice for her. But she's got a lot on her plate right now. The inn, her family, and figuring out what comes next." He paused, choosing his next words carefully. "She needs friends more than anything."

"And you're offering to be that friend," Dave said.

"We were friends before. We can be friends again."

Everyone around the table absorbed this, and Jim watched understanding move across his family's faces in different ways. Rebecca looked like she wanted to say something to make him elaborate more. Anna looked amused. Sarah looked thoughtful. Mike just nodded, and Jim wondered if his widowed brother understood better than the others what it meant to need someone to simply be present without expectations.

"Uncle Jim?" Lizzie's voice piped up from across the table. "Is Grace your girlfriend?"

"No, sweetheart. She's just a friend."

"But she used to be your girlfriend, right? Daddy just whispered and told me you dated her in high school."

Jim shot Mike a look. Mike shrugged. "She asked who Grace was, and I answered."

"That was a long time ago," Jim told Lizzie. "We were just kids then."

"So she's not your girlfriend now?"

"No."

"Do you want her to be your girlfriend?"

"Lizzie," Mike put a gentle hand on his daughter's arm. "That's not a polite question to ask."

"Why not?"

"Because some things are private."

Lizzie considered this, her small face scrunched in thought. "Okay. But I think she should be your girlfriend again."

The table went quiet, and Jim felt heat creep up the back of his neck. Leave it to a six-year-old to say out loud what everyone else was thinking.

"Who wants dessert?" Olivia asked brightly, pushing back from the table. "I made apple pie."

The conversation shifted, and Jim gave his mother a look of gratitude. Around him, his family began the familiar ritual of clearing dishes. Sarah and Rebecca gathered plates. Anna collected silverware. Dave started consolidating the serving dishes. Jim rose to help, Boone padding along behind him as he carried the roast beef platter to the kitchen.

His mother was already at the counter, pulling out dessert plates, when he set the platter beside the sink. She glanced at him, then back at the plates.

"She's newly divorced, Jimmy." Olivia's voice was soft enough that only he could hear. "That's tender ground."

"I know."

"You went through it yourself. You remember what those first months were like."

Jim remembered all too well. The confusion, the self-doubt, and the way Amanda's words had echoed in his head for months afterward. *You and this little town will never be enough for me.* She had told him. He had rebuilt himself slowly, piece by piece, and he had come out the other side stronger. But the rebuilding had taken time.

"I'm not trying to rush anything," he said. "I just want to be there for her. The way people were there for me."

Olivia studied his face for a long moment, and Jim saw something shift in her expression. Understanding, maybe. Or acceptance.

"Your father was right," she said finally. "Grace is a good woman. And you're a good man. And you both have history together." She said as she patted his arm. "Just be careful with both your hearts."

Jim nodded, not trusting himself to speak.

Chapter 9

Jim eased the flatbed truck backward along the parking lot that ran beside the Mountain Laurel Inn, one hand on the steering wheel and the other resting on the back of the passenger seat as he watched the side mirrors. Boone sat beside him, ears perked forward, watching the scene unfold through the windshield with the focused attention of a dog who took his riding-along duties seriously.

The back of the inn came into view as Jim maneuvered the truck closer to where Sarah's crew was working. The old porch was completely gone now, nothing left but the exposed foundation and a skeleton of support beams waiting for the new structure. Sarah stood near the work area, directing two of her employees who were measuring and marking the ground.

Jim put the truck in park and killed the engine. Boone immediately pressed his nose against the window, eager to get out and investigate.

"Hold on," Jim told him. "Let me come around."

He climbed out of the cab and walked around to the passenger side, opening the door so Boone could hop down. The dog's nose went immediately to the ground, investigating the new smells with immense curiosity.

Sarah was already walking toward him, and Jim could see the questioning look in her eyes.

"Well, well." She stopped a few feet away, her arms crossed over her chest. "My big brother is making a delivery himself. That's not something you see every day."

"I had time. Figured I'd come out and see what's going on with the project." He kept his voice casual, already moving toward the back of the truck to start unstrapping the load. "How's it coming along?"

"It's coming." Sarah watched him work at the tie-downs for a moment. "You know my crew can unload this. You don't have to help."

"I know."

"So why are you here, really?"

Jim glanced at her, then back at the straps he was loosening. "Can't a guy deliver lumber to his sister's job site without getting the third degree?"

"A guy can. You can't." Sarah's smile was knowing, but she didn't push further. "Go on inside and say hi to Grace. We've got this."

Jim straightened, brushing his hands on his jeans. "I was planning to."

"I'm sure you were."

He chose not to respond to that. Instead, he whistled for Boone, who had wandered toward the exposed foundation, and started walking toward the front of the inn. The paved parking area ran alongside the building, and Jim followed it around the corner, Boone trotting beside him with his tail swinging.

Jim hadn't been inside this building since he and Grace had dated in high school. The wraparound porch showed its age now, the white paint peeling in places, but the bones of the building were still beautiful. The stone columns, the wide steps, and the original oak doors with their beveled glass panels.

Jim climbed the porch steps and stepped inside the inn through the open front doors, Boone at his heels.

He could hear the sounds of work coming from somewhere deeper in the building. The clatter of tools, the low murmur of voices, the occasional thud of something heavy being moved.

Grace stood on a stepladder near the far wall in the parlor, a scraper in her hand, working at something on the wall's surface. The floral wallpaper was gone, every bit of it stripped away, leaving bare walls that showed the evidence of years of adhesive.

Boone had no hesitation. He walked straight into the parlor and sat down at the base of the ladder, looking up at Grace with his tail thumping against the floor.

Grace glanced down, and Jim watched her face transform when she saw the dog. A smile spread across her features, genuine and surprised and pleased all at once. Then her gaze lifted and found Jim standing in the doorway, and her smile grew.

"Jim." She lowered the scraper, steadying herself on the ladder. "What are you doing here?"

"Lumber delivery. Sarah's crew is unloading it now." He stepped into the parlor, his eyes moving across the room as he took in the progress she'd made. The furniture had been pushed to the center and covered with drop cloths. The built-in bookcases flanking the fireplace were draped in plastic sheeting to protect them from dust. Every inch of wallpaper had been stripped away, leaving the walls bare and ready. "I figured I'd come inside and say hello while I was here."

"That was nice of you." Grace climbed down from the ladder, wiping her hands on the old jeans she was wearing. There was a smudge of something on her cheek, probably adhesive residue, and her hair was pulled back in a messy ponytail.

"You've been busy," Jim said, gesturing at the walls. "This room looks completely different from what I remember."

"Three days of scraping will do that." Grace bent down to scratch behind Boone's ears, and the dog leaned into her touch with obvious pleasure. "The glue residue from that old wallpaper has been a real challenge."

"Always is. The older the paper, the worse the adhesive."

"I'm learning that the hard way." She straightened and pushed a loose strand of hair behind her ear. "I was just about to take a break. Want some coffee?"

"Coffee sounds great."

Grace smiled and headed toward the back of the inn. Boone followed without being asked, his nails clicking on the hardwood floor. The sounds of construction grew louder as they passed the entrance to the kitchen, where Jim caught a glimpse of Tom Reeves directing his crew as they removed the old cabinets from the walls.

Grace's private quarters were through a door at the end of the hall, separate from the rest of the inn. She pushed it open and stepped inside, and Jim followed her into a small living room that looked like it had been frozen in time.

Boone had no hesitation about making himself at home. He walked straight to the couch, hopped up onto the cushions, and settled down with a contented sigh, his head resting on his paws.

"Boone." Jim started toward the couch, embarrassed. "Get down. That's not—"

"It's fine." Grace waved him off, already reaching for two mugs from the cabinet above the kitchenette counter. "Really. I don't mind. He looks comfortable."

"He looks like he owns the place."

Grace poured coffee into both mugs and handed one to Jim. "Cream? Sugar?"

"Black is fine."

She poured cream into her own cup and stirred it, then sat on one end of the couch. Jim took the other end of the couch, with Boone sprawled between them. The dog shifted slightly, inching closer to Grace's side of the cushions.

"So," Grace said, wrapping her hands around her mug. "What do you think? Of the inn, I mean. You haven't been here in a while."

Jim let his gaze travel around the room again, taking in the details. "It still feels like the Mountain Laurel. Like Ellie's place."

"That's what I'm trying to preserve. The feeling of it." Grace took a sip of her coffee. "The bones are good. It's just the cosmetics that need work. And the kitchen. And the bathrooms. And the electrical panel. And probably the plumbing."

"And this?" Jim gestured at the floral wallpaper and the mauve carpet.

Grace laughed. "This is bothering me more and more each day. Every time I walk in here, I just want to rip it all out. But the actual inn itself has to come first. I can worry about my personal space later."

"That makes sense. But it's important to like where you're living too. It helps a place feel more like home when you enjoy your surroundings."

Grace looked at him for a moment, something unreadable in her expression. "That's... a nice way to put it."

"I mean it. You're going to be working hard on this renovation. You deserve a space that feels like yours and makes you happy."

Boone shifted again, his nose now resting on the cushion mere inches from Grace's knee. She reached down absently and scratched behind his ears, and the dog's eyes closed in bliss.

"Aside from my personal space, I've been thinking about the main kitchen," Grace said, changing the subject. "And the bathrooms. I need new cabinets, new appliances, and new fixtures. Do you carry that kind of thing at the store?"

"Some of it. I've got a display area with fixtures for kitchens and bathrooms. For cabinetry, I carry catalogs from several manufacturers. I can place orders for anything you need."

"That's good to know." Grace's expression brightened. "I'd rather shop local if I can. Giving you the business would make me happy."

"I'd appreciate that." Jim took a sip of his coffee. "What look are you going for?"

"Warm. Cozy. Something that fits the style of the inn." Grace's eyes drifted toward the window, her mind clearly working through the possibilities. "The original kitchen was beautiful in its day, but it was designed for a different era. I want to modernize it without losing the character of the building, and it has to be efficient."

"That's doable. There are some great options that would work with the Craftsman style. Shaker cabinets, maybe. Simple lines, quality materials."

"I want simple... nothing flashy or too modern." Grace turned back to him. "Would it be okay if I came by the store tomorrow? To look at what you have and some catalogs?"

"Any time that works for you. I'm there most of the day."

"I'll plan on it then."

They talked for a while longer; the conversation flowing easily between them. Jim asked about the timeline for the kitchen renovation, and Grace explained what Tom had told her about the scope of work.

She asked about cabinet lead times, and Jim walked her through the ordering process. Boone dozed between them, occasionally lifting his head when one of them laughed.

Jim's phone buzzed in his pocket. He pulled it out and glanced at the screen.

Sarah: *Truck's unloaded. You can stop pretending you came just to deliver lumber now.*

He typed a quick response. *Thanks. Be there in a minute.*

"Everything okay?" Grace asked.

"That was Sarah. The truck's unloaded." Jim stood, and Boone lifted his head with a questioning look. "I should get back to the store."

"Of course." Grace rose from her chair and walked with him toward the door. "Thanks for stopping by. And for the delivery."

"Any time." Jim paused in the doorway and whistled for Boone. The dog didn't move. He lay on the couch, looking at Jim with an expression that clearly said he had no intention of going anywhere.

"Boone. Come."

Nothing.

Grace laughed. "I think he likes it here."

Jim looked at his dog, then at Grace, then back at Boone. "Can't really blame him."

The words hung in the air for just a moment, and Jim watched Grace's expression flicker with something he couldn't quite name. Then she smiled, and the moment passed.

"Boone," Jim said again, his voice firmer this time. "Let's go."

The dog finally rose, stretching elaborately before hopping down from the couch and padding toward the door. He paused beside Grace and looked up at her, tail wagging slowly.

"I'll see you tomorrow," Grace said, reaching down to give Boone one final pat.

"Tomorrow," Jim agreed.

He walked out of her living room with Boone at his side, but he could feel Grace watching from the doorway.

Chapter 10

Grace stood at the counter in the back corner of Hartwell Hardware, Tom's handwritten list spread out beside a thick catalog of cabinet options, and tried to focus on the task at hand instead of the man standing next to her.

Jim had been patient for the past forty-five minutes. More than patient. He had walked her through three different catalogs, pulled up manufacturer websites on the computer set up at the end of the counter, and answered every question she asked without a hint of impatience or condescension. He treated each question as if it mattered, like her opinions mattered, and like this decision was worth taking seriously.

Lee would have handled this differently. The thought arrived out of nowhere, and it shocked her. Lee would have been checking his phone by now. Lee would have told her which cabinets to choose and then acted annoyed when she wanted to look at other options. Lee would have made her feel like she was wasting his time, even when he was supposed to be helping her.

Jim just waited. He let her think. He pointed out details she might have missed and then stepped back to let her process.

"What about this one?" Jim turned the catalog toward her, his finger resting on a page she hadn't seen yet. "Shaker style, solid oak, natural finish. Simple lines, but the craftsmanship is excellent. It would fit the Craftsman character of the inn."

Grace leaned closer to study the image. The cabinets were undoubtedly what she had been trying to describe but couldn't quite articulate. Clean and classic. Warm without being fussy. The kind of cabinets that would look like they had always belonged in the Mountain Laurel Inn, even though they were brand new.

"Yes." She reached out without thinking and put her hand on Jim's arm, her fingers pressing against the fabric of his sleeve. "Jim, these are perfect. This is exactly what I've been looking for."

She felt him go still beneath her touch, and suddenly she was aware of what she had done. Her hand was on his arm. The warmth of him through the cotton. The way he was looking at her with an expression she couldn't quite read.

Grace pulled her hand back and tucked it against her side, heat rising to her cheeks.

"Sorry," she said quickly. "I just got excited. Those cabinets are exactly right."

"Don't apologize." Jim's voice was easy, casual, as if nothing unusual had happened. But there was something in his eyes, a flicker of warmth, that made Grace look away. "I'm glad you found what you wanted. Let me get the order form, and we can figure out quantities."

He moved to the other end of the counter to retrieve a clipboard, and Grace let out a deep breath. What was wrong with her? She didn't go around touching people. She had spent the past year learning to keep her distance, to protect herself, and to trust no one but herself.

And here she was, grabbing Jim's arm in the middle of his hardware store like they were still seventeen years old.

A cold nose pressed against her hand, and Grace looked down to find Boone gazing up at her with those soulful brown eyes. He had been lying quietly on the floor near the cabinet displays for most of their conversation, but apparently he had decided he'd been patient long enough. His tail swept across the floor in a slow wag, and he nudged her hand again, more insistently this time.

"Hey, you." Grace crouched down and scratched behind his ears, grateful for the distraction. "Feeling left out?"

Boone's tail picked up speed. He leaned into her touch, his eyes half-closing with pleasure. There was something uncomplicated about a dog's affection. No hidden agendas. No second-guessing. Just a pure and simple choice of wanting to be close.

"He's been watching you this whole time," Jim said, returning with the clipboard. "Every time you moved to look at something different, his head followed you."

"He's sweet."

"He's spoiled." But Jim was smiling as he said it, and Grace noticed the way his entire face changed when he looked at his dog. Softer. More open. The kind of smile that came from somewhere real.

She straightened up and turned her attention back to the catalog, but she could still feel the lingering warmth where her hand had touched his arm. Could still see that flicker in his eyes when she had reached for him.

Stop it, she told herself firmly. *He's being helpful. That's all this is.*

They worked through Tom's list together, counting upper and lower cabinets, corner units, and drawer bases. The kitchen at the Mountain Laurel Inn was substantial, designed for an era when inns served full breakfasts to a dozen guests and needed storage for everything from cast iron skillets to china serving pieces. By the time they finished tallying the order, two pages of the order form had been filled with quantities and measurements.

"This will be a big order," Jim said, reviewing the numbers. "Lead time is usually three to four weeks for this manufacturer. But I can put a rush on it if you need it sooner."

"Three weeks should work. Tom said the plumbing and electrical need to be finished before the cabinets go in anyway." Grace signed the bottom of the order form and set down the pen. "Thank you for taking so much time with this. I know you have other customers."

"Tuck's handling the front. I told him I'd be back here for a while." Jim tucked the order form into the clipboard. "Ready to look at fixtures?"

They walked together toward the front of the store, where a large display wall showcased kitchen and bathroom fixtures in various styles and finishes. Grace had passed this section when she came in, but she hadn't stopped to look closely. Now she took her time, studying the options while Jim explained the differences between manufacturers and price points.

He knew his inventory inside and out. Every question she asked, he had an answer. Not the rehearsed patter of a salesman trying to close a deal, but the genuine knowledge of someone who understood his products and wanted his customers to make informed decisions. He pointed out which brands had the best warranties, which finishes held up longest, and which styles would complement the cabinets she had chosen.

Lee had never cared about details like this. Lee cared about appearances, about what things looked like to other people, and about whether a choice made him seem successful or sophisticated or important. He would have steered her toward the most expensive option without bothering to explain why.

Jim was showing her a mid-range faucet with a lifetime warranty and excellent reviews. "This one's my personal recommendation," he said. "I have the same model in my kitchen. Three years, no problems, and it's used every day."

"You cook?"

The question slipped out before Grace could stop it, and she immediately felt foolish. Of course, he cooked. Everyone cooked. Why had she asked it as if it were surprising?

But Jim just smiled. "Enough to keep myself fed. Nothing fancy. My mom tried to teach all of us the basics, and some of it stuck." He paused. "Why? You seem surprised."

"I don't know. I guess I just..." She trailed off, not sure how to finish the sentence. Lee had never cooked. Lee had considered the kitchen her domain, her responsibility, even when they both worked full-time. The idea of a man who had learned to cook because his mother taught him, all of it felt foreign and familiar at the same time.

"I'm not surprised," she said finally. "I'm just... it's nice. That's all."

Jim held her gaze for a moment, and Grace felt that flutter again, the one she kept trying to ignore. Then Boone appeared between them, wedging himself against Grace's legs with determined affection.

"Boone." Jim's voice carried a note of exasperation. "Give her some space."

"I don't mind." Grace reached down to pat Boone's head, and the dog's tail wagged so hard his whole body moved with it. "I think he's decided we're friends."

"He's decided something, that's for sure."

They moved on to bathroom fixtures, and Grace pulled out the second list Tom had prepared. Twelve bathrooms total. Two on the first floor, seven on the second, and three on the third. Each one needed faucets for the sink, hardware for the shower and tub, and various other pieces that Tom had specified in his careful handwriting.

"So many choices... this is gonna be tough." The words came out quietly, almost to herself, as she studied the list and then looked up at the display wall in front of her.

"You've got this; take your time and make sure you get exactly what you want," Jim said simply.

Grace looked up at him. He wasn't watching her with pity. He wasn't uncomfortable. He was just standing there, patient and steady, waiting for her to tell him what she wanted.

Something loosened in her chest. A knot she had been carrying for so long that she had forgotten it was there. She didn't have words for what she was feeling, couldn't have named it if someone asked, but she knew it was something like relief. Like being trusted to know her own mind.

"Okay. Let's do this."

They worked through the bathroom list methodically, Grace making decisions and Jim writing them down. She chose brushed nickel for all the fixtures, a classic choice that would work with multiple design directions. Jim showed her options on the computer when the display didn't have exactly what she was looking for, and twice he suggested alternatives that were better quality at the same price point.

By the time they finished, Grace had spent more than three hours in Hartwell Hardware. Her feet ached from standing, and she had made more decisions than she cared to count. Her mind was spinning from the experience.

"I'll get all of this ordered today," Jim said, gathering the paperwork. "The fixtures should arrive within a week. The cabinets will take longer, but I'll call you as soon as they come in."

"Thank you, Jim. Really." Grace meant it more than she could express. "This would have taken me forever on my own. And I probably would have made at least three wrong decisions."

"You wouldn't have. You know what you want. You just needed someone to show you the options."

He said it like it was obvious. Like he had complete faith in her ability to make good choices. Like her judgment was something to be trusted, not questioned.

They walked toward the front of the store together, Boone trotting alongside Grace as if he belonged there. Jim held the door open for her, and she stepped out onto Main Street, blinking in the afternoon sunlight.

"I'll see you soon," Jim said. "Call me if you have any questions about the orders."

"I will."

Grace walked to her SUV and climbed inside, but she didn't start the engine right away. She sat there for a moment, her hands resting on the steering wheel, replaying the afternoon in her mind. The cabinets. The fixtures. The way Jim had listened to her, really listened, like what she had to say mattered.

She caught her reflection in the rearview mirror and realized she was smiling. A real smile, not the polite one she had been wearing like armor for the past year. She looked lighter. Younger. More like the confident woman she had been before Lee had made her doubt everything about herself.

Jim Hartwell was a good man. She'd always known that, even when they were teenagers sneaking into old theaters and holding hands in the dark. He was steady and kind and patient, and he made her feel like she could trust her judgment and decisions again.

Grace started the car and glanced up to see Jim still standing in the doorway of the hardware store, Boone at his side.

She waved and backed out of the parking spot.

Chapter 11

Boone was gone.

Jim stood in the middle of Hartwell's Hardware with a box of replacement drawer pulls in his hands and an empty space where his dog should have been. No soulful brown eyes watching everything. No tail thumping against the floor when a regular customer walked in.

Jim set down the drawer pulls and checked the back storage room. Nothing but stacked boxes of inventory. He checked his office. No Boone. He walked back to the front of the store, to the sunny patch by the front window where Boone liked to nap on slow afternoons. Empty. He walked the width of the store, glancing down each aisle. No Boone in sight.

"Tuck." Jim kept his voice calm, but something uncomfortable had started to twist in his gut. "Have you seen Boone?"

Tuck looked up from the register where he was helping Mrs. Carter with a bag of birdseed. "Not in the last thirty minutes or so. He was by the door earlier. Why?"

"He's not here."

"What do you mean he's not here? He's always here."

That was the problem. Boone had spent four years at Jim's side. He came to work every morning, greeted customers, supervised the aisles, and went home with Jim every night. He didn't hide; he enjoyed being in the middle of all activity. He didn't wander. He didn't run off. He was the most reliable presence in Jim's life, more predictable than the weather and twice as loyal.

Jim walked to the front door and pushed it open, scanning Main Street in both directions. The April afternoon was mild and bright, the kind of day that brought people out of their homes and into the shops along the square. He spotted Phyllis, one of his sister's employees, in front of the Fluff & Curl Beauty Shop, sweeping the sidewalk. A couple of teenagers on bicycles. Several people were window shopping along with others leisurely strolling in front of businesses.

No Boone.

Jim's mind cycled through possibilities. Someone had left the door open too long. A customer had come in, and Boone had slipped out behind them. But even that didn't make sense. Boone had never shown any interest in escaping. He liked being in the hardware store. He liked greeting people. He liked being exactly where Jim was.

Jim stepped out onto the sidewalk, ready to start a search, and that's when he saw them.

Grace was walking toward him from the direction of Cedar Street, and trotting happily beside her, tail swinging like a metronome set to "completely satisfied with himself," was Boone.

The dog spotted Jim and picked up his pace slightly, but he didn't look guilty. He looked pleased. Proud, even. Like he had accomplished something important and expected to be congratulated for it.

Jim met them halfway down the block. "Boone. What in the world?"

Grace was trying very hard not to laugh. He could see the effort it was costing her, the way her lips pressed together and her eyes sparkled with barely contained amusement.

"I believe this belongs to you," she said.

"I am so sorry," Jim crouched down to Boone's level, looking his dog in the eye. Boone gazed back at him with an expression of complete innocence. "He's never done anything like this before. I have no idea how he even got out."

"He showed up at the inn a little while ago. I had my front door open for fresh air. I went into my private quarters to get a cup of coffee, and there he was on my couch."

Jim stared at his dog. "Your couch."

"My couch. Head on a throw pillow and everything."

Boone's tail thumped against the sidewalk. No shame. No remorse. Just the quiet satisfaction of a dog who had done exactly what he intended to do.

"I don't know what to say." Jim straightened up, shaking his head. "I'm mortified. He's never wandered off before. Not once in four years."

"Don't be mortified. He was a perfect gentleman." Grace reached down and scratched behind Boone's ears, and the dog leaned into her touch with obvious pleasure. "A little presumptuous, maybe. But sweet."

"Presumptuous is one word for it." Jim looked at Boone, who was now gazing up at Grace like she hung the moon and stars. "I think he's decided you're his new favorite person."

"Well, I'm flattered." Grace gave Boone one more pat and straightened. "Tom and his men said they saw him walk straight into my living area like he owned the place."

"Seriously?"

"That's what Tom said. Boone walked in and completely ignored them when they tried to get his attention... like they weren't even there. Very dignified about it, too. Didn't break stride."

Jim laughed and shook his head. Grace was watching him with that almost-smile still playing at the corners of her mouth, and the afternoon felt suddenly lighter than it had a few minutes ago.

"How's the renovation going?" he asked. "Besides unexpected canine visitors."

"Chaotic. Dusty. Loud." Grace tucked a loose strand of hair behind her ear. "But we're making progress. It's satisfying in a destructive sort of way."

"There's something therapeutic about demolition."

"That's exactly what Tom said." She glanced back toward Cedar Street, then at him again. "I should probably get back. They're waiting on a decision about bathroom tile, and I've been putting it off for two days because I can't decide between three options that all look exactly the same to me."

Jim saw his window. It was small, but it was there. "Can I buy you a cup of coffee? As an apology for my dog's home invasion. Later this afternoon, maybe?" He nodded toward the coffee shop on the corner of Main Street.

Grace hesitated. He watched the yes form on her lips, saw it in the way her posture shifted slightly toward him, and the brief softening in her expression.

Then something changed. A door closing behind her eyes. The softening disappeared, replaced by something more guarded.

"I really shouldn't," she said. "I have a million things to do."

"Of course." Jim nodded, keeping his expression easy and his tone light. No disappointment. No pressure. "Another time, then."

He meant it. He could see that she was protecting something, that the walls she'd built weren't coming down just because his dog had decided to adopt her. And he had apparently gained an ally in Boone, who was looking between the two of them now with an expression that Jim would swear was disappointment.

I brought her right to you, those soulful eyes seemed to say. *What more do you want from me?*

Grace noticed the look. "I think your dog is judging us."

"He does that. He has opinions about everything."

She laughed, and the sound of it did something warm to Jim's chest. "Well. Thank you for not being weird about me bringing him back. Some people would have been embarrassed."

"Oh, I'm embarrassed," Jim said. "I'm just hiding it well."

Another laugh. Lighter this time, more relaxed. She was charming when she laughed, all the careful composure dropping away to reveal something brighter underneath.

"I'll see you around, Jim." She turned to go, then paused and looked back at him. "And Boone? Next time you want to visit, maybe let me know you've arrived so you don't startle me."

Boone's tail wagged once, slowly, as if he was considering her suggestion and finding it unworthy of serious attention.

Jim watched her walk back toward Cedar Street, her ponytail swinging with each step. Boone sat down heavily beside him and let out a long, theatrical sigh.

"Don't look at me like that," Jim told him. "You're the one who escaped and invaded her house."

Boone turned his head and gazed up at Jim with an expression that managed to convey both affection and mild exasperation.

She said no to coffee, the look seemed to say. *That's on you, not me. I did my part.*

Jim reached down and rubbed Boone's ears. "Come on. Back to work."

They walked together toward the hardware store, Boone's nails clicking on the sidewalk. At the door, Jim paused and looked back toward Cedar Street one more time.

Grace had already disappeared around the corner.

Boone nudged his leg impatiently.

"Yeah, yeah." Jim pulled open the door and let his dog go in first.

Chapter 12

The Daily Grind smelled like fresh-brewed coffee and cinnamon, and the moment Grace stepped through the door, she relaxed. The coffee shop occupied a corner spot on Main Street, warm and welcoming in a way that had nothing to do with the decor and everything to do with the atmosphere. Comfortable seating was arranged in clusters throughout the space, inviting people to linger rather than grab and go. A handful of customers occupied various spots: an older man reading a newspaper near the window, two women deep in conversation at a table by the wall, and a younger guy with a laptop and earbuds taking up residence in a corner booth. The morning rush had passed, leaving behind the quieter energy of mid-morning regulars.

Grace spotted Molly at a corner table near the back, and fourteen years collapsed in an instant.

Molly Brennan looked the same but different. Older, yes, with fine lines around her eyes that hadn't been there at eighteen. But still bright-eyed, still smiling like she meant it, still radiating that particular warmth that had made her Grace's closest friend all through childhood and high school. She stood the moment she saw Grace, and the hug she pulled her into was fierce and familiar.

"I'm so glad you moved back home," Molly said into Grace's shoulder.

"Me too."

They settled into their seats, and Molly pushed a coffee cup toward Grace. "I ordered for you. Vanilla latte with an extra shot. That's still your drink, right?"

Grace laughed. "Well... I don't drink it as much as I used to, but I still do love it occasionally."

Molly wrapped her hands around her own cup and smiled. "I have to admit, when I saw you at church on Easter, I almost tackled you right there in the sanctuary. Tuck had to physically restrain me."

"I saw you mouth 'Call me.' I wanted to come find you after the service, but..." Grace trailed off, not sure how to explain why she'd gone to lunch with Jim instead of staying for fellowship.

"But you had a lunch date with Jim Hartwell." Molly's eyes sparkled. "Tuck told me."

Of course he had. Grace felt heat creep into her cheeks. "It wasn't a date. We just caught up. Old friends."

"Mmhmm." Molly's expression said she wasn't buying it, but she let it go. "Anyway, I'm glad you texted. I've missed you, Grace. I really have."

"I've missed you too." Grace took a sip of her latte. "I'm sorry we lost touch. I didn't mean for that to happen."

"Life gets busy. You were building a career, I was having babies, and somehow the years just slipped away." Molly shrugged, but there was no accusation in her voice. "What matters is you're here now."

Grace nodded, grateful for the grace in that statement. She had been terrible at keeping in touch. Christmas cards that arrived late or not at all. Birthday texts she meant to send and then forgot. The distance between Atlanta and Serenity Crossing had felt like more than miles sometimes. It had felt like a different world entirely.

"So tell me everything," Molly said, leaning forward. "What's going on with the inn? Tuck says there's a whole army of contractors over there tearing things apart."

"It feels that way some days." Grace smiled despite herself. "The kitchen is completely gutted. Sarah Hartwell's crew is rebuilding the back porch and installing a gazebo for me. Tom Reeves is handling most of the interior work. It's chaos, but it's the good kind of chaos."

"And you're planning to open by the Heritage Festival, I heard?"

"That's the goal. Twelve weeks from when I started. Well, eleven now." Grace wrapped her hands around her cup. "It's ambitious. Maybe too ambitious. But I need a deadline, or I'll just keep finding things to fix forever."

"That sounds like you. You always did need a goal to chase." Molly studied her for a moment. "How are you really doing, though? Not the inn. You."

The question landed somewhere tender. Grace had been asked versions of it by her mother, her sisters, and various well-meaning relatives since she'd arrived. But there was something about the way Molly asked it that made deflection feel impossible.

"I'm okay," Grace said slowly. "Better than I expected to be, honestly. The divorce was final a month ago, but the marriage was over long before that. I filed over a year ago. So I've had time to process everything."

"That doesn't mean it doesn't still hurt."

"No," Grace looked down at her coffee. "It doesn't."

Molly waited, giving her space to say more or not. That was some-thing Grace had always loved about her. Molly knew how to hold silence without making it awkward.

"The hardest part isn't missing Lee," Grace said finally. "I don't miss him. I'm not sure I even really knew him, not the real him. The hardest part is not trusting myself anymore." She looked up at Molly. "I'm an architect. I'm trained to notice details, to see what other people miss. And I spent two years married to a man who was lying to me constantly, and I didn't see any of it. Everyone else saw it. I was the last to know."

"That's not your fault."

"Isn't it? I should have seen the signs. I should have trusted my instincts when something felt off instead of convincing myself I was being paranoid."

Molly reached across the table and covered Grace's hand with her own. "You didn't see it because he was hiding it. That's on him, not you. You can't blame yourself for trusting your husband."

"I know. Logically, I know that." Grace pulled in a breath. "But it's hard to trust my judgment about anything now. About the inn, about my decisions, about... moving forward. I question everything..." She stopped herself.

"About Jim?" Molly finished gently.

Grace felt her face flush again. "We're just friends."

"Okay." Molly withdrew her hand and picked up her coffee, but her expression remained knowing. "So tell me about being friends with Jim."

"There's nothing to tell. He's been helpful with the renovation. He recommended Sarah and Tom. He helped me pick out cabinets and fixtures a few days ago." Grace heard herself and winced. "That sounds like a lot when I say it out loud."

"It sounds like a man who's finding reasons to spend time with you."

"He's being nice. That's just who Jim is."

"Yes, it is." Molly nodded. "Jim Hartwell is one of the genuinely good ones. Tuck has been his best friend since they were six years old. I've known Jim almost as long as I've known Tuck. He's steady. He's kind. He doesn't play games. He's a gentleman,"

"I know." Grace stared at her cup. "That's what makes it complicated."

"Why complicated?"

"Because I like him... still after all this time." The admission came out before Grace could stop it. "More than I should for a newly divorced woman. And I don't trust myself to know if what I'm feeling is real or if I'm just latching onto the first decent man who's been nice to me since my marriage fell apart."

Molly was quiet for a moment. "Can I tell you something?"

"Please."

"The fact that you're asking yourself those questions means you're not just latching on blindly. You're being thoughtful. You're being careful." Molly leaned forward. "And for what it's worth, you said it yourself... your marriage had been over for some time, so the fact that you're 'newly divorced,' as you said, is irrelevant. Sure, you may have just signed your name on the divorce papers, but in reality, your marriage was over long ago."

Grace didn't have an answer for that.

They sat in silence for a moment, and Grace found her thoughts drifting to Easter Sunday. The church had felt both familiar and strange. She had grown up in those pews, sung those hymns, and listened to sermons every week of her childhood. But somewhere along the way, she had let that part of herself slip away.

"Can I ask you something?" Grace said.

"Anything."

"Do you still go to church every Sunday? You and Tuck?"

"We do. The boys are in Sunday school now, which is an adventure." Molly smiled. "Why do you ask?"

Grace hesitated. "I stopped going regularly. It wasn't a conscious decision at first; it just happened. It started when I was in college and became a habit from there. I just got busy with life. With my career in Atlanta, and then later, Lee never wanted to go, and it was easier to sleep in on Sundays." She traced the rim of her cup. "Being back here, sitting in that sanctuary on Easter, it felt like something I'd lost without realizing it was gone."

"That happens to a lot of people. Life pulls you away, and faith gets put on a shelf." Molly's voice held no judgment. "The good news is, it's always there when you're ready. You don't have to figure it out all at once. Just show up. That's what faith is most of the time, anyway. Just showing up, even when you're not sure about anything in life anymore. Listen, we've all struggled with faith; you're not alone." Molly reached for her hand again. "And if you want company, I'm there every Sunday. Third pew on the left. Come sit with us if you want."

"Thank you."

"That's what friends are for." Molly squeezed her hand and released it. "Now. Tell me more about the inn and all you have planned."

Grace laughed, and the conversation shifted to lighter things. Cabinet hardware and paint colors and the ongoing saga of the plumbing that may or may not need to be replaced. Molly listened with genuine interest, asked good questions, and made Grace feel like her renovation plans were exciting rather than overwhelming.

By the time their coffee cups were empty, an hour had passed without Grace noticing.

"We need to do this again," Molly said as they gathered their things. "Regularly. I'm claiming you as my coffee date every week."

"I'd like that."

They hugged again at the door, and Molly held on for an extra moment. "You're going to be okay, Grace. Better than okay. I can see it in you. Trust your instincts, my friend, and trust in God and what he has planned for you."

Chapter 13

The Mountain Laurel Inn looked like a construction zone had exploded across its front porch.

Jim spotted the mess from half a block away as he and Boone made their way down Cedar Street. Sawhorses. Stacked lumber. A fine layer of dust coated the porch railings. And there, sitting on the top step with her head in her hands, was Grace.

He had told himself he was just out for a walk. Saturday morning, beautiful weather, no reason to spend the whole day inside the hardware store when Tuck and his other employees could handle things perfectly well on their own. The fact that his walk had taken him in the direction of Cedar Street was purely coincidental.

Grace looked up as they approached, and Jim could see the dark circles under her eyes. Hair escaping from her ponytail in a dozen different directions. Dust on her cheek and her shirt and probably places she hadn't discovered yet. She looked exhausted in a way that went deeper than physical tiredness.

"Hey," she said, and even her voice sounded worn thin.

"Hey yourself." Jim stopped at the bottom of the porch steps while Boone immediately climbed up to greet her, tail wagging. "Rough morning?"

Grace let out a sound that was halfway between a laugh and a groan. "The crew hit an unexpected problem with the electrical. Tom's in there now trying to figure out how bad it is. Meanwhile, Sarah's team is doing something loud on the back porch, and I think I'll be breathing sawdust and other debris for the rest of my life."

"So you came out here to escape."

"I came out here because if I didn't get five minutes of peace, I was going to lose my mind." She scratched behind Boone's ears, and the dog settled beside her like he belonged there. "What brings you to this side of town?"

Jim could have made up an excuse. Could have said he was running an errand or checking on something for a customer. Instead, he told the truth. "Nice day. Felt like a walk. Boone agreed, and well, here we are."

Grace glanced down at Boone, who was now resting his head on her knee. "He seems to have strong opinions about where your walks should take you."

"He's developed those recently." Jim climbed the first two steps and leaned against the porch railing, putting himself closer to her level. "When's the last time you took an actual break? Not five minutes on the porch. A real break."

Grace opened her mouth, closed it, and frowned.

"That's what I thought." He held out his hand. "Come walk with me. Get away from all of this for an hour. The sawdust will still be here when you get back."

She hesitated. He could see her mind working through all the reasons she should say no. The electrical problem. The contractors were waiting for decisions. The endless list of things that needed her attention.

Then she looked at Boone, who was gazing up at her with those soulful brown eyes, and something in her expression shifted.

"One hour," she said, and took his hand.

Her fingers were warm against his palm. Jim helped her to her feet and let go before the contact could become something he'd have to think about too carefully. Boone jumped up, tail wagging with enthusiasm, clearly pleased that his humans had finally made the right decision.

They walked east on Cedar Street toward Main, the sounds of construction fading behind them with every step. The April afternoon was warm without being hot, the kind of day that made people remember why they loved living in the mountains. Sunlight filtered through the trees lining the street, and somewhere nearby a cardinal was singing.

"I forget sometimes," Grace said as they walked, "how pretty this town is. In Atlanta, everything was concrete and glass and traffic noise. Here, you can actually hear birds."

"That's one thing that hasn't changed. The birds, I mean, and the peace and quiet. The town's grown some since you left, but it's still pretty much the same place."

They reached Main Street and turned left, following the sidewalk that ran along the east side of the town square. The white gazebo sat at the center of the green space, and a few families had spread blankets on the grass for picnics. An older couple sat on one of the benches, feeding pigeons from a paper bag.

"Mr. and Mrs. Holloway," Jim said, nodding toward the couple. "They've been feeding pigeons and the other birds every Saturday for as long as I can remember."

"I think they were doing that when I was in high school," Grace said. "Some things really don't change."

They walked past Heritage House Antiques, where a new display of vintage furniture filled the front window. Grace slowed to look, her eyes moving over the pieces with interest.

"See something you like?"

"That sideboard." She pointed to a carved oak piece near the back of the display. "It would be perfect for the dining room at the inn. If I had an unlimited decorating budget, which I definitely don't."

"Margaret gives good deals to locals. You should ask her."

Grace made a noncommittal sound, and Jim watched as she took a photo of the sideboard with her phone before they moved on.

Boone trotted between them, occasionally veering off to sniff something interesting before returning to his spot. He seemed content in a way that Jim recognized. This was Boone at his happiest: outside, walking, with his favorite people nearby.

Both of them. His favorite people.

Jim didn't examine that thought too closely.

They passed The Book Nook, where Miranda McKenna, Grace's sister, was arranging a display of new releases in the window. She spotted them through the glass and waved enthusiastically. Grace waved back, and Jim caught the small smile that crossed her face.

"Miranda's doing well with the shop," Grace said. "Mom says she's turned it into a real gathering place. Book clubs, author events, that sort of thing."

"She has. Rebecca drags me to the mystery book club sometimes. I'm usually the only man there, which Rebecca finds hilarious."

Grace laughed. "Rebecca would."

They continued around the square, passing Hawthorne Mercantile and The Daily Grind, where a few customers sat at the outdoor tables enjoying the weather. Jim nodded to people he knew, which was most of them. Mrs. Carlisle from the dry cleaner. Pastor Davis walking toward the bakery with his wife. Danny Whitfield, Minnie's grandson who worked part-time at the hardware store, was heading somewhere with his earbuds in and his head bobbing to music no one else could hear.

"Everyone knows you," Grace observed.

"Small town. Everyone knows everyone. You must have forgotten about that."

"They know you differently, though. The way they look at you." She paused, seeming to search for the right words. "It's like everyone in this town is one big happy family... I really have forgotten what it's like to live in a small, close-knit community."

Jim wasn't sure how to respond to that. He'd never thought about it in those terms. He just lived here, worked here, and tried to be helpful when he could.

"I guess you're right; we are sort of one big family. Everyone knows everyone else," he said finally.

They had reached the south side of the square, where Oak Street branched off toward the quieter part of downtown. Jim steered them in that direction without really thinking about it, and it wasn't until they turned onto Beech Street that he realized where his feet had taken them.

The Granville Theater sat halfway down the block, its old marquee dark and its windows covered with paper announcing the restoration project that had been "coming soon" for the past three years. The building itself was beautiful, an Art déco gem from the 1930s that had been the center of Serenity Crossing's social life for decades before the multiplexes in Pigeon Forge and Gatlinburg drew audiences away.

Grace stopped walking. "The Granville."

She stood there studying the building, and Jim watched her expression shift into something more focused. More professional. The architect in her was taking over, her eyes tracing the lines of the facade, the decorative molding above the entrance, the geometric patterns etched into the stonework.

"What a shame," she said quietly. "A building like this, just sitting here. Do you know how rare original Art déco architecture is? Most of it got torn down in the sixties and seventies when everyone decided modern was better."

"It's been empty for years now. Every once in a while someone talks about doing something with it, but nothing ever happens."

Grace tilted her head, still examining the details. "The bones are incredible. Look at those window frames. And the marquee, even faded like that, you can tell how beautiful it was."

"What would you do with it?" Jim asked. "If you bought it?"

She laughed, but her eyes stayed on the building. "Probably exactly what it was meant to be. Fix it up, restore all the original details, and reopen it as a theater. Maybe add some modern touches behind the scenes, better sound system, comfortable seating, but keep everything visible exactly as it was." She shook her head slowly. "Buildings like this tell stories, Jim. They're part of a town's history. You can't replace that with something new."

"I've heard through the grapevine there's been some interest lately. Some company from out of state, supposedly. But so far, nothing's come of it."

"An outside company?" Grace wrinkled her nose. "They'd probably gut it and turn it into condos or a chain restaurant."

"Probably."

She turned to look at him then, and the professional focus in her eyes softened into something warmer. "This town deserves better than that. Serenity Crossing deserves people who understand what makes it special."

Jim held her gaze, struck by the certainty in her voice. Standing here on this quiet street with the afternoon light turning golden around them, watching Grace talk about preserving something beautiful because it mattered, Jim knew she belonged here. She had always belonged here; she just had to figure it out in her own time.

He had known what he wanted when he was eighteen years old as well. He had let her go then because she needed to chase her dreams, and he had no right to hold her back. But she was here now, and he wasn't a man who made the same mistake twice.

They walked back toward Main Street without needing to fill the air with conversation, Boone padding along between them. Grace looked more relaxed than she had when they'd started their walk. The tension had eased from her shoulders. The worry lines had smoothed from her forehead.

Jim made a decision and stopped walking.

"Have dinner with me tonight."

Grace's steps faltered. She turned to look at him, and he could see the question forming in her eyes before she asked it.

"The 1887 Room," he added. "Seven o'clock."

This wasn't coffee at Minnie's. This wasn't a casual lunch between old friends. The 1887 Room had white tablecloths and candlelight and was the kind of place you took someone when you wanted them to know you were serious, they were special, and you wanted to spend time with them.

Grace knew it. Jim could see in her face that she knew exactly what he was asking.

She was quiet for a long moment. Long enough that Jim felt his chest tighten, felt the first whisper of doubt creep in. Maybe he'd misread things. Maybe she wasn't ready. Maybe he'd pushed too hard, too fast, and now—

"Okay," Grace said. "Yes."

Two words. Just two small words.

Jim had never heard anything better in his life.

Chapter 14

The woman in the mirror looked like someone Grace used to know.

She stood in the small bathroom of the innkeeper's quarters, studying her reflection with a critical eye. The navy-blue dress she'd chosen was simple but elegant, with a fitted bodice and a skirt that fell just below her knees. She'd bought it in Atlanta two years ago for a company event and had worn it exactly once before it disappeared into the back of her closet. Tonight, she'd pulled it out on instinct, and when she'd slipped it on, she felt like a new woman—feminine.

She looked good. Not just acceptable, not just presentable, but genuinely good. The dress hugged her curves in all the right places. The color brought out the green in her eyes. Her hair fell in soft waves past her shoulders, and the simple gold earrings she'd chosen caught the light when she moved.

For the first time in months, Grace felt like herself again. Not Lee's wife. Not Lee's ex-wife. Not the woman who had been too blind to see the truth in front of her face. Just Grace. A woman getting ready for a dinner date with a man who made her laugh and didn't make her feel small.

She applied a final touch of lipstick and stepped back to take in the full picture. The woman in the mirror smiled back at her, and Grace realized with a start that the smile was real. Not the polite mask she'd worn for so long, but genuine anticipation for what the evening might hold.

A knock sounded at the front door of the inn.

Grace grabbed her clutch from the bed and walked through the parlor to the main entrance. Through the beveled glass panels, she could see Jim's silhouette on the porch. She took a breath, smoothed her dress one final time, and opened the door.

Jim stood on the threshold in a charcoal gray suit that fit him like it had been tailored specifically for his broad shoulders. A deep burgundy tie added a splash of color against the crisp white of his dress shirt, and his dark hair was neatly combed in a way that made him look distinguished without seeming stuffy. He'd even shined his shoes, she noticed. The effort touched her more than it should have.

But it was the expression on his face that made her breath catch. He was looking at her like she was something extraordinary, something worth taking time to appreciate. Not with hunger or possession, but with genuine admiration.

"Grace." Her name came out like a breath. "You look beautiful."

"Thank you." She felt warmth rise to her cheeks and didn't try to hide it. "You clean up pretty well yourself."

Jim smiled, and the nervousness she'd glimpsed in his eyes softened into something warmer. "Ready?"

"I am."

She stepped onto the porch and pulled the door closed behind her, checking to make sure it locked. The evening air was cool but pleasant, carrying the faint sounds of the town settling into its Saturday night rhythm. Music drifted from somewhere in the distance, and the streetlights had begun to flicker on along Cedar Street.

They walked side by side down the porch steps and onto the sidewalk, passing the darkened windows of the Mountain Light Studio. The photography studio was closed for the evening, its window displays showcasing portraits of local families and scenic mountain landscapes. Grace had walked past it a dozen times since moving into the inn, but tonight she barely noticed it. Her attention was fixed on the man beside her and the way her pulse quickened with each step.

"I made reservations for us," Jim said. "Hopefully we shouldn't have to wait too long to be seated. I'm definitely hungry."

"I forgot to eat lunch, so I'm starving."

Jim gave her a look of mild concern. "You forgot to eat lunch?"

"The electrical situation sort of took over everything else."

"We'll have to fix that. The forgetting to eat part, I mean. Not the electrical situation. Although I could probably help with that too, if it comes to that."

Grace laughed. "I might take you up on that. Tom looked pretty grim this evening when he finished up for the day."

They reached the corner and paused at the edge of the street. The 1887 Room occupied a stately brick building on the opposite side of Cedar, its windows glowing with soft golden light. Even from here, Grace could see the elegant simplicity of the restaurant's exterior, the careful restoration that had preserved its historic character while making it feel warm and inviting.

Jim offered his arm. "Shall we?"

Grace slipped her hand into the crook of his elbow, feeling the solid warmth of him through the fabric of his suit jacket. They crossed the street together, and she was acutely aware of how natural it felt to walk beside him like this. Like they'd done it a hundred times before. Like they might do it a hundred times again.

The entrance to The 1887 Room was framed by tall windows draped in burgundy velvet, and a polished brass plate beside the door announced the restaurant's name in elegant script. Jim held the door open for Grace, and she stepped inside.

The interior took her breath away.

Exposed brick walls rose toward tin ceilings pressed with intricate patterns that caught the light from vintage chandeliers. Rich hardwood floors gleamed beneath her feet, and antique furnishings were arranged throughout the space with careful attention to both beauty and comfort. Historic photographs lined the walls, images of Serenity Crossing through the decades, and glass display cases held artifacts and memorabilia donated by the town's founding families. The restaurant felt like a living museum, a place where history and hospitality merged into something special.

A hostess in a black dress approached them with a welcoming smile. "Good evening. Do you have a reservation?"

"Hartwell," Jim said. "Party of two, for seven o'clock."

The hostess consulted her book and nodded. "Right this way, Mr. Hartwell."

She led them through the main dining room, past tables occupied by couples and small groups engaged in quiet conversation. The lighting was soft and warm, provided by candles on each table and the glow from wall sconces designed to look like gas lamps. White tablecloths covered every surface, and fresh flowers in small crystal vases added splashes of color throughout the room.

Their table was tucked into a corner near a window that looked out onto Cedar Street. The hostess pulled out Grace's chair, and she settled into it while Jim took the seat across from her. Menus were placed in their hands, and the hostess informed them that their server would be with them shortly before disappearing back toward the front of the restaurant.

Grace looked around, taking in the details she'd missed on the walk-through. A fireplace dominated one wall, its mantel decorated with framed photographs and what appeared to be a collection of antique books. The table beside theirs was empty, giving them privacy, and the murmur of other diners provided a pleasant backdrop without being intrusive.

"This place is incredible," she said.

"It opened about eight years ago. The building used to be the town's first mercantile store, back when Serenity Crossing was just getting started. When they restored it, they tried to preserve as much of the original character as possible." Jim gestured toward the photographs on the nearest wall. "Those are all real. Donated by families who've been here for generations."

Grace studied the images: a group of men standing in front of what might have been this very building, a woman in Victorian dress posed beside a horse-drawn carriage, and children playing in a town square that looked remarkably similar to the one just down the street. The past felt close here, present in a way that was both comforting and humbling.

"I love that they kept all of this," she said. "So many places would have modernized everything, stripped out the character to make it feel more contemporary."

"That's what I appreciate about it. The food is excellent, but it's the atmosphere that makes it special."

A server appeared at their table, a young man with a friendly demeanor who introduced himself as William and asked if they'd like to start with drinks. Grace ordered sparkling water with lemon, and Jim asked for the same. William nodded and promised to return shortly to take their dinner orders.

When he was gone, Grace opened her menu and scanned the options. The selections were elegant but not pretentious: pan-seared trout, herb-crusted chicken, and beef tenderloin with seasonal vegetables. Everything sounded delicious.

"Any recommendations?" she asked.

"The trout is incredible. They get it fresh from a farm just outside of town. But honestly, I don't think you can go wrong with anything on the menu."

Grace decided on the trout. Jim chose the beef tenderloin. When William returned with their waters and a basket of warm bread, they placed their orders and settled back into their seats.

The bread was still warm from the oven, its crust golden and its interior soft and yielding. Grace tore off a piece and spread it with butter from a small ceramic dish, and the first bite was good enough to make her close her eyes in appreciation.

"Okay," she said. "You were right. This place is special."

Jim smiled across the table at her. "I'm glad you like it."

They talked as they waited for their food, an easy conversation that flowed without effort. Jim asked about the renovation timeline, and Grace filled him in on the latest developments. The kitchen demolition was complete. Sarah's crew was making excellent progress on the back porch and gazebo, and if everything stayed on schedule, she might actually make her Heritage Festival deadline.

"That's impressive," Jim said. "You've accomplished a lot in just a couple of weeks."

"I've had good help. Sarah knows what she's doing, and Tom has been a lifesaver with the interior work." She paused, considering her next words. "And you've been helpful too. More than you probably realize."

Jim tilted his head slightly. "How so?"

"The contractor recommendations. The supplies. The advice about the cabinets." Grace turned her water glass in her hands, watching the light catch the bubbles rising through the liquid. "You've made things easier. And you've done it without making me feel like I need help. There's a difference."

"You're more capable than you give yourself credit for, Grace. You always have been."

Their meals arrived before she could respond. William set the plates before them with practiced grace, and the presentation was as beautiful as the restaurant itself. Grace's trout was perfectly seared, resting on a bed of wild rice and seasonal vegetables, while Jim's tenderloin was sliced and fanned across the plate with elegant precision.

Jim reached his hand across the table, palm up. "Shall we say grace?"

The gesture surprised her in the best way. Grace placed her hand in his, feeling the warmth of his fingers closing gently around hers. Jim bowed his head, and she followed.

"Lord, we thank You for this food and for this evening. We thank You for bringing Grace home to Serenity Crossing and for the blessing of old friendships made new. Watch over us and guide our paths. Amen."

"Amen," Grace echoed softly.

Jim released her hand, but the warmth of his touch lingered against her palm. They began to eat, and the food was every bit as excellent as Jim had promised. The trout was tender and flavorful, the vegetables perfectly seasoned, and Grace realized she'd been hungrier than she thought.

For a while, they focused on their meals, exchanging occasional comments about the food and the atmosphere. But as the plates emptied and the initial hunger faded, the conversation began to shift. Grace felt it happening: the gradual descent from surface-level pleasantries into something deeper and more honest.

"Can I ask you something?" Jim said, setting down his fork.

"Of course."

"Your divorce. You said it was finalized a month ago, but it sounds like things ended long before that. What happened?"

Grace had known this question was coming. She'd been preparing for it, in some way, since she agreed to this dinner earlier this afternoon. But sitting here now, with Jim's steady gaze on her face and the candlelight flickering between them, she realized that preparing and actually speaking were two very different things.

"Lee was unfaithful," she said. The words came out more evenly than she expected. "Not once. Not a mistake he regretted. It was a pattern. Multiple women, multiple affairs, spanning our entire marriage."

Jim's jaw tightened, but he didn't interrupt. He just listened.

"The worst part wasn't the betrayal itself. I mean, that was awful, don't get me wrong. But the worst part was that everyone around me that I associated with knew. Everyone at the firm, everyone in our social circle. They all knew, and they all kept it from me. That hurt. That made me feel so betrayed not only by Lee but by everyone my life revolved around." Grace set down her own fork, no longer interested in the remaining food on her plate. "I'm an architect, Jim. I'm trained to notice details, to see what other people miss. I design buildings by paying attention to things that most people overlook. And I spent two years married to a man who was lying to me constantly, and I didn't see any of it. The people I thought were friends lied to my face as well and betrayed me. It's like I had blinders on. I keep asking myself how I could have missed the signs."

"Grace." Jim's voice was gentle but firm. "That's not your fault."

"Isn't it? Shouldn't I have known? Shouldn't I have seen something?"

"You didn't see it because he was hiding it. Because he was good at hiding it. And because you were doing what you were supposed to do in a marriage. You were trusting your husband. And sad as it is to say, there are men in this world who take a woman's love and devotion for granted and have no respect for the one person they should be entirely devoted to." Jim leaned forward slightly, his eyes never leaving hers. "You're not broken because he betrayed you. He's broken because he couldn't see what he had. You were too good for him, Grace."

The words hit somewhere deep, in a place she'd been protecting for over a year. She felt her eyes sting and blinked against the threat of tears. She was past crying about Lee. She'd told herself that a hundred times. But this wasn't about Lee. This was about someone finally saying out loud what she'd needed to hear.

"Thank you," she said quietly.

Jim nodded, accepting her gratitude without making a bigger thing of it than it needed to be. That was something she was re-learning about him. He said what needed to be said, and then he let it be.

Grace took a sip of her water and steadied herself. "What about you? What happened with Amanda?"

Jim was quiet for a moment, and she watched emotions move across his face like clouds crossing a mountain. He wasn't someone who hid what he felt, but he also wasn't someone who spoke carelessly. When he finally answered, his voice was measured and honest.

"Amanda came to Serenity Crossing about eight years ago. She was visiting friends, fell in love with the town, or so she said. We met at a community event, started dating, and got married within a year." He paused, turning his water glass in his hands the same way Grace had earlier. "For three years, I thought we were happy. I thought we were building something together. I was wrong."

"What happened?"

"She got restless. At first, I didn't notice it. Or maybe I noticed and convinced myself it was something else. But she started pulling away, spending more time away from home, making comments about how small the town was and how limited our options were." Jim's voice was steady, but Grace could hear the old wound beneath the words. "One day she sat me down and told me she was leaving. Just like that. No warning, no discussion. She'd already packed her things. She'd already made her decision. She'd already filed the paperwork."

"Jim." Grace reached across the table without thinking about it. Her fingers found his, and she felt him tense briefly before relaxing into her touch.

"The words she used are what stayed with me," he continued. "She said, 'You and this little town will never be enough for me. I need more.'" He let out a breath that seemed to carry the weight of years. "She didn't leave because I failed. She left because I wasn't enough for her. That's what hurt the most, Grace. Being told that who I am, at my core, wasn't enough. That alone nearly destroyed me."

Grace understood those words in a way that cut straight to her bones. Different wound, same shape. Lee had betrayed her trust; Amanda had rejected Jim's very essence. Both of them had been found insufficient by the people who should have loved them most.

"How did you get through it?" she asked.

"It took time. A lot of time. And honestly, I'm not sure I would have made it without my faith." Jim turned his hand over beneath hers, his fingers interlacing gently with her own. "Church helped. Having somewhere to go where people knew me and expected nothing from me. It was an anchor when everything else was shifting. I sat in those pews every Sunday, even when I wasn't sure I believed anymore, and somehow that consistency held me together."

Grace thought about her own distance from faith, the years she'd let slip away without even noticing.

"And Boone," Jim added, and something in his expression lightened. "I believe God put that dog in my life exactly when I needed him. He showed up at the hardware store one day, skinny and scared and looking at me like I was the answer to some question he'd been asking his whole life. I fed him, and he never left my side." Jim smiled, a real smile that reached his eyes. "It sounds strange, maybe, but having something... no, someone who needed me, someone that was happy just to be near me, that helped more than I can explain. Boone isn't your ordinary dog; he's almost human-like at times. Boone didn't care that Amanda thought I wasn't enough. To him, I was everything."

Grace felt tears prick at her eyes again, but this time she didn't fight them. She let one fall, a single track down her cheek that she wiped away with her free hand.

"That doesn't sound strange at all," she said. "That sounds like grace... and that is beautiful."

"It was." Jim squeezed her fingers gently. "And I think maybe this is too. You being here. Us sitting across from each other after all these years." He held her gaze with an openness that made her breath catch. "I'm not saying I have it all figured out. I don't. But I believe God works in ways we don't always understand. And I believe He brought you home for a reason."

William appeared at their table with two plates of chocolate mousse, elegantly plated with fresh berries and a drizzle of raspberry sauce. He set them down and asked if there was anything else they needed. Jim thanked him, and William retreated once more.

The desserts sat untouched between them.

Grace looked at Jim across the candlelit table, at the man who had listened without judgment, who had shared his own pain without expecting her to fix it, who had held her hand through a prayer and kept holding it because neither of them wanted to let go.

"I'm scared," she admitted. The words came out before she could stop them. "Of this. Of what it might mean. Of trusting myself to see clearly when I've been so wrong before."

"I know," Jim said. "I'm scared too."

"You are?"

"Grace, you're the first woman I've wanted to have dinner with since Amanda left. The first woman I've thought about when I wake up in the morning. The first woman who's made me wonder if maybe I could try again." He paused, and his thumb traced a gentle circle against her palm. "That's terrifying. But it's also the most alive I've felt in four years."

She didn't have words for what she felt in that moment. So she simply held his hand and let the silence speak for both of them.

Eventually, they tried the mousse, which was rich and decadent and exactly what the evening needed. They talked about lighter things, about Boone's antics and Miranda's bookshop and the ongoing drama of small-town life. The heaviness of their earlier conversation eased into something warmer, something that felt like the beginning of a new chapter.

When the check came, Jim insisted on paying despite Grace's protests. "I asked you out on this date. You can get the next one," he said, and the assumption that there would be a next one made her smile.

They gathered their things and made their way back through the restaurant. The dining room had filled even more since their arrival.

Grace shivered slightly as they stepped onto the sidewalk outside the restaurant; the evening air was a bit cooler now. Jim noticed immediately.

"Cold?"

"A little. I should have brought a jacket."

Without hesitation, Jim shrugged off his suit jacket and draped it over her shoulders. The fabric was warm from his body and carried a faint trace of his cologne, something clean and subtle that she hadn't noticed until now. She pulled the lapels closer around her.

"Thanks."

"Can't have you freezing on the walk home." He offered his arm with the same easy grace he'd shown earlier. "Shall we?"

Grace slipped her hand into the crook of his elbow and looked up at him with a smile.

"Would you mind taking a walk around town first?" she asked.

"Not at all, I'm not quite ready for this evening to end."

Chapter 15

Jim pulled his truck into the parking lot behind Serenity Crossing Community Church and cut the engine.

Through the windshield, he watched families making their way toward the white-steepled building, children tugging at collars and women adjusting hats against the April breeze.

This morning felt different. Something had shifted in his world after dinner at The 1887 Room, after holding Grace's hand across a candlelit table and admitting things he hadn't said out loud in years. He had walked with her around town after dinner, enjoying the time they spent together, then walked her home and said goodnight on the porch of the Mountain Laurel Inn with a restraint that had cost him more than he wanted to admit.

He climbed out of the truck and straightened his tie, a navy-blue one his mother had given him last Christmas. His Bible was tucked under his arm, the leather cover worn soft from years of use. He had inherited it from his grandfather, and the margins were filled with notes in two different hands: his grandfather's careful script and his own looser scrawl.

The morning air carried the green smell of new growth and the faint sweetness of the dogwoods blooming along the cemetery fence. Jim followed the stone path toward the church's main entrance, nodding to friends and exchanging brief greetings with people he had known his entire life.

Inside, the sanctuary was filling steadily. Sunlight poured through the stained glass windows, casting patterns of gold and blue and rose across the wooden pews. The organist was playing something quiet and contemplative, and the low hum of conversation created a backdrop of community that Jim had never taken for granted.

He paused just inside the double doors and let his gaze travel across the room.

His family was already seated in their usual spot. His mother caught his eye and lifted her hand in a small wave. Dave was there beside her, and Rebecca, as well as the rest of his siblings and his father, was at the end of the pew, looking dignified in his Sunday suit. They had saved him a seat. They always did.

But Jim's attention had already moved to the right side of the sanctuary, where the McKenna family occupied two full pews near the front. Bruce and Jean sat at the center, surrounded by their children and extended family.

Grace sat near the aisle, her chestnut hair falling in soft waves past her shoulders, wearing a dress the color of spring leaves. She was looking down at something in her lap.

He walked down the center aisle, past his family's pew, without stopping. He walked with purpose, with the kind of quiet confidence that came from knowing exactly what he wanted and being unafraid to reach for it.

When he reached the McKenna pews, he stopped beside Grace and waited until she looked up.

Her green eyes widened slightly when she saw him standing there.

"Morning," Jim said, keeping his voice low enough not to disturb the people around them. "Room for one more?"

Grace blinked. Then a smile tugged at the corner of her mouth, and she slid toward her sister to make space.

Jim settled into the pew beside her. He was aware of Jean McKenna's gaze from a few seats down, warm and knowing. He was aware of Bruce's brief nod of acknowledgment. He was aware that half the congregation was probably watching and drawing conclusions.

Let them watch. Let them conclude.

Grace leaned toward him slightly. "This is a surprise."

"Good surprise or bad surprise?"

"I haven't decided yet."

But she was smiling, and that was answer enough.

Pastor Davis stepped up to the pulpit, and the sanctuary settled into attentive quiet. The pastor was a man who had earned his gray hair honestly, with decades of shepherding this community through births and deaths, weddings and funerals, ordinary Sundays and extraordinary ones.

"Good morning, church," he said, his voice carrying easily through the room. "It's good to see so many familiar faces. Let's begin with prayer."

Jim closed his eyes and listened to the pastor's words, but his attention kept drifting to the woman beside him. The warmth of her presence. The rhythm of her breathing was steady and calm despite the flush he had noticed on her face.

The prayer ended, and the congregation rose for the opening hymn. Jim reached for the hymnal in the rack in front of them at the same moment Grace did. Their fingers brushed against the worn spine, and Grace pulled back quickly, letting him take it.

They stood shoulder to shoulder as the organ swelled into the familiar melody of "Great Is Thy Faithfulness." Jim found the page and held the hymnal so Grace could see, positioning it closer to her side than his own.

Her voice was soft but clear, blending with the surrounding voices. He had heard her sing in high school, in the choir that performed at school assemblies and community events. Her voice hadn't changed. It was still lovely.

The hymn ended, and they sat together as Pastor Davis moved into the morning's announcements. Committee meetings. A potluck next Wednesday. The ongoing collection for the food pantry. The ordinary business of a church family going about its ordinary life.

Then the pastor opened his Bible.

"Turn with me to John, chapter twenty-one," Pastor Davis said. "We're going to look at what happened after the resurrection. Not the empty tomb. Not the appearances. But what came next, when the disciples had to figure out how to live in a world that had been turned upside down."

Jim found the passage and angled his Bible so Grace could read along with him. She leaned slightly closer, and he caught the faintest trace of something floral and clean, but he kept his focus on the page in front of them.

Pastor Davis read the scripture aloud, the familiar story of Peter and the other disciples returning to their fishing boats after everything that had happened. They fished all night and caught nothing. Then, at dawn, a figure appeared on the shore and told them to cast their nets on the other side. When they did, the nets were so full they could barely haul them in.

"I want you to notice something," Pastor Davis said, looking up from his Bible. "These men had just witnessed the most extraordinary event. They had seen their teacher crucified. They had seen him rise from the dead. And what did they do next? They went back to work. They went fishing."

Jim turned that over in his mind. The ordinariness of it. The way life continued even after everything changed.

"Some people read this passage and think Peter was giving up," the pastor continued. "Going back to his old life because he didn't know what else to do. But I don't think that's quite right. I think Peter was doing what all of us do when we're trying to make sense of something bigger than ourselves. He was returning to what he knew. To the familiar rhythms of daily work."

Grace shifted beside him, and Jim wondered what she was thinking. She had come back to Serenity Crossing. She had returned to what she knew, to the familiar rhythms of a place that had shaped her.

"And here's the beautiful part," Pastor Davis said. "Jesus didn't scold them for going fishing. He didn't tell them they should have been doing something more spiritual, more important. Instead, he met them right there, on the shore, in the middle of their ordinary work. He cooked them breakfast. He ate with them. He showed them that his presence wasn't confined to mountaintop moments. He was with them in the boat. He was with them on the shore. He was with them in the breaking of bread."

"Faith isn't only lived on holy days," Pastor Davis said. "It isn't something we put on for Sunday mornings and take off when we walk out those doors. Faith is lived in the ordinary moments. In the work we do with our hands. In the meals we share with the people we love. In the daily choice to show up, to keep casting our nets, to trust that Christ is present even when we can't see him clearly."

Jim thought about the hardware store. About the customers who came in with broken things that needed fixing. About the satisfaction of helping someone find exactly what they needed. About the ordinary, faithful work of being useful to his community.

He thought about Grace, working day after day on the inn, pouring herself into the restoration of something her grandmother had loved. Ordinary work. Faithful work.

The sermon continued, but Jim found his attention divided between the pastor's words and the woman beside him. At one point, Grace reached up to tuck a strand of hair behind her ear, and her elbow brushed against his arm. She glanced at him with an apologetic smile, and he shook his head slightly to let her know it was fine.

More than fine.

When the final hymn was sung and the benediction offered, the congregation began to stir. People gathered their things, greeted their neighbors, and made plans for the afternoon. The sanctuary filled with the comfortable noise of community doing what community did.

Jim stood and offered Grace his hand to help her rise from the pew. She took it, her fingers cool and slender in his grip, and he held on a moment longer before letting go.

"That was a good sermon," Grace said as they made their way toward the center aisle.

"It was. Pastor Davis has a gift."

They walked together down the aisle, moving with the slow flow of the congregation toward the double doors at the back of the sanctuary. The April sunlight was bright when they stepped outside, and Jim squinted against it as they descended the stone steps.

"What are your plans for the afternoon?" he asked as they turned onto the path that led toward the fellowship hall.

"More work at the inn. I thought I'd tackle some of the painting in the library. The trim needs at least two coats, and I want to get it done before the crews show back up tomorrow."

"You're painting trim on a Sunday afternoon?"

"It needs to be done, and today's just as good as any other day." Grace shrugged.

"You should take breaks. Even God rested on the seventh day."

"I'll rest when the inn is open."

Jim laughed. "That sounds like something my grandfather used to say. He worked six days a week at the hardware store until he was seventy-three years old."

"And then he retired?"

"Yes, after my grandmother threatened to lock him out of the store if he didn't."

Grace smiled at that. "Smart woman."

"She knew what she wanted."

They had almost reached the fellowship hall when footsteps sounded behind them, quick and purposeful. Jim turned to see Jean McKenna approaching with that particular expression mothers wore when they had something on their minds.

"Jim," she said warmly. "I'm so glad I caught you. Bruce and I would love to have you join us for Sunday dinner this evening. Nothing fancy, just family. Grace will be there, of course." She smiled at her daughter. "We'd enjoy your company."

The invitation was casual, the tone friendly and welcoming, and he didn't hesitate to respond.

"Yes ma'am. I'd like that."

Jean's smile widened, satisfaction and affection warming her features. "Wonderful. We eat at six."

She patted Jim's arm and continued toward the fellowship hall, leaving him standing on the path beside Grace.

Jim turned to look at her.

Grace was watching him with an expression he couldn't quite read. There was surprise there, certainly. And maybe something like pleasure, though it was tangled up with something else. Uncertainty, perhaps. Or the particular kind of fear that came with wanting something and being afraid to believe it might actually happen.

"You don't have to come," she said quietly. "If she put you on the spot, I can make an excuse for you."

"Grace." Jim held her gaze, letting her see that he meant every word. "I want to come. I wouldn't have said yes if I didn't."

She studied his face for a long moment, searching for something. Whatever she found must have satisfied her.

Chapter 16

Grace watched Jim charm her family, and she wasn't sure what to do with the feelings rising in her chest.

He sat at the long farmhouse table in the seat her mother had directed him toward, right across from Grace, where she couldn't avoid looking at him even if she tried. Which she wasn't trying. That was part of the problem.

The dining room was full tonight. Bruce sat at the head of the table with Jean at his right hand. Faith had taken the chair beside Grace, and the rest of her siblings filled in the remaining seats in their usual configuration. Logan, quiet and watchful at the far end. Josie was beside him, babbling on about some of the work she had to do this coming week on the farm. Graham beside her, steady and solid. Cain had come straight from his shift at work, still wearing his uniform. Miranda was telling some story about a customer at the bookshop, her hands moving as she talked. Chad and Mandy rounded out the group, and the noise level had reached that particular pitch that only happened when all the McKenna siblings gathered in one place.

Jim looked completely at ease.

Grace remembered him joining their family for Sunday dinner the first time when she was seventeen. He had been nervous then, sitting stiffly in this same dining room while her father asked questions about his plans for the future and her mother plied him with food. He had won them over eventually, the way Jim won everyone over, with his steady kindness and his genuine interest in the people around him.

Years later, his nervousness was gone. He leaned back in his chair and listened to Miranda's story, laughing at the right moments and asking follow-up questions that made her youngest sister beam with pleasure.

"So this woman," Miranda continued, "she comes up to the counter with a stack of romance novels and asks me, completely serious, if I can guarantee that all of them have happy endings. And I said, 'Ma'am, that's literally the definition of the genre.' And she looked at me like I'd just revealed the secrets of the universe."

"Some people don't know about the rules," Mandy said. "I had a guest at the inn last month who was genuinely surprised that checkout was at eleven. She thought it was more of a suggestion and didn't apply to her."

"Everything's a suggestion if you're confident enough," Josie said dryly.

"That's not how rules work," Logan pointed out.

"That's exactly how rules work for some people." Cain shook his head. "You wouldn't believe the excuses I hear on traffic stops."

The conversation flowed around the table, easy and overlapping, and Grace found herself watching Jim more than participating. He caught her eye at one point and smiled, just a small curve of his lips, and she felt warmth spread through her that had nothing to do with the food.

Faith nudged Grace's elbow under the table. When Grace glanced at her sister, Faith raised one eyebrow slowly, deliberately. She said nothing. She didn't need to. The look on her face said everything.

"Jim," Bruce said during a lull in the cross-talk, "how's the lumber mill doing these days? I heard your father expanded the operation."

"Yes, sir, he did. Added a new sawmill and hired three more workers. Business has been steady. All the construction happening in the county keeps them plenty busy."

"I remember when your granddaddy started that mill. Must have been, what, forty years ago now?"

"Forty-three. He always said the hardware store was the family business, but the lumber mill was his passion project."

Bruce nodded, appreciation in his eyes. "Your granddaddy was one tough character. He had this business mind that was way ahead of his time. I remember him saying many times, A man needs something to build. Something that outlasts him."

"That's what he believed." Jim glanced around the dining room, taking in the farmhouse that Bruce and Jean had built together over three decades. "I think you understand that better than most, Mr. McKenna."

"Bruce," Grace's father corrected. "You're not seventeen anymore, son. I think we can drop the formalities."

"I can do that, sir," he replied.

Jean rose from her seat and began collecting empty plates. Grace stood automatically to help, gathering the serving dishes that had been picked clean over the course of the meal.

"That cornbread was delicious, Mrs. McKenna," Jim said as Jean reached for his plate. "Best I've had in quite some time. Would it be too much trouble to ask for the recipe? My mom's been looking for a new one."

Jean's face lit up the way it always did when someone complimented her cooking. "I'll write it down for you before you leave. And tell Olivia I expect her to call me this week. We haven't had lunch in nearly a month, and I'm starting to think she's avoiding me."

"I'll pass that along." Jim grinned. "Though I'm pretty sure she's just been busy with the church auxiliary. They're planning something big for the summer social."

"That woman takes on too much. Just like someone else I know." Jean shot a pointed look at Grace, who pretended not to notice.

Grace followed her mother into the kitchen, arms full of dishes, while the conversation continued in the dining room behind them. Through the doorway, she could hear Chad asking Jim about a fishing spot on the Rolling River and Jim's voice as he described the best places to cast a line this time of year.

"He fits right in," Jean said quietly as she set the dishes in the sink. "Always did."

Grace didn't respond. She wasn't sure what to say.

"I remember the first time you brought him home." Jean turned on the water and began rinsing the plates. "You were so nervous. You kept asking me if the house looked okay, if I'd made enough food, and if your father was going to interrogate him."

"Dad did interrogate him."

"Your father asked perfectly reasonable questions about his intentions." Jean smiled at the memory. "I remember Jim answered every one of them without flinching. That impressed Bruce more than anything else could have."

Grace began loading the dishwasher with the rinsed dishes. The rhythm was familiar, something they had done together hundreds of times in the past. It should have been soothing. Instead, Grace felt a knot forming in her stomach that she couldn't quite explain.

"He still looks at you the same way, you know." Jean's voice was gentle, almost offhand. "After all these years. The way his eyes follow you around the room. It's sweet."

Grace's hands stilled on the plate she was holding.

"Mom."

"I'm not prying." Jean continued rinsing, her attention seemingly fixed on the task. "I'm just making an observation. A momma notices these things."

"I don't know what I'm doing." The words came out before Grace could stop them. "With Jim. With any of this. I just got divorced. I'm supposed to be focusing on the inn, on rebuilding my life, on figuring out who I am without..." She trailed off, not wanting to say Lee's name in this kitchen.

Jean turned off the water and dried her hands on her apron. Then she turned to face Grace fully, her expression soft but serious.

"Sweetheart, you've spent the last year taking care of everything yourself. The divorce, the move, the inn. You've been so determined to prove you can handle it all alone that you've forgotten something important."

"What's that?"

"You don't have to." Jean reached out and tucked a strand of hair behind Grace's ear; the gesture was so maternal that Grace felt her throat tighten. "Letting someone in doesn't mean you're weak. It means you're brave enough to try again."

Grace looked down at the plate in her hands, blinking against the sting behind her eyes.

"What if I'm wrong again? What if I can't see clearly, and I make another mistake, and I end up right back where I started?"

"Then you'll get through it. With family, and faith, and the stubborn McKenna determination that won't let you quit." Jean smiled and patted Grace's cheek. "But for what it's worth, I don't think you're wrong about Jim. I've known that boy since he was in diapers. He's one of the good ones, Grace. He always has been."

From the dining room came a burst of laughter. Something Cain had said, from the sound of it, followed by Jim's voice joining in.

"Now," Jean turned back to the counter and picked up the strawberry cake she had prepared earlier. "Grab some dessert plates, and let's go enjoy the rest of our evening. And Grace... let yourself be the young, lovely woman that you are. Enjoy the attention of that wonderful man who is so clearly still in love with you. God's got this... stop worrying."

Grace followed her mother back into the dining room, carrying a stack of small plates and forks. The conversation had shifted while they were gone. Graham was telling a story now about something that had happened on the farm this past week, and Jim was listening with the same genuine attention he had shown Miranda earlier.

Jean began cutting slices of cake, and the table fell into a brief, anticipatory quiet as plates were passed around.

"Before we dig in," Bruce said, "I'd like to say grace again."

Heads bowed around the table.

"Lord, we thank You for this food and for the hands that prepared it. Thank You for bringing us together around this table, for the blessing of children, and for the joy of watching them grow into who they were meant to be. Thank You for this wonderful life You've given us. Thank You for old friends and new beginnings. Watch over this family, Lord. Keep us in Your care. Amen."

"Amen," the table echoed.

Grace opened her eyes and found Jim looking at her across the table. His expression was soft, unguarded in a way that made her breath catch. She held his gaze for a moment longer than she probably should have, then looked away and reached for her fork.

The cake was sweet and perfect; the strawberries were fresh from the first early crop. The conversation resumed, lighter now as the meal wound down. Miranda mentioned a book club meeting coming up. Josie complained about a piece of equipment that needed replacing. Chad talked about a training exercise his search and rescue team had scheduled for next month.

Jim contributed where it felt natural and listened when it didn't. He belonged here. That was the thing Grace kept circling back to. He fit into the spaces between her siblings as if he had never left.

Eventually, the cake was finished, and the hour had grown late. Jim pushed back from the table and thanked Jean for the meal with the kind of genuine warmth that made mothers want to adopt grown men on the spot.

"You're welcome here anytime," Jean told him, pressing a folded piece of paper into his hand. "That's the cornbread recipe. Don't let Olivia change a thing about it."

"Yes ma'am. I wouldn't dare."

Grace walked him to the front door while her siblings began the familiar chaos of cleanup behind them. The evening air was cool when they stepped onto the porch, carrying the smell of fresh earth that had recently been turned over in the fields and the distant sound of frogs singing somewhere near the creek.

They stood together at the top of the porch steps, and Grace found herself not wanting him to go.

"I'm glad you came," she said. "You didn't have to."

"I wanted to." Jim turned to face her, his expression serious in the soft light spilling from the windows. "I had a great time tonight. Your family is..."

"A lot?"

"Wonderful," he smiled. "They're wonderful, Grace. You're lucky to have them."

"I know."

They stood there for a moment; the silence filled with everything neither of them was saying. Then Jim reached for her hand.

His fingers wrapped around hers, warm and solid and sure. He didn't pull her closer. Didn't try for anything more. He just held her hand and squeezed gently.

"Thank you for letting me back into your life, Grace; it means more to me than you realize."

Then he let go of her hand, turned, and walked down the porch steps toward his truck.

Grace watched him go, her hand still tingling where his fingers had been. She stood on the porch until his taillights disappeared down the long gravel drive, until the night sounds swallowed the rumble of his engine, until she was alone with the stars and questions spinning through her mind.

Chapter 17

The cursor blinked at Grace from her laptop screen, patient and unimpressed by her indecision.

She had been sitting on the front porch of the Mountain Laurel Inn for the better part of an hour, her to-do list growing longer with every thought that crossed her mind. Website development. Social media presence. Online reservation system. Hiring staff for cooking. Hiring staff for cleaning. The list stretched down the document like a road with no visible end, and Grace felt the familiar tightness in her shoulders that came from realizing she had underestimated something important.

The inn itself was coming together. That much was true. But the inn was only half the battle. The other half was everything that came after: the business of running a business, the practical realities of turning a restored building into a functioning hospitality operation. She had spent so much mental energy on construction timelines and paint colors and cabinet selections that she had pushed these other concerns to the back of her mind, telling herself she would deal with them later.

Later had arrived, and it had brought a spreadsheet full of tasks.

Grace scrolled through her notes, trying to organize her thoughts into something resembling a plan. She needed a website that looked professional but felt warm and welcoming. She needed a reservation system that was easy for guests to use and easy for her to manage. She needed social media accounts that would help people find the inn and give them a reason to book a stay. She needed staff, at least two people, someone to help with breakfast service and someone to handle housekeeping, because even with her ambitious work ethic, she could not cook and clean and manage guests and maintain the property all by herself.

The admission stung, even in the privacy of her own thoughts. She had come back to Serenity Crossing determined to prove she could do this alone. She had needed to show herself that she was capable of building something without anyone else's help. That she could trust her own judgment and her own abilities. That she didn't need to rely on anyone else to succeed.

But the truth was more complicated than that.

She had already hired professional painters to handle the guest rooms on both upper floors of the inn. That decision had come a few days ago, after she spent an entire day painting a single bathroom and realized that at her current pace, she would still be rolling walls in August. The painters had already started, and after only two days had transformed several guest rooms into a fresh, welcoming space while Grace focused on other tasks. It had been the right choice. It had also been humbling.

A wet nose pressed against her bare ankle, and Grace startled so hard she nearly knocked her laptop off her lap.

She looked down to find Boone gazing up at her with those soulful brown eyes, his tail sweeping slowly across the porch boards. He had climbed the steps without her noticing, too absorbed in her own thoughts to hear his approach. Now he rested his chin on her knee and looked at her with an expression that seemed to say he had been waiting for this moment all day.

"Hey, you," Grace said, reaching down to scratch behind his ears. "Did you escape again?"

Boone's tail picked up speed, and he pressed closer, settling his weight against her leg like he belonged there.

Grace looked up from the dog and smiled.

Jim was walking toward her, carrying a cardboard tray with two cups and a small paper bag. He wore jeans and a button-down shirt with the sleeves rolled to his elbows.

"I brought reinforcements," he called out as he reached the porch steps. "Coffee from The Daily Grind and scones from Sweet Surrender Bakery. Cinnamon sugar. I remembered you used to love those."

Cinnamon sugar. He remembered. After fourteen years, he still remembered what she liked.

"You didn't have to do that," she said as he climbed the steps and settled into the wicker chair beside hers.

"I know." Jim handed her one of the cups and set the paper bag on the small table between them. "I wanted to. Figured you could use a break."

Boone had not moved from his spot at Grace's feet. If anything, he had pressed closer, his chin now resting fully on her knee as though staking a claim.

"I'm starting to think Boone really likes me," Grace said.

"He's been restless all afternoon. He kept looking at the door as if he were waiting for something. I finally gave in and took him for a walk."

"And your walk ended up here... with coffee and scones in hand?"

"Apparently so." Jim's eyes met hers, and something in his gaze made her stomach flutter. "What can I say? Boone has good taste."

Grace laughed as she reached for the bag. The scones inside were still warm, their cinnamon sugar coating slightly sticky against the wax paper wrapping. She pulled one out and took a bite, and the sweetness melted on her tongue.

"These are incredible," she said.

"Ida Mae's baked goods are the best, always have been."

They sat together on the porch, eating scones and drinking coffee while the afternoon stretched golden around them. A soft breeze carried the fresh scent of spring blooms from the trees lining the street, and somewhere down the block a wind chime rang soft and random. From inside the inn came the distant sound of Tom's crew working, but out here the noise faded into background rhythm, easy to ignore.

Jim nodded toward her laptop. "What were you working on? You looked pretty focused when I walked up."

Grace sighed and turned the screen so he could see her document. "Business planning. All the things I haven't figured out yet. Website, reservations, social media, staffing." She shook her head slowly. "I spent so much time thinking about the renovation that I forgot I'd actually have to run this place once it was finished."

"That's a lot to tackle all at once."

"It is." Grace took a sip of her coffee, gathering her thoughts. "I've had to adjust my expectations about what I can realistically handle alone. I hired professional painters to do all three floors. I thought I could do it myself, but..." She trailed off, then forced herself to finish the sentence. "Reality set in."

Jim was quiet for a moment, and Grace braced herself for some kind of comment about her stubbornness or her need to control every-thing. But when he spoke, his voice was gentle.

"That sounds like wisdom to me. Not defeat."

Grace looked at him, surprised by how much those words meant.

"The renovation's mostly on schedule," she continued, feeling the need to prove that she had not completely lost control of the situation. "There were some delays with the plumbing, and the electrical work took longer than expected, but Tom and Sarah's crews handled everything. Nothing major."

"That's impressive. So, you're still on track for a soft opening at the end of June?"

"Assuming nothing else goes wrong."

"Nothing else will go wrong." Jim said it with such certainty that Grace almost believed him. "You've got this."

Grace wanted to argue, to list all the ways things could still fall apart, but she stopped herself. Maybe he was right. Maybe she could trust that the rest would work out.

"I could help," Jim said. "With the business planning. The website. I maintain the hardware store's website myself, and I've picked up a few things about online marketing over the years. Our website's not fancy, but it works."

"You'd do that?"

"Of course. On one condition."

Grace raised an eyebrow, her guard going up slightly. "What condition?"

Jim's lips curved into a smile that made her pulse quicken. "Play hooky with me tomorrow."

"Play hooky?"

"Take the day off. The farmer's market opens at eight. We could walk through, pick up some fresh produce, and then head out to my place. I'll cook lunch. We could go for a hike if you want, or just watch a movie. Whatever sounds good." He paused, and his expression softened. "Just enjoy a day off, Grace. You've earned it."

She should say no. She had a thousand things to do.

But looking at Jim, sitting beside her on this porch with the afternoon light warming his face and Boone dozing contentedly at her feet, Grace realized she didn't want to say no. She wanted to say yes. She wanted to walk through the farmer's market with him and spend a whole day doing nothing productive at all.

The wanting surprised her. Not the fact of it, but the strength of it. Somewhere in the past few weeks, spending time with Jim had shifted from pleasant to necessary, from something she enjoyed to something she looked forward to with an anticipation that bordered on eagerness.

Thank You, she thought, the prayer rising unbidden and natural. For this. For him. For things going well when they could have gone so wrong.

"You haven't taken a real day off since you got here," Jim added. "And honestly, neither have I. Not in years. We both deserve a break."

Grace looked at him, at the hope in his eyes and the way he was trying so hard not to pressure her, and she made her decision.

"Okay," she said.

Jim's smile widened, and something warm and bright bloomed in Grace's chest at the sight of it.

"I'll be here at eight in the morning then," he said. "Now, what do you want to work on first: a website or building out your business plan?"

"Let's work on a website... something easy that I can maintain and nothing fussy."

"We can do that. I use a basic website builder for the hardware store. It has drag-and-drop type features, so it's simple to use even if you've never built a website before."

Jim pulled his chair closer to hers so he could see her laptop screen better, as Boone continued to snooze between them on the porch.

Grace glanced at Jim as he leaned forward, focused on helping her navigate the website builder he had pulled up on the laptop screen. He made it look easy. He made everything look easy. And somewhere in the back of her mind, a quiet thought took shape: this was what it felt like to have someone in your corner. Not taking over. Not telling her what to do. Just showing up and offering to help carry the load.

She turned back to the screen and let herself enjoy the moment.

Chapter 18

Grace held a strawberry up to the light like she was examining a gemstone.

Jim stood beside her at the produce booth, watching her turn the berry slowly between her fingers, inspecting it from every angle. Her brow furrowed slightly as she considered its merits.

He had never seen anyone take strawberry selection so seriously.

"You know they're all going to taste the same once we get them home," he said.

Grace shot him a look of mock offense. "They absolutely will not. See this one?" She held up another berry from the basket she was holding. "The color is deeper. That means it's sweeter. And the leaves are still bright green, which means it was picked recently."

Jim smiled. "I'm just giving you a hard time, you know that, right?"

She grinned up at him, and something in his chest loosened at the sight of it. This was the Grace he remembered from high school, the one who threw herself fully into whatever she was doing, whether it was a school project or selecting the perfect piece of fruit. Atlanta hadn't erased that quality. It had just been buried for a while.

The morning sun fell warm across the town square, catching the highlights in Grace's hair and turning them to copper. She wore a simple sundress in a shade of pale yellow that made her look like she belonged in a painting, something pastoral and peaceful. Jim had picked her up at the inn an hour ago, and they'd walked to the farmer's market, which was located in the center of town. Since then they had been wandering around, moving from booth to booth without any particular hurry. No schedules. No renovation deadlines. Just the two of them and a morning that stretched out ahead like a gift.

Grace seemed satisfied with her selection and handed the basket of berries to the vendor, a young woman with a friendly smile who weighed the berries and named a price. Grace reached for her wallet, but Jim was faster.

"I've got it."

"Jim, you don't have to pay for everything."

"I know I don't have to." He handed over the bills and accepted the paper bag the vendor offered. "I want to."

Grace looked like she might argue, but something in his expression must have convinced her to let it go. She tucked her wallet back into her bag and fell into step beside him as they moved on to the next booth.

Boone walked between them, his leash slack in Jim's hand. The dog had been on his best behavior all morning, staying close and calm despite the crowds and the tempting smells drifting from every direction. A child ran past with a sticky cinnamon roll in hand, and Boone's nose twitched with interest, but he held his position. Every few minutes, though, Boone would drift closer to Grace's side, pressing his shoulder against her leg or nudging her hand with his nose until she reached down to scratch behind his ears.

Jim understood the impulse entirely.

The town square was alive with the particular energy that only a farmer's market could create. Vendors had set up tables and canopies around the rectangular space, their displays overflowing with fresh produce, homemade preserves, artisan breads, and crafts of every description. The air carried layers of scent that shifted as they walked: fresh-baked bread from one direction, the fresh smell of cut herbs from another, and the sweet perfume of early spring flowers from a booth near the gazebo. Families wandered through with children in tow, stopping to sample honey or admire handmade jewelry. An older couple sat on one of the benches near the war memorial, sharing a bag of kettle corn and watching the activity around them with contented expressions.

The white gazebo at the center of the square stood empty for now, its white paint bright against the surrounding lawn. Later in the summer it would host musicians and community events, but today it served as a landmark, a fixed point around which the market swirled.

Jim had been coming to this market since he was a kid, tagging along with his mother while she filled her basket with ingredients for Sunday dinner. The faces behind the tables had changed over the years, some of them at least, but the feeling remained the same. Community. Connection. The simple pleasure of buying something directly from the hands that had grown or made it.

"We should get salad ingredients," Grace said, pausing at a booth piled high with leafy greens. The farmer behind the table was arranging heads of butter lettuce in neat rows, their pale green leaves still beaded with water from a recent misting. "Something fresh to go with the steaks."

"Good thinking. And we could grab some potatoes for baking."

"Perfect. I saw a booth with some beautiful russets a few rows back."

They made their way through the market together, collecting what they needed. Lettuce and tomatoes from one vendor, an older gentleman who insisted they try a sample of his heirloom variety before they bought. A cucumber and some radishes from another; a young mother with a toddler balanced on her hip who managed to make change one-handed with practiced ease. Four large russet potatoes from another booth. The farmer recognized Jim immediately and asked after his parents with the easy familiarity of someone who had known the Hartwell family for decades.

"Tell your daddy I've got those garden seeds he wanted to try whenever he wants to pick them up," the farmer said as he bagged the potatoes.

"I'll let him know. Thanks, Earl."

Grace picked out a container of homemade pasta salad from a woman selling prepared foods, declaring it too good to pass up after sampling a bite. She held the small tasting spoon out to Jim, and he leaned in to try it, his eyes meeting hers over the plastic container.

"That is good," he admitted.

"Told you." Grace added it to their growing collection with a satisfied nod.

At some point, Jim's hand found the small of Grace's back as they navigated a particularly crowded section near the baked goods. People pressed in on all sides as they tried to reach the popular booth at the end, where the smell of fresh cinnamon rolls drew customers like moths to a flame. His hand had simply moved there to guide her through. A natural gesture. Instinctive. The warmth of her through the thin fabric of her dress registered against his palm, and he found himself in no hurry to let go.

Boone stayed close to Grace's other side, creating a protective barrier between her and the press of people. The dog seemed to have appointed himself her guardian for the morning, and Jim felt a surge of affection for his loyal companion.

They emerged from the crowd near a booth selling fresh flowers; the buckets overflowing with tulips and daffodils and the first early roses of the season. Grace paused to admire a bouquet of pale pink peonies, her fingers hovering over the petals without quite touching them.

"Jim! Grace!"

The voice carried across the market, and Jim turned to see his parents approaching. His father walked with his characteristic steady stride, a reusable shopping bag already half full in his hand. His mother moved beside him, her face bright with the particular pleasure she took in running into people she loved in public places.

"I thought that was you two," Olivia said as she reached them. She hugged Grace first, holding on for an extra moment before releasing her, then Jim, then bent down to give Boone an affectionate pat on the head. The dog's tail wagged in recognition. "What a beautiful morning for the market."

"It really is," Grace agreed. "We're picking up a few things for lunch."

"Jim mentioned he was planning to fire up the grill." Bill nodded at the bags they were carrying, his eyes crinkling with approval. "Looks like you found everything you need."

"Steaks are waiting at home. We just needed the sides," Jim said as he shifted the bags in his hands.

Olivia turned to Grace. "You two should come by the house later if you have time. We're not doing anything special, just a quiet day at home. But you're always welcome. It'd be fun to catch up. I'd enjoy hearing about how your progress at the inn is going."

"We might," Jim said, glancing at Grace. "We'll play it by ear and see where the day leads us."

"I'd love to catch up with you sometime, Mrs. Hartwell. I've really missed you," Grace said.

"Now, Grace, call me Olivia. I'll have none of that Mrs. Hartwell stuff." His mother waved her hand dismissively. "And I've missed you as well, sweetie. I was just talking to your momma on the phone this morning, and we were reminiscing about when you two were teenagers. Ahh, those were the good old days. How fast time has flown."

"It really has. The years flew by so fast."

"Well, you two drop by the house later if you want." Olivia turned to Jim and patted his arm, her touch lingering for just a moment. The look she gave him said more than words could have. She approved. She was happy for him. She wanted this to work out for him. "Enjoy your day, son. It's good to see you out and about enjoying yourself."

Bill nodded to both of them. "Nice to see you, Grace. Don't let this one burn the steaks."

"I've never burned a steak in my life," Jim protested.

"There's a first time for everything." His father's eyes crinkled with amusement. "Take care, son."

They parted ways; his parents continuing toward the vegetable vendors while Jim and Grace turned in the opposite direction. Boone trotted alongside Grace now, having apparently decided that her side was preferable to Jim's for the moment.

"Your parents are wonderful," Grace said as they walked.

"They like you."

"They're just being polite."

"Grace," Jim stopped walking and turned to face her. Around them, the market continued its cheerful bustle, but for a moment it all faded into background noise. "My parents have known you since you were a little girl. They watched us date in high school. They saw how happy you made me back then." He paused, weighing his next words, wanting to get them right. "And they can see how happy you make me now. They're not being polite. They're being honest."

Grace held his gaze for a long moment. Something moved through her expression, too quick to name, and then she smiled. It was a real smile, the kind that reached her eyes and softened every line of her face.

"You make me happy too."

Jim felt those words settle into him, warm and welcome. He wanted to say something in return, something that captured what this morning and the time spent with her meant to him, but before he could find the right words, a familiar voice cut through the moment.

"Well, look who it is!"

Minnie Whitfield appeared beside them as if she had materialized from thin air, a large basket hooked over one arm and overflowing with vegetables. Tomatoes and cucumbers and bunches of fresh herbs poked out from the top, evidence of a thorough shopping expedition. Her silver hair was pinned up in its usual twist, and her eyes sparkled with the particular delight of someone who had just discovered something interesting. If there was news to be gathered, Minnie would find it. And if there was news to be spread, she would spread it faster than the town newspaper.

"Jim Hartwell and Grace McKenna shopping together at the farmer's market." Minnie looked between them with obvious pleasure. "Isn't this lovely?"

"Morning, Minnie," Jim said. "Stocking up for the diner?"

"Fresh salads tonight. I refuse to serve anything that came out of a bag when I can get the real thing right here." She hefted her basket higher on her arm, the vegetables shifting with the movement. "Had to fight Mrs. Morris for the last of the good romaine, but I won. She'll just have to make do with iceberg." Minnie's eyes twinkled with competitive satisfaction. "What about you two? Planning something special?"

"Just lunch," Grace said. "Jim's going to grill steaks."

"Is he now?" Minnie's eyebrows rose with interest, and Jim could practically see her filing this information away for later distribution. "You two have fun with your 'just lunch.' And Grace, honey, you stop by the diner soon. I want to hear all about how the inn is coming along. Tom and his crew came for lunch yesterday, and they told me all about this lovely new kitchen you have planned. Your grandmama, God rest her soul, would be so proud of what you're doing with that place."

"Thank you, Minnie. That means a lot."

"I mean every word." Minnie reached out and squeezed Grace's arm with genuine affection. "Your grandmama was one of my dearest friends. Seeing that inn come back to life, knowing it's in good hands, well, it does my heart good." She released Grace's arm and took a step back, her expression shifting back to its usual brightness. "Now, I'd better get moving. I have a few more things to pick up, and then I need to hustle back to the diner and get ready for the evening crowd."

Minnie bustled off toward another vendor, her basket swinging with each purposeful stride, and Jim caught Grace watching her go, grinning while she shook her head.

"She's something else," Grace said.

"She really is. Half the town's news travels through her diner. The other half travels through my sister Rebecca's beauty shop."

"Between the two of them, I imagine nothing stays secret for long."

"Not a thing. But they mean well. They both do."

They continued through the market, their pace unhurried. The crowd had thinned slightly as the morning wore on, making it easier to move between the booths. Jim found himself noticing small things. The way Grace tilted her head when something caught her interest. The way she laughed at a display of hand-painted signs with corny sayings. The way Boone kept pressing close to her side, his tail wagging whenever she looked down at him.

Near the gazebo, they encountered Pastor Davis and his wife, Mary. The pastor was carrying a bouquet of fresh flowers, a cheerful mix of yellows and purples. Mary herself carried a bag of homemade breads; the paper wrapping doing little to contain the warm, yeasty scent.

"Jim, Grace." Pastor Davis's smile was warm and genuine, the kind of smile that made you feel welcomed without any effort at all. "Beautiful morning, isn't it?"

"It really is," Jim agreed. "Looks like you found some nice flowers."

"Mary's weakness. We can't walk past a booth plumb full of flowers without her finding something she has to have."

Mary swatted his arm playfully, her own smile matching her husband's. "You're the one who insisted we stop. You said they'd look nice on the kitchen table."

"Did I say that? I don't recall."

"Warren Davis, you are a terrible fibber."

Pastor Davis chuckled, the sound easy and familiar, then turned his attention to Grace. "How are you settling in? The inn keeping you busy?"

"Very busy." Grace shifted the bag she was carrying to her other hand. "But it's good work. Meaningful work. It's been a bit of an adjustment being back home after so long, but I'm happy to be home."

"I imagine it's quite a change from Atlanta."

"It is. In the best ways, mostly." Grace paused, and Jim watched something thoughtful move across her face. "I forgot how much I missed being part of a community like this. Where people know your name and actually care about the answer when they ask how you're doing."

Pastor Davis nodded slowly, his expression kind. "That's one of the gifts of a small town. We're all in each other's business, for better or worse." He smiled. "Grace, if you ever have time, I'd love for you to stop by the church. Just to catch up. And of course, if you ever want to talk about anything, my door is always open."

"Thank you, Pastor. I appreciate that."

"I mean it. Anytime. You know where to find me."

They exchanged a few more pleasantries, Mary complimenting Grace on her sundress and asking after her mother, before parting ways. The pastor and his wife headed toward the parking area while Jim and Grace turned back toward Main Street.

"He's a good man," Grace said as they walked.

"One of the best. I can't imagine our church without him. He's baptized half the town and married the other half."

"He baptized me. When I was twelve."

Jim glanced at her. "I remember. I was there."

Grace looked up at him.

"You were wearing a white dress, and you looked terrified. Your hands were shaking when Pastor Davis led you into the water. But when you came up out of the water, you were smiling like you'd just discovered something wonderful."

Grace was quiet for a moment, and Jim wondered if he'd said too much. If he'd revealed too clearly how much attention he had paid to her, even back then, even before they started dating. Then she reached over and took his hand, threading her fingers through his.

"You remember that," she said softly.

"I remember a lot of things."

They walked hand in hand toward Main Street, Boone trotting beside them. The morning sun warmed their shoulders as they crossed the street and onto the sidewalk that ran in front of the businesses lining the square. The familiar storefronts passed on their right: The Daily Grind with its chalkboard sign advertising the day's specials, The Book Nook with Miranda's latest window display, and Hawthorne Mercantile with its old-fashioned charm.

They turned into the narrow passage between Hartwell's Hardware and the Smoky Mountain Soapery, following it toward the alley behind the buildings. Jim's truck was parked in its usual spot, the extended cab gleaming in the late morning light.

He opened the back door and loaded the grocery bags onto the seat, arranging them so the strawberries wouldn't get crushed and the pasta salad wouldn't tip. Then he walked around to the passenger side and opened the door for Grace.

She paused before climbing in, turning to look at him.

"This has been a perfect morning. I'm glad you suggested we play hooky from being responsible adults."

"We haven't even gotten to the good part yet. The steaks are waiting."

Grace laughed, the sound bright and easy, and climbed into the truck. Jim closed the door gently behind her.

He walked around to the driver's side and opened the door. Boone hopped up into the cab and settled himself in the middle of the bench seat. The dog looked between them with an expression of pure contentment, like this was precisely where he was supposed to be.

Jim climbed in, pulled his door closed, and started the engine. He let it idle for a moment and glanced over at Grace. She was looking out the windshield, a small smile playing at the corners of her mouth, her hand resting on Boone's back. The sunlight coming through the window caught the curve of her cheek, the line of her jaw, and the soft fall of her hair against her shoulder.

He could get used to this.

Chapter 19

T he truck rounded the final curve in the driveway, and the trees fell away on both sides like curtains being drawn back from a window. Sunlight flooded the cab after the cool shade of the forest, and Jim squinted against the brightness as the clearing opened before them. Boone's ears lifted, his nose twitching toward the gap where Grace's window was cracked open, catching the familiar scents of home.

The cabin stood at the far end of the clearing, log walls warm against the green of the surrounding forest, and afternoon light glinted off the windows. Beyond the roofline, the mountains and ridgelines rose in staggered layers, each one paler than the last until the farthest peaks faded into the haze that hung over the Smokies.

Grace turned to look at him, her lips parted, her eyes wide.

"Jim." Grace's voice was barely above a whisper. "This is incredible."

He eased off the gas and let the truck roll forward at a crawl, watching her take in the property. Her gaze swept from the treeline on the left to the open meadow on the right, then back to the cabin, then up to the mountains, like she couldn't decide where to settle her attention.

"We used to hike through here," Grace said, and there was wonder in her voice. "Remember? This whole area. We'd ride four-wheelers through these woods with all our friends."

"I remember."

"I never imagined anyone would build a house back here. It always felt so wild. So untouched."

"That's why I chose it. Mom and Dad offered me and each of my siblings a piece of their property a few years ago, and I picked this portion without hesitation." Jim pulled the truck to a stop near the front of the house and put it in park. "I spent months walking the land before I even started drawing plans. Figuring out where the light would fall. Where the best views were. How to position everything so the house would feel like it belonged here instead of intruding."

Grace turned to look at him. "You designed this yourself... without any help?"

"With help. I worked with an architect in Knoxville on the technical details, the engineering, the permits, and all that. But the vision was mine. Every room, every window, every choice about how it would sit on the land." He nodded toward the house. "Sarah and her crew built it. I helped whenever I could get away from the store."

Grace's gaze returned to the cabin, and Jim watched her take in the details. The structure rose two stories, built from logs that had been milled from trees harvested on Hartwell land. A stone chimney climbed the eastern wall, the rocks gathered from the creek that ran behind the property. The wraparound porch extended across the front, along both sides, and around to the back, supported by thick timber posts that anchored the house to the earth.

"It's beautiful," she said. "The proportions are perfect. The way it sits in the clearing, the way the roofline echoes the slope of the mountains behind it. This isn't just a house, Jim. This is architecture."

"Come on." He opened his door and stepped out. "Let me show you the inside."

They retrieved the grocery bags from the back seat. Boone bounded ahead of them up the porch steps, his tail wagging as he waited at the front door.

Jim unlocked the front door and pushed it open, stepping aside to let Grace enter first.

The great room opened before them, two stories of space anchored by a massive stone fireplace that climbed to the vaulted ceiling. The logs that formed the walls had been left natural on the interior; their honey-gold color was warm in the afternoon light that poured through the tall windows. Exposed timber beams crossed overhead, supporting the upper floor and the peaked roof above. The floors were wide-plank oak, darkened with age to a rich amber tone.

Grace stood just inside the doorway, the grocery bag forgotten in her hands, her eyes traveling slowly around the room.

"Jim." She shook her head slowly, and he could see her professional mind cataloging details even as her personal response showed on her face. "This is extraordinary."

"Let me take that." He lifted the bag from her hands and carried all the groceries toward the kitchen, which opened off the great room through a wide archway.

The kitchen was generous, designed for someone who actually cooked rather than just reheated. Custom cabinets lined the walls, built from the same oak as the floors and finished with simple iron hardware. A large island occupied the center of the space, its butcher-block top scarred from years of meal preparation. The countertops were granite, dark with flecks of gold that caught the light. Windows ran along the back wall, offering a view of the backyard and the tree line beyond.

Jim set the groceries on the island and turned to find Grace standing in the archway, her gaze moving from the cabinets to the windows to the ceiling and back again.

"The light in here must be spectacular in the morning," she said.

"It is. The sun comes up over that ridge." He pointed toward the windows. "First thing in the morning, this whole room and the back portion of the living room fill with light. It's my favorite area of the house, besides the porch, honestly. I spend more time in this kitchen or the living room than anywhere else."

"The cabinet work in here is beautiful. Who did the millwork?"

"A guy out of Gatlinburg that does custom work. Sarah recommended him, and I'm glad she did. His work is outstanding."

Grace moved into the kitchen, running her fingers along the edge of the island. "The joinery is excellent. You can always tell quality craftsmanship by the details people think no one will notice." She crouched down to examine where the cabinets met the floor. "Perfect scribing. No gaps."

"You really do see things others miss."

She stood and smiled at him. "Occupational hazard. I spent years designing buildings and then watching contractors cut corners. You learn to look for the places where quality either shows or doesn't." Her smile widened. "This kitchen was built by someone who cared about doing it right."

"I'll pass that along to Sarah. She'll appreciate hearing it."

"She should be proud. This is excellent work."

Jim led her back through the great room, Boone padding along behind them. He showed her the study off the main living space, a smaller room lined with built-in bookshelves that held his collection of novels, history books, and a few treasured volumes that had belonged to his grandfather. A leather chair sat near the window, positioned to catch the afternoon light, with a reading lamp beside it and a small table for his coffee.

"This is where I disappear on winter evenings," he said. "Fire going in the main room, a book, maybe some music playing. Boone curled up at my feet."

"It's perfect." Grace ran her hand along the spine of a book, her touch gentle. "A quiet space... a room for thinking."

"That's exactly what I wanted it to be."

They climbed the stairs to the second floor, where a wide hallway connected the bedrooms. Jim pointed out the guest rooms first, four of them, each with its own bathroom and windows that framed different views of the property. The furniture was simple but well-made; the beds were covered with quilts his mother had given him as housewarming gifts.

"The quilts are beautiful," Grace said, pausing in the doorway of the second guest room. "Your mother's work?"

"She made one for each room. Said a house isn't a home without something handmade in it."

"She's right."

The master bedroom occupied the far end of the hall, larger than the guest rooms and positioned to capture the best of the mountain view. A wall of windows faced east, framed by curtains Grace's fingers lingered on as she passed. The bed was a four-poster made from reclaimed barn wood, something Jim had commissioned from a local craftsman after seeing a similar piece at a furniture show in Asheville.

"The view from here must be incredible at sunrise," Grace said, standing at the windows.

"It is. I enjoy watching the sun rise over the mountains."

She turned slowly, taking in the rest of the room. The stone-topped dresser. The comfortable chair in the corner with a small book-shelf beside it. The bathroom visible through an open door, with its claw-foot tub and walk-in shower.

"You've created something special here, Jim. Every room has an intention behind it. Purpose. It's not just beautiful. It's thoughtful."

"I had a lot of time to think about what I wanted." He leaned against the doorframe, watching her. "When you're designing a home from scratch, you get to ask yourself what really matters. What do you need? What do you want? How do you want to feel when you're in each space?"

"Those are the good questions." Grace moved toward him, and they walked together back toward the stairs. "Most people don't think that deeply about their homes. They buy what's available or build what's expected. But you built something that reflects who you are."

They descended the stairs and returned to the great room, where Boone had already claimed his favorite spot on the large rug in front of the fireplace, his chin resting on his paws as he watched them with obvious satisfaction.

"He looks happy," Grace said.

They made their way to the kitchen to unpack the groceries. Grace was quiet as they worked, her gaze occasionally drifting toward the windows or around the room. He could tell something was on her mind.

"Can I ask you something?" She said finally. "I don't mean to sound nosy or like I'm prying. But this house is large. Very large for a man and his dog." She paused, and he could see her choosing her words carefully. "Why build something this size?"

"I didn't build it just for myself. When I drew up the plans, when I sat down with that architect and worked through every detail, I was imagining more than this. I imagined a family. Kids running through that great room. Bedrooms full instead of empty. Sunday mornings with noise and chaos and people I loved filling every corner."

Grace was silent, watching him.

"I started planning this house about six years ago. Started building it about five years ago. Amanda and I were married when the foundation was poured." He kept his voice even. "She filed for divorce while Sarah's crew was still framing the first floor."

"Oh, Jim. I'm so sorry I asked. I didn't know," Grace's voice was soft.

"Most people don't, and you don't need to apologize. It's not something I talk about much." He straightened and moved to the island, resting his hands on the butcher-block surface. "I finished the house, anyway. Partly because I'd already invested too much to walk away. Partly because I still believed in what I was building, even if the person I thought I was building it with was gone."

"That took courage."

"It took stubbornness, mostly." He allowed himself a small smile. "But the house is finished now. It's mine. And whatever I imagined when I started, this is what it became. A good home. A quiet life. Boone and I are making the best of it."

Grace crossed to where he stood and placed her hand over his on the countertop. Her touch was warm, her grip firm.

Jim turned his hand over beneath hers, their palms pressing together. "The past is the past. I've made my peace with it." He met her eyes, letting her see the truth of what he was saying. "What I care about now is right here. This afternoon. You. That's what matters to me."

Grace held his gaze and nodded.

"So," Jim said, squeezing her hand gently before releasing it. "I don't know about you, but I'm starving. What do you say we get those steaks on the grill?"

Grace smiled, and the weight of the conversation lifted. "I thought you'd never ask."

Chapter 20

Grace prepared the cucumber in clean, even slices, each one falling away from the blade with a satisfying sound against the butcher-block surface. Country music drifted from a small speaker mounted in the corner of the kitchen near the ceiling, something with fiddles and a steady beat, the kind of song that made you want to sway without realizing you were doing it.

Jim stood at the island across from her, his attention focused on the two ribeye steaks laid out on a wooden cutting board. He had already rubbed them with olive oil and was now applying a generous coating of garlic, salt, and pepper, his movements practiced and unhurried.

Boone had claimed his spot on the large dog bed tucked into the corner near the pantry door. His chin rested on his paws, but his eyes followed every movement in the kitchen with the focused attention of a dog who knew that cooking meant the possibility of dropped food. His tail gave an occasional lazy thump against the floor whenever Jim or Grace looked his way.

"You're putting a lot of salt on those," Grace observed, glancing up from her cucumber.

"Trust me. Steaks need salt. It's not optional."

"I'm just saying, if we have to drink a gallon of water each after dinner, I'm blaming you."

Jim grinned and reached for another pinch of salt, adding it to the steaks with exaggerated deliberateness. "Noted."

Grace shook her head and turned her attention back to the vegetables. The lettuce they had picked up at the farmer's market that morning sat in a colander near the sink, already washed and waiting to be torn into pieces. The tomatoes from the older gentleman's booth were deep red and perfectly ripe, and she had sliced them into wedges that now filled a small bowl. The radishes added splashes of bright pink and white to the cutting board.

This was nice. More than nice. It was the kind of afternoon she had forgotten existed during her years in Atlanta, where weekends meant catching up on work, and dinners were usually takeout eaten standing at the kitchen counter or out at a restaurant.

"The potatoes should go in soon," Jim said, checking the clock on the microwave. "They'll need about thirty minutes in the microwave."

"I'll get them ready if you want to get the grill going for the steaks."

"Deal."

Grace used a fork to puncture the skins of the russet potatoes they had bought from Earl's booth and made a small cut in each to insert a pat of butter.

Jim grabbed the platter of seasoned steaks. "Be right back. Grill master duties call."

"Try not to burn anything."

"Have a little faith, woman."

He headed for the back door, Boone scrambling up from his bed to follow. The dog apparently considered grill supervision to be part of his job description. Grace watched them go, smiling at the way Boone's tail wagged as he trotted after Jim onto the wraparound porch.

She turned back to the salad, tearing the lettuce into bite-sized pieces and adding them to a large wooden bowl she had found in one of the cabinets. The cucumber slices went in next, then the tomato wedges and radishes. She located a bottle of ranch dressing in the refrigerator door and set it on the counter alongside the container of homemade pasta salad they had picked up at the market.

Through the windows, she could see Jim standing at the built-in grill on the back porch, Boone sitting attentively at his feet. The smoke rose in lazy spirals, carrying the smell of searing meat that made her stomach growl in anticipation. Beyond the porch, the backyard sloped gently toward the tree line, and she could hear the faint sound of the creek that ran through the property through the open windows.

She set two places on the dining table near the back windows. Napkins, forks, knives. The salt and pepper shakers she found on a shelf near the stove.

Jim returned with the steaks eventually, the meat resting on the platter with those perfect grill marks that spoke of someone who knew what he was doing.

"Those smell amazing."

"Told you to trust me." He set the platter on the counter and moved to check on the potatoes, opening the microwave door to poke one with a fork. "These are getting close. Another five minutes, maybe."

Grace leaned against the counter, the music shifting to a slower song with a woman's voice singing about coming home to someone she loved.

"Can I ask you something?"

Jim turned to look at her, his expression open and attentive. "Of course."

"What if we'd never broken up?"

Jim's hands stilled on the dish towel he had been using to wipe down the counter.

"I think about that sometimes," he said finally as he looked up at her. "More than I probably should."

"Go on."

"Grace." His voice was gentle but firm. "I didn't want to break up with you back then. Not really. You were the one who thought it was best, and I followed your lead because I loved you enough to let you go. But I never wanted to."

The floor felt as if it had shifted beneath her feet.

"I thought it was mutual," she said slowly. "I thought we both agreed that long distance wouldn't work, that we were too young to limit our futures."

"That's what I told myself too. That's what I let you believe because you seemed so sure it was the right thing." Jim set down the dish towel and turned to face her fully. "But if I could go back and do it over again, I would have fought harder. I would have found a way to make it work. Long distance, visiting on weekends, whatever it took." He paused, and something raw moved through his eyes. "I should have followed you to Virginia if that's what it took to keep you."

Grace's throat tightened. She had carried a certain version of their breakup in her memory for fourteen years. Two teenagers who loved each other but were sensible enough to know that first love rarely survived the transition to adulthood. A clean ending that honored what they had without trying to force it to be something it couldn't sustain. A mutual decision made by two people who wanted the best for each other.

But that wasn't what had happened at all. Jim had let her go because she had asked him to. He had stepped back because she had stepped away first. He had pretended the breakup was what he wanted because that's what she needed to believe to feel okay about leaving.

"Jim." His name came out barely above a whisper. "Why didn't you say anything?"

"Because you had dreams, Grace. Big dreams that Serenity Crossing couldn't give you. Architecture school at Virginia Tech. A career in a city where people actually needed architects for more than barn conversions and farmhouse additions." His smile was soft, tinged with an old sadness that she was only now seeing clearly. "How was I supposed to ask you to give all that up for a boy who loved this town and only ever wanted to run his grandfather's hardware store?"

"You wouldn't have been asking me to give anything up. You would have been asking me to include you in my future."

"I know that now. I didn't know it then." He took a step closer, close enough that she could see the flecks of gold in his brown eyes. "I was eighteen years old, and I thought the most loving thing I could do was let you fly without making you feel guilty for leaving. That's one of the big regrets of my life, Grace. Letting you go without fighting for us."

She felt tears prick at her eyes and blinked them back. This man. This steady, patient, good man who had loved her enough to set her free and then spent fourteen years wondering what might have been.

"I had no idea," she said softly.

"How could you? I never told you. I thought I was being noble." He laughed quietly, the sound rueful. "Turns out noble feels a lot like lonely when you're lying awake at three in the morning wondering if she's happy without you."

Grace reached out and laid her hand on his arm. She could feel the warmth of his skin through the fabric of his sleeve, the solid strength of muscle beneath. He covered her hand with his own, his fingers wrapping gently around hers.

"For what it's worth," she said, "I wasn't happy. Not in the way I thought I would be. College was tough, and missing you made it worse. Then I had the career and the city and all the things I thought I wanted, and none of it ever felt quite right." She met his eyes, letting him see the truth of what she was saying. "I kept comparing everyone I met to a boy from Serenity Crossing who used to open doors for me and remember what kind of scones I liked. Nobody ever measured up."

"Grace."

"It's true. Every relationship I had after you, I was always looking for what we had. I just didn't admit to myself that's what I was doing until I came home and saw you standing in the hardware store looking at me like no time had passed at all."

Jim lifted his free hand and brushed his thumb across her knuckles. "Time passed. A lot of it. But some things don't change."

The microwave timer beeped, breaking the moment. Jim released her hand and walked to the microwave. Grace took a breath, steadying herself, feeling the new shape of their history settling into place inside her mind.

They plated the food together. Jim took care of the steaks while Grace added the potatoes, splitting each one open and adding more butter and a sprinkle of salt. She spooned pasta salad alongside and set the wooden bowl of green salad between their places at the table.

"Shall we eat outside?" Jim asked, nodding toward the back porch. "The view's better."

"I'd like that."

They carried their plates through the back door and settled into the chairs on the wraparound porch. Boone followed them out and took up his position between their chairs, his nose twitching at the smell of the food but his manners too good to beg outright.

The view was everything. The backyard stretched toward the tree line in a gentle slope, the grass green with new spring growth. Beyond the trees, the mountains rose in layered ridges, their peaks softened by the haze that gave the Smokies their name. The creek was visible now, a ribbon of silver winding through the property, its gentle sound providing a constant backdrop to the birdsong and the rustle of wind through the leaves.

Grace cut into her steak and took a bite. The meat was perfectly cooked, tender, and flavorful, the salt exactly right despite her earlier teasing. She told Jim so, and his pleased smile made something warm bloom in her chest.

They ate slowly, savoring the food and the view and the simple pleasure of each other's company. The conversation drifted through easier topics now. Jim told her about a customer who had come into the hardware store last week looking for a part that hadn't been manufactured since 1975. Grace described her latest battle with trying to decide on the best bed linens to purchase for each of the rooms at the inn.

"Sarah mentioned the porch and gazebo are almost finished," Jim said, spearing a piece of tomato from his salad. "She's proud of how it's turning out."

"She should be. The design is exactly what I wanted. And her crew has been incredible. They show up on time, they work hard, and they actually clean up after themselves." Grace shook her head. "You have no idea how rare that is. Some of the contractors I worked with in Atlanta would leave job sites looking like disaster zones."

"Sarah wouldn't tolerate that. She learned from our dad, and he learned from his dad. Hartwells don't do sloppy work."

"It shows."

Grace set down her fork and leaned back in her chair, letting the beauty of the moment wash over her. The food was delicious. The company was better. And the revelation from earlier, the truth about their breakup that Jim had carried alone for fourteen years, had shifted something fundamental in how she understood not just their past but their present.

He had loved her enough to let her go. He had loved her enough to pretend he didn't want her to stay. He had loved her enough to give her the freedom to become whoever she was going to become, even though it meant watching her walk away.

That was the kind of love no other boyfriend or ex-husband from her past had ever been capable of. That was the kind of love Grace had spent years searching for without knowing what she was looking for.

And here it was. Sitting beside her on a porch in the mountains, asking if she wanted more pasta salad.

"I think I'm good," she said. "But thank you."

"Room for strawberries later?"

"Always room for strawberries."

"I'll take our plates inside and clean up a bit."

Grace insisted on helping with the dishes despite Jim's protests that she was a guest. She started filling the sink with warm, soapy water while he gathered the serving dishes.

"We could use the dishwasher," Jim offered.

"For this many dishes? That's a waste." Grace turned on the faucet and adjusted the temperature. "I'll wash, you dry."

"Bossy."

"Efficient."

Jim laughed and grabbed a dish towel from the drawer, positioning himself beside her at the sink.

The dishes didn't take long. A few plates, the serving bowls, the knives, and forks. Grace washed each one methodically while Jim dried and put them away, moving around his kitchen with the ease of someone who knew exactly where everything belonged. The domestic rhythm of it felt natural in a way that surprised her.

"So," Jim said as he dried the last fork and set it in the drawer. "What would you like to do? We could go for a hike or sit on the porch and do nothing but enjoy the day. Or I have a decent movie collection if you'd rather stay inside."

Grace rinsed her hands and reached for the towel he held out to her. "A hike sounds perfect. I've been cooped up at the inn for so long, and it's such a beautiful afternoon. I'd love to stretch my legs and enjoy the fresh air."

"I know a trail that follows the creek and then goes up in the mountains. The views are worth the hike."

"That sounds wonderful."

Jim nodded, but he didn't move toward the door. He was looking at her with an expression she had been learning to recognize over the past few weeks. The intensity beneath the steadiness. The want that he held so carefully in check, always waiting for her to set the pace.

Grace realized she was still holding the dish towel. She set it on the counter beside her and took a step closer to him.

Jim reached up and brushed a strand of hair from her face. His fingers were gentle, unhurried, tracing a path from her temple to her jaw. Grace's breath caught, but she didn't pull away. She leaned toward him, drawn by a gravity.

The kiss was slow. Deliberate. His lips met hers with a tenderness that made her heart ache, asking nothing and offering everything. Grace's eyes closed, and she let herself sink into the moment, into the warmth of him, into the rightness of being exactly where she was.

When they finally pulled apart, her eyes were bright and her pulse was racing. Jim was looking at her like she was something precious, something worth waiting for, and something he had been hoping to find again for fourteen years.

Grace smiled, her voice soft when she spoke.

"I was hoping you'd do that."

Chapter 21

The trail wound along the creek, dappled sunlight filtering through the canopy of oak and hickory overhead. fork; Jim was acutely aware that Grace had not let go of his hand since they crossed the small wooden bridge that spanned the creek behind his cabin.

Her fingers were laced through his, warm and sure, as they walked side by side on the packed earth path. Boone ranged ahead of them, nose to the ground, then circled back to check on his humans before bounding off again to investigate some new scent that demanded his attention. The sound of the creek provided a constant backdrop, water tumbling over rocks and fallen branches on its way down the mountain.

Jim glanced at Grace. She was watching Boone with an amused expression, her ponytail swinging with each step.

"This connects to the state park trails, doesn't it?" Grace asked, looking around at the familiar terrain. "The ones that run behind your parents' property?"

"It does. I had the bridge built over the creek a few years ago so I could access it without having to drive over to the main trailhead or go over to Mom and Dad's house."

Grace's steps slowed as recognition dawned on her face. "Jim. This is the trail we used to hike in high school. With Tuck and Molly and everyone else."

"The very same."

She stopped walking and turned in a slow circle, taking in the trees, the slope of the hillside, and the way the creek curved around a large boulder that jutted out from the bank. "I can't believe I didn't realize it sooner. We spent so many Saturday afternoons out here."

They continued walking, and the memories of those long-ago hikes rose up around Jim like friendly ghosts. A dozen teenagers tramping through these woods with backpacks full of sandwiches and sodas, arguing about nothing important, laughing at jokes that probably weren't as funny as they seemed at the time. Grace had always walked beside him, just like this, her hand sometimes finding his when the trail narrowed or the footing got tricky.

"Do you remember the time Tuck tried to impress Molly by climbing that big oak near the ridge?" Jim asked.

Grace burst out laughing. "Oh my gosh, yes. He got about twenty feet up and then couldn't figure out how to get back down."

"We had to talk him through it for thirty minutes. Step by step. 'Put your foot on that branch. No, the other branch. Your left foot, Tuck.'"

"And Molly just stood there at the bottom, hands on her hips, telling him he was an idiot."

"She wasn't wrong."

Grace shook her head, still grinning. "He was so determined to show off for her."

"She made him buy her a milkshake at Minnie's and carry her books to class for a week after that. I think she called it compensation for emotional distress."

"I remember that."

The trail began to climb, the grade gentle but steady as it wound up the mountainside. Boone had found a stick somewhere and was carrying it proudly, his tail wagging as he trotted ahead of them like a scout leading an expedition.

"What about the time you tried to teach me to skip rocks at Hawthorne Lake?" Grace asked. "That was a disaster."

Jim groaned at the memory. "You kept throwing them straight down into the water. Like you were trying to punish the lake for something."

"I was doing my best!"

"Your best involved splashing me in the face a million times."

"That was intentional. You were being smug about how good you were at it."

"I was trying to demonstrate proper technique."

"You were showing off." Grace bumped her shoulder against his arm playfully. "Just like Tuck with his tree climbing. You Serenity Crossing boys and your need to impress girls with your outdoor skills."

Jim laughed, the sound echoing through the trees. "Did it work? Were you impressed?"

Grace tilted her head, pretending to consider the question. "I was impressed by how patient you were. Most guys would have given up after my third attempt."

"I'm a persistent man."

"I'm starting to figure that out."

They walked in easy quiet for a while, the only sounds their footsteps on the trail and the creek below and Boone's occasional snuffling as he investigated the underbrush. The air smelled of pine and damp earth and fresh growth, the scent of spring settling into the mountains.

"Are you up for going to the waterfall?" Jim asked as they approached a fork in the trail. "It's another mile or so, but the view is worth it."

Grace's face lit up. "Serenity Falls? I haven't been there in years."

"Then we're definitely going."

They took the left fork, the trail growing steeper as it climbed toward the falls. Grace's grip on his hand tightened slightly on the inclines, and Jim shortened his stride to match her pace, in no hurry to reach their destination when the journey itself was this good.

"Tell me about college," he said as they navigated around a section of trail where tree roots had broken through the surface. "I've always wondered what it was like. Living in a dorm, taking classes, all of it."

"You never ended up going away to college?"

"I thought about it, but taking business courses at the community college made more sense. I could work during the day and go to class at night and pick up a few business skills." He shrugged. "It wasn't glamorous, but it gave me what I needed."

"That's practical. Very you."

"Is that a compliment or an observation?"

"Both." Grace smiled up at him. "College was... an adjustment. I'd never lived away from home before, never shared a room with someone who wasn't a sibling. My freshman roommate was this girl from New Jersey named Stephanie who talked on the phone with her boyfriend until two in the morning every single night."

"Every night?"

"Every. Single. Night. I learned to sleep with a pillow over my head."

Jim winced sympathetically. "That sounds miserable."

"It was, for about three months. Then they broke up, and suddenly Stephanie wanted to be best friends. She'd come back from class and sit on my bed and tell me every detail of her day while I was trying to study." Grace laughed at the memory. "I spent a lot of time in the library that semester."

"Did you end up friends?"

"We did, actually. She calmed down eventually, and we stayed roommates through junior year. She's a lawyer in Philadelphia now."

The trail leveled out briefly before beginning another climb, and Jim could hear the falls in the distance, the low roar of water that grew louder as they approached. Boone had already disappeared around the next bend, probably investigating the source of the sound.

"What about you?" Grace asked. "What was it like staying here while everyone else went off to school?"

Jim considered the question, searching for the honest answer rather than the easy one. "Lonely, sometimes. That first year, especially. You were gone, and Tuck was at UT Knoxville, and half our friend group had scattered to different colleges. I'd go to work at the lumber mill in the morning and help out at the hardware store in the afternoon, and by evening, if I wasn't in class at the community college, I was too tired to do much besides eat dinner and fall into bed."

"That sounds exhausting."

"It was. But it was also good, in a way. I learned a lot about the business side of the hardware store and about what it takes to run a company day after day. My grandfather was still alive then, and he'd sit with me on the porch after work and tell me stories about the early days, about building the store from nothing." Jim felt the familiar ache of missing his grandfather, softened by time but never entirely gone. "Those conversations were worth more than any college class I could have taken."

"I miss him; he was such a good, kindhearted man."

"He was. He told me once that you had good sense and pretty eyes."

Grace squeezed his hand. "I wish I'd spent more time with him... isn't that always a regret of youth, though? Our younger selves never realize how important it is to spend time with our elders until it's too late."

"So true... I miss him terribly."

The trail made a final turn, and suddenly the trees opened up, and there it was: Serenity Falls, cascading fifty feet down a rock face into a pool that sparkled in the afternoon light. Mist rose from where the water hit the rocks, creating rainbows that appeared and disappeared depending on the angle of the sun. The rocky ledge beside the pool was dry and warm, perfect for sitting and taking in the view.

Boone was already at the water's edge, lapping from the pool with enthusiasm. He looked up when they approached, water dripping from his jowls, his expression one of pure canine satisfaction.

"It's just as beautiful as I remember," Grace said softly.

They settled onto the rocky ledge side by side, their shoulders touching, their hands still linked between them. The sound of the falls filled the air, loud enough to make conversation require effort but not so loud that it overwhelmed. Jim leaned back on his free hand and let the spray cool his face, watching Grace watch the water.

She looked happy. Truly happy, in a way he hadn't seen much of since she'd come home. The tension she carried in her shoulders had eased. The worry lines that appeared between her eyebrows when she talked about the inn were nowhere to be seen. She looked young and free, the way she used to look when they were seventeen and the whole world was a possibility.

"Thank you for bringing me here," she said, turning to look at him. "I needed this more than I realized."

"A good hike and being outdoors does a body good."

"I've been so focused on the inn, on the renovation, and on proving to myself that I can do this massive thing alone. I forgot what it feels like to just... stop. Enjoy a beautiful day. Be present."

Jim watched the play of light on her face, the way the mist caught in her hair like tiny jewels. An idea had been forming in the back of his mind since they left the cabin, and now it pushed its way forward, demanding to be spoken.

"Grace. Your private quarters at the inn. The wallpaper and the carpet you hate."

She blinked at the change of subject. "What about them?"

"Let me help you fix them. Next week. I'll take time off from the store, and we'll tackle the whole space together. Get rid of that wallpaper, pull up the carpet, and paint the walls. Make it somewhere you actually want to come home to at the end of the day."

Grace stared at him. "Jim, I can't ask you to do that. You have a business to run."

"You're not asking. I'm offering."

"But the store—"

"Tuck can handle the store without me. My other employees are great as well; they can handle it. I'll be close by if anything comes up, but honestly, the place won't fall apart just because I take a few days off." He turned to face her more fully, wanting her to see that he meant every word. "I haven't taken real time off in years, Grace. I'm overdue. And I want to spend that time helping you."

"Why?" The question was quiet, searching. "Why would you do this?"

Jim reached over and tucked a strand of hair behind her ear, the same gesture he'd made in the kitchen before he kissed her. "Because you deserve to have a space that feels like home. Because I know that wallpaper and carpeting are driving you crazy. Because the thought of you trying to relax in your personal space after a long day of working on the inn bothers me more than it probably should." He held her gaze, letting her see the truth of what he was feeling. "Because helping you matters to me... making you happy matters to me."

Grace studied his face for a long moment, her green eyes moving over his features like she was trying to memorize them. "You still care about me enough to take a week off from work, only to spend it working and fixing up my living space?"

Jim lifted her hand to his lips and pressed a gentle kiss against her knuckles.

"I never stopped caring about you, Grace."

She didn't say a word. She just looked at him, her eyes bright with something he couldn't name but recognized all the same, as if he was the most wonderful man she had ever known.

Chapter 22

"The wallpaper goes first," Grace said, gesturing at the floral pattern covering the living room walls. "Every single inch of it. I look at those roses every morning, and I promise you, they're mocking me."

Jim stood beside her in the middle of her private quarters, a small notebook in one hand and a pen in the other. He had shown up at the inn an hour ago, ready to start planning the renovation of her living space, and Grace had been talking almost nonstop since she let him in. She couldn't seem to stop herself. The vision for this space had been building in her mind for weeks, and now the words tumbled out faster than she could organize them.

"Wallpaper removal," Jim said, writing it down. "Got it. Carpet?"

"Gone. All of it." Grace crouched down and tugged at a corner where the mauve carpet met the baseboard. "I'm almost positive there's hardwood underneath. The bedroom has the original floors, and so do the kitchenette and bathroom."

"Only one way to find out." Jim knelt beside her and helped her pull the corner back further. Beneath the carpet padding, the unmistakable grain of oak appeared, dusty but intact. "There you go. Looks like it matches the rest of the inn."

Relief washed through Grace. She had been worried that she would pull up the carpet and find subflooring or water stains or some other disaster. But so far, the wood looked good. It would need refinishing, just like the floors throughout the rest of the building, but it was there.

"When the contractors do the floors throughout the inn, they can do these too," she said, letting the carpet fall back into place.

They stood and moved through the small living room into the bedroom. The brass bed frame held a mattress she had determined was acceptable, and the blue and cream striped wallpaper on the walls was less offensive than the florals in the living room but still needed to go.

"This room is lower priority," Grace said. "The wallpaper isn't great, but I can live with it for now. The living room and the kitchenette are what really need attention."

Jim made a note and followed her back through to the kitchenette, a cramped space with cabinets that had seen better days. Grace opened one of the doors, and the hinge protested with a squeak that made them both wince.

"These cabinets are falling apart," she said. "And the refrigerator doesn't work. I've been using the old fridge that was in the inn's kitchen, and I now have that plugged in and running in the library. But once the inn opens, I'd like to have my own small fridge here in my private space."

"What kind of cabinets are you thinking of?"

"Nothing fancy. I don't need custom millwork in here. Just something functional that I can paint or stain to match whatever color scheme I end up with."

"I keep builder-grade cabinets in stock at the store. Oak, unfinished, solid construction. They're not going to win any design awards, but they'll last for years, and you can do whatever you want with them."

"That sounds perfect."

Jim wrote it down. "What about the countertop?"

Grace ran her hand along the scarred laminate surface that currently occupied the space. "This needs to be replaced."

"And the refrigerator?"

"Small. Apartment-sized. Just enough for basics."

"I can check what we have in stock at the store. If not, I can order one for you."

They moved into the bathroom, where Grace pointed out the fixtures she wanted to update. The pedestal sink was fine, but the hardware was tarnished and dated. The claw-foot tub was charming, but the showerhead attached to the wall above it was the kind of cheap chrome that belonged in a budget motel.

"I want a rainfall shower head," Grace said. "I've always wanted one. It seems silly, maybe, but standing under one of those after a long day sounds like heaven."

Jim didn't laugh or tell her it was silly. He just nodded and added it to the list. "What size? They come in different diameters."

"Eight inches? Ten? I'm not sure what's standard."

"Well, you can look at what I have in stock at the store and decide on the size. If none of those make you happy, we can order what you want."

They returned to the living room, where Grace stood in the center and tried to articulate what she wanted this place to become.

"I want comfort," she said finally. "Cozy. Warm tones. I want it to feel like a retreat, not a showroom. Nothing sleek or modern or cold." She paused, searching for the right words. "When I was working in Atlanta, everything I designed had sharp edges and clean lines and spaces that photographed well. I don't want that here. I want a home."

Jim looked up from his notebook. "That makes sense. This should be the place where you get to stop working and just be."

"Exactly. Antique or a simple, clean style of furniture, eventually. Soft fabrics. Maybe some of my grandmother's things displayed eventually. She had this beautiful quilt that used to hang in the parlor, and I think it would look perfect in here."

"I remember that quilt. The one with the blue stars?"

"You remember my grandmother's quilt?"

"I remember a lot of things about this inn, Grace. I spent enough time here when we were dating."

"Grandma liked you. She told me once that you were a keeper, and I'd be a fool to let you go," Grace said before she turned away and walked to the window. She looked out at the side garden, where the rhododendrons were threatening to take over the walkway. "I really miss her. I wish I had taken time off from work and come home to spend time with her and my family. I have so many regrets now, looking back. I was always so focused on work and pushing toward the next big project."

"Tell me more about your work in Atlanta," Jim said from behind her. "The buildings you designed. What are you proudest of?"

The question caught her off guard. People didn't usually ask about her career in those terms. They asked what firms she had worked for, what projects she had been assigned to, and how many square feet she had under her belt. Nobody asked what she was proud of.

Grace turned back to face him. "There's a community center on the south side of Atlanta. The Meadowbrook Center. It serves a neighborhood that hadn't had any real investment in decades. When I got the project, the brief was basically 'functional and cheap.' That was what the developer wanted. Something that would meet the requirements and nothing more."

"But that's not what you built."

"No." Grace moved to the small couch against the wall and sat down, her hands folded in her lap. "I fought for that building. I redesigned it three times until I found a way to make it beautiful without exceeding the budget. I used natural light instead of expensive fixtures. I specified local materials that cost less than imports. I spent my own time researching grants that could cover the difference."

Jim sat down beside her, his notebook forgotten on the cushion between them. "What happened?"

"It got built. The way I designed it." Grace could still remember the first time she had seen the finished structure. She had cried openly. "For a month after it opened, I drove past it every single day on my way to work. Just to look at it. Just to remind myself that I had made something real and something that the people in that depressed area of Atlanta could feel proud of and enjoy being in."

"I think I read about that building," Jim said slowly. "There was an article. Something about how it was revitalizing the neighborhood, bringing people together, and parents felt safe letting their children attend activities there."

"There were a few articles. It won some awards. Small ones, local recognition mostly, but it meant something." Grace looked down at her hands. "Kids have their birthday parties in that space. Seniors take exercise classes in the main gym. People gather there for meetings and events, and celebrations. I created something that matters to a community that was fighting to stay alive, and that matters to me."

"Grace." Jim's voice was quiet. "You walked away from your career. From all of it. Why?"

The question settled into the room like a physical presence. She knew that she would have to explain the rest of her story one day. The parts she had glossed over. The parts that still hurt to examine too closely.

"The firm I worked for in Atlanta," she began. "Bennett and Associates was Lee's firm. I was his employee before I was his wife."

Jim's expression shifted as understanding dawned. "He was your boss."

"He owned the company. Every project I worked on, every promotion I earned, every success I had... it all went through him. For years, I ignored his advances, and then one day, I agreed to have dinner with him. Then we were dating. Then we got married. Two years later... I filed for divorce." Grace felt the old anger rise up, the frustration and humiliation that she had spent months trying to process during the year it took to finalize their divorce. "People at the firm always wondered if I'd gotten where I was because of talent or because the boss favored me. And honestly? By the end, I wondered the same thing."

"Grace, no. That community center you just described, that wasn't about who you were married to. That was skill. That was dedication."

"I know that. Logically, I know that." She pulled in a breath. "But when I found out about Lee's affairs, when I realized that everyone at the firm had known and no one had said a word to me, something broke. Not just my marriage. My trust in everything I had built there. Every relationship, every professional connection, and every achievement. It all felt tainted by the fact that my husband had been lying to me and the people I worked with had helped him do it."

Jim didn't say anything. He just listened, his attention focused entirely on her.

"The day I signed the divorce papers, I went straight to his office, and I quit. Walked in, told him I was done, and walked out. I didn't give notice. I didn't clean out my desk. I just left." Grace felt the emotions of that day settle over her again, the strange mix of liberation and terror. "I spent the next week trying to figure out what to do next. I could have found another job at a different firm. I had the credentials and the portfolio. But every time I thought about going back into that world, all the corporate politics and the long hours and the stress, I felt sick. I literally felt sick to my stomach."

"So you came home."

"I came home." Grace met his eyes. "I sold the condo. I packed everything I cared about into a trailer. And I drove back to the one place that had always been home." She gestured around the room with its floral wallpaper and mauve carpet. "This inn. This town. A life that actually belongs to me."

"Do you miss it? The architecture?"

Grace considered the question honestly. "I miss the designing. I miss the satisfaction of solving problems, of taking someone's needs and translating them into spaces that work. But I can do that here eventually if I want. Maybe open a small firm someday, take on residential projects, and help people in Serenity Crossing build houses and renovate buildings." She shrugged. "Or maybe I just run this inn, and that's enough. I haven't figured it all out yet. But I knew I needed to stop the way I was living. I needed to breathe. I needed space to become someone other than Lee Bennett's ex-wife. I needed to fix myself and figure out who I was and what I wanted from life."

Jim reached over and took her hand. His fingers wrapped around hers, solid and warm. "Some things don't need fixing. They just need space to be."

Grace looked at him as he stood and drew her to her feet. He lifted her hand to his lips and pressed a kiss against her knuckles, the same gesture he had made at the waterfall yesterday. Then he met her eyes with an expression that made her breath catch.

"Come on," he said softly. "Let's go pick out what you need to make this place feel more like home."

Chapter 23

Grace carried a gallon of paint and a bag of painting supplies as she entered her private quarters. Jim followed behind with two bags full of bathroom fixtures, including the rainfall showerhead she'd spent twenty minutes selecting from the display at Hartwell's Hardware. Boone trotted in last, having appointed himself supervisor of the entire operation.

"That's the last of it," Jim said, setting his bags down next to the builder-grade oak cabinets they had carried in earlier. The small living room looked like a staging area now, cluttered with paint cans, drop cloths, brushes, rollers, wallpaper removal supplies, and everything else they would need to transform this space starting Monday morning.

Grace surveyed the collection with satisfaction. "I can't believe we got all of this in one trip."

"Benefits of having a truck." Jim stretched his arms above his head, working out the stiffness from loading and unloading.

The doorbell chimed from the front of the inn; the sound carried through the empty building.

"That'll be the pizza," Jim said.

"Perfect timing. I'm starving. Let's eat on the front porch. It's too nice an evening to stay inside."

Jim headed toward the main entrance to pay for the delivery while Grace grabbed a roll of paper towels and two bottles of water from the case she kept near the kitchenette. Then she made her way through the parlor and out onto the porch. The evening air held that particular coolness that came as the sun began its descent below the mountains, and she could already hear crickets beginning their chorus somewhere in the rhododendrons. She settled onto the top step and set the water bottles and paper towels beside her, leaving room for Jim and the pizza.

Boone sat down next to Grace and looked up at her with hopeful eyes.

"Don't give me those sad puppy-dog eyes," she told him. "You'll get your share when there's crust."

His tail wagged as if she had just made a binding promise.

Jim lowered himself onto the step beside her, setting the box between them. The smell that rose when she lifted the lid made Grace's stomach growl audibly. Pepperoni, sausage, mushrooms, green peppers, onions, and extra cheese, still bubbling from the oven.

"Oh my gosh... I'm so hungry," she said.

Jim reached for her hand before she could grab a slice. "Let's say grace before you melt away from starvation."

She bowed her head as his fingers wrapped around hers.

"Lord, we thank You for this food. Thank You for good company and this blessing of life that you've given us. Bless this meal and bless the hands that made it. Amen."

"Amen," Grace echoed.

They released hands and reached for the pizza simultaneously, pulling slices onto paper towels and eating in hungry silence for the first few minutes. The cheese stretched in long strings, and the crust was perfect: thin and slightly crispy, with just enough chew to hold everything together.

"This is so much better than anything I ever found in Atlanta," she said around a mouthful.

"The Pizza Palace is the best I've ever had."

Grace swallowed and reached for another slice. "Is that the place we used to hang out at?"

"Same place, same recipes. Pat and Shirley retired a few years back, but two of their grandchildren took over. Alex and Cameron. They've modernized things a bit and expanded the menu, but all the traditional pizzas are still made exactly the way Pat and Shirley always made them."

"That's amazing." Grace looked down at the slice in her hand with new appreciation. "Multiple generations keeping the same recipes alive. There's something really special about that."

Boone nudged her elbow, and she tore off a piece of crust and offered it to him. He accepted it with the dignity of a dog who had been expecting this tribute all along.

"I agree. Alex told me once that he grew up in that kitchen. He said he could make the dough in his sleep by the time he was twelve."

Grace turned to look at Jim. "Could you see yourself doing that someday? Retired from the hardware store, watching your grandchildren run it?"

Jim was quiet for a moment, his gaze drifting out toward Cedar Street, where the streetlights were beginning to flicker on. "That's hard to imagine right now. But yeah, it's a hope of mine. Passing something good on to the next generation. Knowing that what my grandfather started, and I helped to continue, will go on after I retire." He glanced at her. "What about you? What do you want your life to look like years from now? Grandkids continuing on with the inn?"

Grace wasn't sure. In the past, she would have had a ready answer: partner at a firm, bigger projects, maybe a feature in an architecture magazine. All the markers of success that were supposed to mean something.

Now those answers felt like they belonged to someone else entirely.

"Simplicity," she said slowly, finding the words as she spoke them. "Peace. A life I can actually enjoy instead of constantly racing toward the next deadline." She pulled her knees up and wrapped her arms around them, watching the last light fade from the sky. "I spent so many years running toward something I thought I wanted and then running away from something that turned out to be all wrong. I just want to be happy and settled."

"And the inn is part of that?"

"The inn is a big part of that, I think. Serenity Crossing is my future for sure. So is being near my family again." She paused. "What about you? What does your future look like in your mind?"

"Family," he said without hesitation. "A big one. I enjoyed my childhood; our house was always full of noise and chaos, and people. I want that for myself someday. Three or four children, maybe more if that's what God has in store. A wife to share it all with." He smiled, a little self-conscious. "I know that probably sounds old-fashioned."

"No... not at all. It sounds honest."

"It's what I've always wanted. Even when I was building my home, I was thinking about filling those bedrooms. It didn't work out the way I planned, but the wanting hasn't changed."

Boone had finished his crust and was now lying between them, his chin resting on his paws, his eyes moving from Jim to Grace and back again as if following their conversation.

"What about you?" Jim's voice was gentle, careful. "Do you want children?"

The question hit somewhere tender, somewhere she had protected for so long that she had almost forgotten it was there.

"I did," she said. "When I was younger, I used to imagine having a big family like the one I grew up in. Our house was never quiet, and I loved that." She watched a firefly blink into existence near the rhododendrons, then disappear again. "But then my career took over. And Lee didn't want children. He made that very clear early on. Said he wasn't interested in the responsibility or the disruption to his lifestyle." She heard the bitterness in her own voice and tried to soften it. "So I stopped letting myself want them. I told myself I was fine with it. I told myself that career success would be enough."

"Was it?"

"No." The admission came out quietly, barely louder than the crickets. "It wasn't enough. None of it was enough. But by the time I realized that, I was so deep into a life I'd built around someone else's priorities that I couldn't see a way out."

Jim reached over and took her hand, threading his fingers through hers. He didn't say anything. He just held on.

"Now?" Grace continued, surprising herself with how much she wanted to answer the question she hadn't let herself ask in years. "Looking at life now, from where I'm sitting?" She let out a breath that felt like it had been trapped inside her for a very long time. "Yes. I still want children. I want to be a mom. I want the noise and the chaos and the full house. I just stopped believing it was possible for so long that I forgot how much I wanted it."

The evening had deepened into proper night, and the stars were emerging one by one above the mountains. Somewhere down the street, a dog barked, and another answered.

Grace realized she was in no hurry to go inside. No hurry to end this conversation this evening this moment of sitting on her grandma's porch with a man who listened without trying to fix things and asked questions without demanding answers.

"Could we take a walk?" she asked. "Around town, maybe? It's such a nice night, and I'm not ready for today to be over."

Jim stood and reached for her hand to help her up. But instead of leading her down the porch steps, he drew her closer. His arms wrapped around her, pulling her against his chest, and she felt him rest his chin on top of her head. She fit there, in the circle of his embrace, like the space had been waiting for her all along.

"I'm so glad you're back in my life, Grace." His voice was low, rough at the edges. "I've missed you."

She didn't answer. She just pressed her face against his shoulder and let herself be held, the night sounds of Serenity Crossing wrapping around them both.

Chapter 24

The small cabinet came free from the wall with a satisfying crack, and Grace pushed it toward Jim, who added it to the growing pile of demolition debris.

"That's the last one," she said, stepping back to survey their progress. The upper and lower cabinets were gone now, leaving behind rectangles of faded paint on the wall where they had hung for decades. The whole space looked stripped and raw, full of possibility.

"Not bad for a morning's work." Jim wiped his forearm across his forehead, leaving a streak of dust on his skin. His flannel shirt had pieces of debris and dust clinging to the sleeves, and there was a smudge of something dark along his jaw. He looked good like this. Relaxed. Happy. Like a man doing exactly what he wanted to be doing.

From somewhere above them came the muffled sounds of Tom's crew working on the bathroom tile, the occasional scrape of a trowel against porcelain, and the low murmur of voices coordinating their efforts. Through the window, she could hear the rhythmic pulse of a nail gun as Sarah's team installed the new windows that had finally arrived this morning, each sharp report followed by the quieter sounds of adjustment and measurement. The inn hummed with activity, with progress, and the steady transformation from neglected building to something beautiful. And here in her private quarters, surrounded by demolition debris and peeling wallpaper, Grace felt more content than she had in ages.

"Ready to tackle the refrigerator?" Jim asked.

Grace eyed the ancient appliance. It sat in the corner of the kitchenette like a stubborn guest who had overstayed its welcome, white enamel yellowed with age and a door that no longer sealed properly against the frame. A faded magnet shaped like Tennessee clung to the front.

"That thing has to weigh a ton."

"Probably. But there's two of us and one of it." Jim grinned at her, that easy expression that crinkled the corners of his eyes. "I like our odds."

They positioned themselves on opposite sides, and on a count of three, they lifted. The refrigerator was awkward more than heavy, its bulk making it difficult to maneuver through the narrow doorway. They shuffled like crabs, Grace walking backward and trusting Jim to guide her around obstacles.

"Left," he said. "No, your other left."

"That's the same left, Jim."

"Then go that way."

She laughed as she adjusted her grip. They cleared the doorway and entered the living room, where the furniture had been pushed aside and covered with drop cloths, creating a strange landscape of lumpy shapes. The radio she had set up on the fireplace mantel played country music at a comfortable volume, a woman's voice singing something about back roads and summer nights, filling the space with melody.

"Watch the corner of the couch," Jim warned.

They navigated around the covered furniture, past the spot where Boone had claimed his observation post near the cold fireplace, and through the doorway into the kitchen area of the inn, then into the parlor. The front door stood propped open to let in the late April breeze, and Grace could smell fresh-cut grass from somewhere nearby mixed with the sharper scent of sawdust and construction.

They made it across the porch and down the steps without dropping it, though there was a close call when Grace's foot caught and she stumbled. Jim steadied the refrigerator while she regained her balance, his grunt of effort the only indication that the maneuver had cost him anything.

"You good?" he asked.

"I'm good. Keep going."

They continued across the walkway and around the side of the building, toward the dumpster. It sat in the parking lot near the service entrance, already half-full with construction debris from the various renovation projects happening throughout the inn. Broken tiles, splintered wood, and twisted metal joined together in a monument to progress.

"On three," Jim said. "One, two..."

They heaved the refrigerator up and over the edge, and it landed with a crash that sent a flock of sparrows scattering from the nearby rhododendrons. The sound echoed off the surrounding businesses, a satisfying punctuation to the morning's work.

"Good riddance," Grace said, brushing her palms against her jeans.

"Amen to that." Jim stretched his arms above his head, working out the stiffness in his shoulders. His shirt pulled taut across his chest with the movement, and Grace looked away before she could think too much about it. "What's next? The wallpaper?"

"The wallpaper for sure. It's time to lay the roses to rest."

They walked back inside together. Boone lifted his head from his spot near the fireplace to watch them pass, his tail giving two slow thumps against the floor in greeting before he settled back down.

Grace retrieved the spray bottles and scrapers from her box of supplies. The wallpaper in this room was the worst of the bunch, a floral pattern in shades of mauve and burgundy that had been fashionable sometime in the early eighties. She had been staring at those roses for weeks now, watching them mock her every time she walked through the door, their faded petals a constant reminder of how much work remained to be done. Today, finally, they were coming down.

She sprayed a section of the wall with the removal solution and waited for it to soak in while Jim did the same on the opposite end of the wall. The chemical smell was sharp but not unpleasant, mixing with the sawdust and the faint sweetness of spring air drifting through the open windows. Outside, she could hear Sarah calling instructions to her crew, something about the window frame in the upstairs hallway.

"Remember when your mom tried to teach me to make her biscuits?" Grace asked, working her scraper under the edge of the wallpaper. A long strip peeled away with a soft tearing sound, revealing the bare wall beneath like a secret finally told. "That Thanksgiving when we were seventeen?"

Jim laughed, the sound warm and easy. "I remember you set off the smoke alarm."

"That was not my fault. The oven ran hot."

"The oven ran exactly the same as it had for twenty years. You just forgot to set the timer."

"Details." Grace pulled another strip of wallpaper free and dropped it into the trash bag at her feet. The paper curled in on itself, those mauve roses finally defeated. "Your mother was very gracious about the whole thing. She didn't even mention it when we sat down to eat."

"My mother loved you. She would have been gracious if you'd burned down the entire kitchen." Jim paused in his scraping, a thoughtful expression crossing his face as he looked over at her.

"Your mom's a sweetheart; she's one of the good ones."

"That she is."

Olivia Hartwell had always been kind to her, treating her like another daughter rather than just her son's girlfriend. Those Sunday dinners at the Hartwell homestead, crowded around a table that somehow always had room for one more, had been some of her happiest memories from high school. Olivia moving through the kitchen with easy confidence, Bill carving a roast or a ham at the head of the table, and the Hartwell siblings talking over each other in their eagerness to share stories from the week.

"Your family game nights were something else," she said. "I'd never seen people get so competitive over Monopoly. We McKenna's were competitive, but not like you all were."

"The Hartwells don't believe in playing games for fun. We play to win." Jim attacked a stubborn section of wallpaper with his scraper, the muscles in his forearms flexing with the effort. "It's in our blood. Dad says his father was the same way. Grandpa Hartwell once didn't speak to his brother for three weeks after losing a chess match."

"Three weeks?"

"Family legend. Could be exaggerated." He grinned. "But probably not by much."

"Do you remember that time when Dave nearly flipped the game board when Sarah bought Boardwalk out from under him? I thought he was going to lose his mind."

"That was a legitimate strategy, and he knows it." Jim's grin widened at the memory. "Sarah saved her money for the entire game, pretending she wasn't interested in the expensive properties. Then she swooped in at the last second and took everything. Dave still brings it up to this day."

"She was ruthless."

"She's always been ruthless. It's why she's so good at business. You should see her negotiate with suppliers." He shook his head in admiration. "They don't stand a chance."

They worked in companionable rhythm, spraying and scraping and peeling, the pile of discarded wallpaper growing steadily larger with each passing hour. The radio played through a string of songs that Grace recognized, the kind of comfortable background music that required no attention but filled the silence nicely. A man sang about fishing with his father. A woman crooned about dancing in a nightclub in Nashville. The ordinary poetry of country music, telling stories about lives that could have been anyone's.

"McKenna dinners were different than what I was used to," Jim said after a while, stepping back to examine his progress on the wall. A large section was stripped bare now, the old plaster beneath showing through like bones beneath skin. "Louder. More chaotic. But in a good way. And the food... my goodness... your mom always cooked enough to feed a small army."

"Nine kids will do that." Grace smiled. "Mom never could figure out how to cook just enough. Even now, with most of us moved out, she still makes enough food to feed half the town. Last Sunday there were only six of us at the table, and she made four different casseroles on top of a turkey and multiple other side dishes. We were all sent home with leftovers."

"I always liked your family dinners. There was so much energy. So much life. Someone was always laughing or arguing or telling a story that everyone else had heard a hundred times but wanted to hear again anyway."

"That's one word for it. Faith used to call it controlled pandemonium." Grace pulled a particularly stubborn section of wallpaper free and felt a surge of satisfaction as it came away in one long piece, those mauve roses surrendering at last. "Growing up with eight siblings was never boring, I'll say that much. There was always someone to play with. Always someone to fight with. Always someone in your business, whether you wanted them there or not."

Jim was quiet for a moment, his scraper stilling against the wall. When he spoke again, his voice had shifted to something more thoughtful, more careful. "Can I ask you something? About your family?"

"Of course."

"Do you ever think about it? Being adopted, I mean. What your life might have been like if things had been different?"

Grace set down her scraper and turned to look at him fully. It wasn't a question people asked her often. Most folks in Serenity Crossing had known her since she was a baby and simply thought of her as a McKenna, the same way they thought of Faith and Miranda and all the rest. The adoption was just a fact of her history, not a defining characteristic. Not something that required examination.

"Sometimes," she admitted. "Not as much as you might think. I was only a year old when Bruce and Jean adopted me. They're all I've ever known. All I remember."

Jim had stopped working entirely now, giving her his full attention with that steady focus that had always made her feel like the most important person in any room. Boone lifted his head from his paws, ears perked as if he sensed the shift in the conversation, the movement from casual banter to something deeper.

"My birth parents died in a car accident," Grace continued, the words coming easier than she expected. She had told this story before, but not often and not to many people. "I was in the vehicle with them when it happened. The child safety seat saved my life." She paused, turning her scraper over in her hands without really seeing it. "I don't remember any of it, obviously. I was too young. But occasionally I wonder what they were like. What their voices sounded like. What my life would have looked like if they had lived."

"That's natural," Jim said quietly. "Anyone would wonder."

"The thing is, I had a good childhood. A really good childhood." Grace looked around the room, at the stripped walls and the covered furniture. "Bruce and Jean never treated me any differently. Logan, as you know, is their only biological son, and I never once felt like he was loved more or valued more than the rest of us. They loved me completely and unconditionally. I never felt like an outsider. I never felt like I didn't belong. I'm truly thankful for Mom and Dad; my life could have turned out so differently if they hadn't chosen me."

"Not all of my siblings can say that," she continued. "Some of them were older when they were adopted. They remembered their lives before. They remembered families that had failed them, situations they had been rescued from, and promises that had been broken. A few of them had a hard time adjusting, trusting that this new family was going to stick. That Bruce and Jean wouldn't give up on them the way others had."

"But not you?"

"Not me." She smiled softly, the expression bittersweet. "I was lucky. I was young enough that the McKennas were all I ever knew. Bill and Jean are the parents that God chose for me. My brothers and sisters are a gift. This town. This life... all of it is a gift." She gestured around the room, at the work they had accomplished and the work that remained, at Boone watching them with those calm eyes, at the mountains visible through the window. "This is who I am. Grace McKenna. Everything else before Bill and Jean came into my life is just... history. Someone else's story that ended before mine began."

Jim crossed the room to where she stood and took her hand in his. His palm was warm and rough, his grip gentle but sure. He didn't say anything for a long moment, just held her hand and looked at her with an expression she couldn't quite name.

"For what it's worth," he said finally, "I'm glad you ended up here. I'm glad you ended up being Grace McKenna. I can't imagine you as anyone else."

"Me too."

They stood like that for a moment, hands clasped, the radio playing softly in the background and the spring breeze carrying the scent of new growth through the open windows. Outside, Sarah's nail gun fell silent, and in the quiet, Grace could hear birdsong and the distant rumble of a truck on Cedar Street.

Then Jim squeezed her fingers once and released her, returning to his section of wall with that easy smile still playing at the corners of his mouth. Grace watched him go, her hand tingling where his had been, and turned back to her own work with a warmth in her chest that had nothing to do with exertion.

The afternoon wore on, marked by the gradual disappearance of the wallpaper and the steady accumulation of debris in the trash bags. By the time the light through the windows had shifted to the honeyed tones of early afternoon, nearly all the wallpaper in the kitchenette had been stripped away and the living room walls were bare. Grace's arms ached pleasantly from the work. There was wallpaper paste under her fingernails and probably in her hair, but looking at the bare walls and the empty spaces waiting to be transformed, she felt a deep sense of accomplishment settle into her bones.

She was standing near the fireplace, surveying their progress with tired satisfaction, when the song on the radio changed.

The opening notes were familiar, achingly so, a gentle melody that seemed to reach through time itself. Grace's breath caught in her throat as the music wrapped around her, pulling her backward through years and miles to a summer before high school graduation. One that smelled like cut grass and tasted like sweet tea. Lazy evenings on a wooden porch swing watching fireflies rise from the meadow in slow, spiraling dances and a boy with a guitar who used to sing to her like she was the only person in the world who mattered.

She looked up and found Jim watching her from across the room, something soft and knowing in his expression. He had stopped working, his scraper forgotten in his hand, his eyes holding hers with an intensity that made her forget to breathe.

"It's our song," he said.

He crossed the room and took her hand, pulling her gently toward the center of the living. His other hand found the small of her back, settling there with a naturalness that made her chest ache with the rightness of it.

And then they were dancing.

It wasn't graceful, not really, not with the debris scattered around them and the chemical smell of wallpaper remover still hanging in the air and Boone watching from his corner with his head tilted in canine curiosity. But Jim led her in a slow circle around the room, their feet finding a rhythm that had nothing to do with skill and everything to do with memory.

Grace tilted her head back to look at him, her throat tight with emotion. "Do you remember singing this to me? That last summer, before I left for college. You used to sit on your front porch with your guitar and play this song for me over and over again."

"I remember." His voice was low, rough at the edges.

"You sang it like you meant every word."

"I did mean every word, Grace. Every single one."

She felt tears prick at her eyes, unexpected and unwelcome but impossible to stop. All those years ago, a boy had sat on his family's porch with a guitar balanced on his knee and sung to her about being wanted, about being needed, and about being loved exactly as she was. She had carried that memory with her through college and career and a marriage that had ended in betrayal, never quite letting go of it, never quite forgetting how it felt to be seen and loved so completely by another person.

"Do you still play?" she asked, her voice barely above a breath. "The guitar, I mean."

"I do."

Jim spun her out gently, her arm extending to its full length, their fingers still intertwined. Then he drew her back to him, her free hand landing against his chest, where she could feel his heartbeat steady and sure beneath her palm. The song continued playing, the singer's voice filling the room with words that had meant everything to her once and meant even more now.

And then Jim started to sing.

His voice was quiet, meant only for her, following the melody on the radio as he held her close and swayed with her across the cluttered floor. He sang about wanting, needing, about the way loving someone could feel like finally finding a place where you belonged. His eyes never left hers, and in them she saw everything he wasn't saying out loud. Everything he had never stopped feeling. Everything that had been waiting for both of them all along through fourteen years and two failed marriages and all the distance they had tried to put between their hearts and this moment.

Grace stopped dancing.

She stood there in the circle of his arms, barely breathing, listening to him sing to her the way he had when they were eighteen and the future was something that happened to other people. His voice surrounded her and held her in a cocoon of emotion.

The song played on, and something inside Grace that had been closed for a very long time began to open.

Chapter 25

Grace lifted her coffee cup and breathed in the steam rising from its surface, letting the morning quiet settle around her. The front porch of the Mountain Laurel Inn had become her favorite place to greet the day; this wooden expanse with its stone columns and the view of Cedar Street stretching toward downtown. The April air carried the fresh scent of spring and the distant sound of birdsong.

She was watching a cardinal hop along the porch railing when she heard the sound of an engine coming up the road. Jim's truck appeared around the bend, and happiness sparked through her, quick and undeniable. Boone's head was visible through the front windshield, ears perked forward with anticipation.

But as she watched, two more vehicles followed Jim and turned into her parking lot. Her parents' truck, a dark green Ford, and behind that, a blue pickup with Bill Hartwell behind the wheel and Olivia sitting beside him.

Grace set down her coffee cup and rose from her chair, confused and curious as she walked to the edge of the porch.

Boone reached her first. The dog bounded across the parking lot and up the porch steps with the enthusiasm of a creature who had been separated from his favorite person for an unbearable length of time, which in Boone's case apparently meant overnight. He pressed his shoulder against her leg and pushed, his tail sweeping wide arcs through the air, his whole body wiggling with joy.

"Good morning to you too," Grace said, reaching down to scratch behind his ears.

Jim was walking toward her with that easy stride she enjoyed witnessing, and behind him came a procession that made her heart squeeze. Her mom, dressed in old jeans and a faded t-shirt, her silver-streaked hair pulled back in a practical ponytail. Her dad, tall and distinguished even in work clothes, was carrying a cooler. Olivia was in paint-spattered overalls that suggested this wasn't her first renovation project. Bill brought up the rear with a toolbox in each hand and a smile on his face.

"What is this?" Grace asked as Jim reached the bottom of the porch steps.

"Reinforcements." His grin was bright with barely contained satisfaction. "I called Mom last night and asked if she and Dad could come help today. Then I called your dad and asked the same thing."

"We were thrilled to be included," Bruce said, setting the cooler down on the porch. He climbed the steps and wrapped Grace in a hug. "Your mom started baking cookies last night as soon as I told her."

"I made two different kinds," Jean added, reaching Grace next and pulling her into an embrace. "Chocolate chip and oatmeal raisin. I know oatmeal raisin is Jim's favorite."

Grace looked over her mom's shoulder at the assembled group, her throat tight with emotion she hadn't expected. Jim stood there, watching her with an expression that made her feel loved.

"You did this for me," she said to him.

"I just made a couple of phone calls."

"Don't let him fool you," Olivia said, climbing the steps with the energy of a woman half her age. "He called us at seven o'clock last night and talked for twenty minutes about all the work you've been doing on this inn and how he wanted you to have your personal living space done and fast so you could close your door at the end of the day and enjoy peace and quiet." She pulled Grace into a hug that was warm and unhesitating. "We've been waiting for an invitation to come help, sweetheart."

The morning unfolded with a rhythm of ease and determination. The men gathered in the living room to tackle the carpet removal, their voices a low rumble of discussion about the best approach and the tools they would need. Grace could hear her father's distinctive laugh mixing with Bill's quieter chuckle and Jim's occasional interjection.

The women claimed the bedroom.

Grace and Jim had stripped the wallpaper from this room late yesterday afternoon. The walls were bare now, ready for the fresh coat of paint that would transform the space from dated to inviting.

"I brought extra paint rollers and brushes from home," Jim said, appearing in the doorway with a bag and two paint cans in his hands. "Soft Linen for the walls and Cloud White for the trim. Let me know if you need anything else."

"We've got everything we need," Olivia assured him. "Go help the men with that carpet. We'll handle things in here."

Jim caught Grace's eye and smiled before disappearing back toward the living room. A moment later, she heard the sound of carpet being pulled away from the floor, followed by her father's exclamation of surprise.

"Would you look at that?" Bruce called out. "Beautiful hardwood."

Grace felt a surge of relief wash through her.

The threesome set to work in the bedroom with the easy efficiency of women who understood the rhythm of labor. Jean took the trim work, her steady hands well-suited to the detailed brushwork around windows and baseboards. Olivia claimed the roller, moving in long, even strokes that covered the walls with surprising speed. Grace worked wherever she was needed, cutting in around the closet door and filling in the spots the roller couldn't reach.

The conversation began slowly, the way good conversations always do, with observations about things around town and the weather, and the progress happening throughout the inn. But as time passed, the talk deepened into something richer.

"This reminds me of painting our first house," Olivia said, stepping back to examine her work. "Bill and I had been married about six months, and we bought this little place on the edge of town that needed a little TLC. We couldn't afford to hire anyone, so we did it all ourselves."

"I remember that house," Jean said from her spot near the window. "The one with the crooked front porch?"

"The very same. Bill spent three weekends trying to level that porch. I told him it added character, but he was determined." Olivia laughed at the memory. "We painted every room in that house together. Stayed up until midnight some nights just to finish a wall before we had to go to work the next morning."

"Bruce and I were the same way," Jean added. "Our first place was a cabin on the back forty of the McKenna property. One bedroom, a kitchen barely big enough to turn around in, and a wood stove that smoked every time the wind changed direction." She dipped her brush in the trim paint and resumed her careful work. "We were so young.

We thought we knew everything about marriage and building a life together. Turns out we knew almost nothing."

"That's how it always is," Olivia agreed. "You learn as you go. You make mistakes, and you figure it out, and you keep showing up for each other even when it's hard."

Grace listened, her brush moving steadily across the wall, absorbing the stories like rain into dry earth. These were the kinds of conversations she had missed during her years in Atlanta, the intergenerational wisdom passed down in ordinary moments. Her mom and Olivia spoke about their marriages with the easy honesty of women who had weathered decades together, who had nothing to prove and everything to share.

"The first year is the hardest," Jean said. "Everyone tells you that, but you don't really understand it until you're living it. You're learning how to be two people becoming one, and that's not as romantic as the songs make it sound."

"It's a lot of compromise," Olivia added. "A lot of choosing your battles. A lot of deciding that being right isn't as important as being kind."

"How did you know?" Grace asked. "How did you know Bill was the right one?"

Olivia paused in her rolling. "I knew because when I imagined my future, he was always in it."

"For me it was different," Jean said. "I knew Bruce was the right one because of how he loved. Not just me, but everyone around him. He had this capacity for seeing people as they really were and loving them anyway. When I watched him with his family, with his friends, with strangers who needed help, I saw the kind of man he would be as a husband and father. And I was right." She smiled softly. "Thirty-four years later, I'm still right."

Grace looked over and smiled at her mom. "I remember Grandma saying that you and Dad were made for each other. She always said, 'God couldn't have created a better match.'"

"That always tickled me when she said that. You know... your grandma would be so proud of you," Jean said quietly. "Ellie loved this inn with her whole heart, but she loved you more. You were her little pride and joy... her 'Graciekins.' Do you remember her calling you that when you were little?"

"I do. I really miss her."

"I know you do, sweetheart. We all do." Jean set down her brush and crossed the room to where Grace stood. She took her daughter's hand and squeezed gently. "But she's here. In every room of this inn, in every memory these walls hold, and in every bit of love you're pouring into this restoration. She's here, and I know with everything in me she's smiling down from heaven. I can just picture that smile of hers. I know she'd be proud of the woman you've become and the happiness you've brought back into this family. I know it in my heart. Grace... just having you home now... our family feels complete again."

Olivia had stopped painting and walked toward them. "While the men are still busy and we women can talk... can I tell you something, Grace? About Jim? It's been on my heart, and I want to share it with you."

Grace nodded.

"After his divorce, he stopped believing he deserved happiness. Not consciously, maybe, but somewhere deep down. He threw himself into work, into the store, into being there for everyone else. But he stopped hoping for himself." Olivia's eyes glistened. "These past few weeks, since you've been home, I've watched my son come back to life. The way he talks about you, the way his face lights up when your name comes up in conversation, the way he's started making plans for the future again instead of just getting through each day." She paused, her voice catching. "You've given him back something I was afraid he'd lost forever. And for that, Grace, I will always be grateful to you. You are a blessing."

The room fell silent except for the distant sounds of work continuing in other parts of the inn. Grace stood still, her brush dripping onto the drop cloth, her heart so full it hurt.

"God's timing is perfect," Jean said softly. "It doesn't always feel that way when we're living through the hard parts. But when you look back, you can see how every piece fit together. Every detour, every delay, every heartbreak that felt unbearable at the time. It was all leading somewhere."

"To here," Olivia agreed. "To now. To exactly where you're supposed to be."

Grace wiped her eyes with the back of her hand, leaving a streak of Soft Linen paint across her cheek. Both mothers laughed gently, and Jean pulled a bandana from her pocket to clean the smudge.

"Now, enough of these tears," Jean said. "Let's get this room finished. I have a feeling the men will be grumbling they're hungry soon."

The work continued, and the conversation flowed lighter now, punctuated by laughter and gentle teasing. Olivia told stories about Jim as a boy, the mischief he and his twin brother Dave used to get into, and the time they'd built a treehouse and nailed their father's brand new ladder to the tree. Jean countered with tales of Grace and her siblings, the joy and chaos of raising nine children, and the creative ways they had found to get into trouble despite her best efforts.

By the time the bedroom walls and trim were finished, Grace's stomach was rumbling and her arms ached with the good kind of tiredness that came from honest work. She stepped back to admire their progress, the fresh paint gleaming in the light from the windows, the room transformed into something clean and welcoming.

"Lunchtime, girls," Bill's voice called from the living room.

The women quickly cleaned their painting tools and made their way to where the men had gathered.

The carpet was gone. Every inch of that mauve monstrosity had been pulled up and removed, revealing a floor beneath that made Grace smile. Oak hardwood, the same as the rest of the inn, and in near pristine shape.

"What do you think?" Jim asked, appearing at her elbow.

"I think I might cry."

"Please don't. I'm not equipped to handle that... women crying tears me up."

She laughed. "I'll do my best."

They gathered in the middle of the living room, settling down on a drop cloth the men had spread out. Olivia unpacked the cooler she had brought, producing ham and turkey sandwiches wrapped in wax paper, the bread thick and fresh, and bottles of sweet tea. Jean added the cookies she had baked and bags of potato chips, and suddenly there was a feast spread across the drop cloth in the middle of the demolition.

"Bruce, would you say grace?" Olivia asked.

They bowed their heads, and Grace felt Jim's hand find hers, his fingers interlacing with her own. Her father's voice filled the space, deep and steady.

"Lord, we thank You for this food and for the hands that prepared it. We thank You for bringing us together today, for the gift of family and friendship, and for work done in service of someone we love. Bless this meal and bless this home and bless the woman who is bringing it back to life. In Your name we pray. Amen."

"Amen," the others echoed.

The meal was simple and perfect. Conversation flowed easily between bites, jumping from topic to topic with the comfortable randomness of people who knew each other well. Jean described the new variety of tulips she was trying to cultivate on the farm. Bruce asked about the inn's opening timeline, and Grace found herself explaining her plans with enthusiasm.

She was reaching for another cookie when it hit her.

It started as a quieting inside her, a gradual falling away of the noise and bustle until all that remained was this moment, this scene, these people. Grace looked around the circle at the faces she loved. Her parents, sitting close together the way they always did, Jean's hand resting on Bruce's knee. Bill and Olivia sat across from her, their shoulders touching, decades of partnership visible in every shared glance. Jim beside her, his presence steady and warm.

They were sitting on a drop cloth in the middle of a construction zone. Carpet dust clung to the men's work shirts. Paint streaked the women's hands and faces.

And yet Grace had never seen anything so beautiful.

The realization hit her with a force that stole her breath. These people had given up their day to be here. They had driven across town, brought food, picked up brushes and tools, and worked beside her without expecting anything in return. They had shown up because they loved her. Because she belonged to them and they belonged to her, and that belonging was worth protecting, worth nurturing, and worth showing up for.

Her throat tightened. Her eyes burned with tears; she didn't bother wiping away.

"Grace?" Jean reached across the space between them and took her daughter's hand. "Sweetheart, what's wrong?"

The room fell silent. Conversations died mid-sentence. Everyone looked at her with expressions of gentle concern, and Grace felt their attention like a warm blanket rather than a burden.

Another tear slipped down her cheek. Then another.

"Nothing's wrong," she managed, her voice thick with emotion. "Nothing at all. I just..." She paused, searching for words that felt inadequate for what she was trying to express. "I'm looking at all of you, sitting here in the middle of this mess, and I feel so loved."

No one spoke. No one moved. They simply listened with the patience of people who understood that some moments required space.

"You all gave up your day to be here," Grace continued, the words tumbling out unpolished and raw. "You brought food and tools, and you worked so hard, and you didn't have to do any of it. But you did. Because that's who you are. That's what family means." She looked at each face in turn, trying to memorize this moment, trying to hold it somewhere safe inside her heart. "I spent so many years in Atlanta feeling alone even when I was surrounded by people. I had colleagues and acquaintances and a husband who was supposed to love me, and none of it felt like this."

Jim squeezed her hand, and she drew strength from his touch.

"Coming home was the easiest decision I've ever made," she said. "Admitting to myself that my marriage had failed, that my life in Atlanta was built on lies, that I needed to start over at thirty-two years old... that was hard. I felt like such a failure. I felt like I had wasted so many years chasing something that was never going to make me happy."

She wiped her cheek with her free hand, but the tears kept coming.

"But sitting here now, I can see it differently. I think God brought me back home for a reason. I think every wrong turn, every heartbreak, and every moment when I felt lost was leading me exactly here. To this town. To this inn. To all of you." Her voice broke on the last word, and she had to pause to steady herself. "I took the long road. The hardest road. But I'm home now, and I'm so grateful. I'm so grateful for each of you, and I don't know how I'll ever be able to thank you enough for loving me just the way I am."

The silence that followed was sacred. Not empty but full, weighted with emotion that words couldn't capture.

Jean moved first. She released Grace's hand only to wrap both arms around her daughter, pulling her into an embrace that felt like safety, like shelter, and like coming home after the longest journey imaginable. Grace buried her face against her mother's shoulder and let the tears fall.

Jean's lips brushed against her ear, and when she spoke, her voice was barely a whisper meant only for Grace.

"God brought you through it, my sweet girl. He brought you home to us. And for that, I will be forever grateful."

Chapter 26

Jim twirled another forkful of lo mein noodles and leaned back against the base of the couch as he sat beside Grace on the hardwood floor of her living room. Paper containers from China Palace sat between them on the drop cloth they'd spread out as an impromptu tablecloth. Boone was stretched out nearby, legs twitching occasionally as he chased something through whatever dream had claimed him. The dog had earned his rest. He'd spent the entire day moving from room to room, supervising every brushstroke and roller pass with the solemn attention of a foreman inspecting his crew's work.

"I still can't believe how much we got done." Grace reached for the container of fried rice and scooped another serving onto her paper plate. "When we started out this morning, I thought maybe we'd finish one room. Maybe two if we really pushed it."

Jim looked around the living room, taking in the transformation. The walls now wore a soft sage green that caught the lamplight and made the space feel larger, brighter, and more alive. The trim work gleamed white and crisp against the new color. Even the ceiling, which had been a dingy off-white that morning, now looked fresh and clean overhead.

"Six people can accomplish a lot when they know what they're doing," Jim said. "And our mothers know what they're doing. I'm pretty sure they've painted more rooms between the two of them than most professional crews."

"My mom finished all the trim in half the time it would have taken me. I watched her cut in around window frames without even using tape." Grace shook her head slowly, a smile playing at the corners of her mouth. "It was honestly a little intimidating. And your mom is amazing. She can definitely roll paint on a wall far better than I can."

"She's had a lot of practice."

Jim watched Grace from the edge of his vision as she ate. Paint flecks dotted her forearms, and there was a smudge of sage green near her left temple that she'd missed when washing up. Her hair was pulled back in a ponytail that had grown increasingly disheveled as the day wore on, loose strands framing her face.

She was beautiful. This was Grace with her guard down, comfortable in her own skin, enjoying life like she once had when they were younger.

Jim loved seeing her like this. He loved watching her come alive as she talked about the inn, loved the way her hands moved when she described her vision for a space, and loved the spark in her green eyes when a plan came together. He loved the woman she was becoming as she shed the weight of her old life and stepped into something new.

"Jim." Grace's voice pulled him from his thoughts. She had set down her paper plate and was looking at him with an expression he couldn't quite read. "I wanted to apologize for earlier. For getting so emotional when everyone was here."

"Grace, you don't need to apologize for that."

"I do, though. Everyone was enjoying lunch, and I just started crying like some kind of..." She trailed off, searching for the word.

"Like someone who's been through a lot and is finally seeing good things happen?"

She met his eyes, and her expression softened. "That's a generous way to put it."

"It's an honest way to put it." Jim set his own plate aside and turned to face her more fully. "You've had a rough year, Grace. Several tough years, from the sounds of it. You're allowed to feel things."

She pulled her knees up and wrapped her arms around them, making herself smaller in a way that tugged at Jim's chest. "Everything hit me all at once today. I could suddenly see my whole life stretching out behind me. All the wrong turns. All the years I spent building something that wasn't real. All the time I wasted."

"And then I looked around at this room that's finally starting to feel like mine, and then our parents and you... sitting around enjoying life, and I thought about how I got here. The divorce. Tossing away everything I thought I wanted. Running home with nothing but a trailer full of boxes and a building that needed more work than I knew how to give it." Grace's voice had grown thick, her eyes fixed on some middle distance Jim couldn't see. "A year ago, I would have told you my life was falling apart. I would have said God had abandoned me or that I'd made too many mistakes to ever find my way back. But today, watching all these people who love me show up to help me... I could see it, Jim. I could finally see that everything happened for a reason. That God was waking me up. Shaking me out of a life that was never going to make me happy and putting me on a path toward something better."

"That's not something to apologize for," Jim said quietly. "That's something to be grateful for."

"I am grateful. That's what made me cry. I'm grateful for the worst year of my life because it brought me here. To this town. To this inn. To you." She looked at him then, her green eyes bright with unshed tears. "I'm grateful for you, Jim."

The words landed somewhere deep in his chest and took root there. Jim reached over and took her hand, threading his fingers through hers.

"I'm grateful for you too," he said. "And I want you to know that I didn't organize today because I felt obligated, or because I thought you needed rescuing, or because I was trying to prove something. I did it because I care very deeply for you, and I knew you'd be happy to get your living space situated. I knew our parents wanted to help, but they didn't want to force themselves on you. So I reached out to them, and they were just waiting to be asked. Grace, there's nowhere else I'd rather be than right here, with you, helping you build the life you deserve."

Grace squeezed his hand, and for a moment neither of them spoke. The lamplight cast soft shadows across her face, and Jim could see the exhaustion there beneath the emotion, the physical toll of a day spent working alongside people who loved her.

"You took a whole week off work," she said. "That's not nothing, Jim. The store is your life."

"The store shouldn't be my life, Grace. The store is fine. Tuck's got it handled, and my other employees know what they're doing. Besides," he added, letting a small smile cross his face, "it turns out there are things more important than inventory counts and supplier orders."

"That's a big admission coming from a man who once told me he dreams about shelf organization."

"I said I had a dream about shelf organization once. There's a difference."

"Is there, though?"

Jim grinned. This was what he loved about being with Grace. The way they could move from deep emotion to easy teasing without it feeling jarring. The way she could make him laugh even when his heart was full of things he didn't know how to say.

They finished their dinner slowly; the conversation drifting through lighter topics. They talked about nothing important and everything important, and the line between the two blurred until Jim couldn't tell where one ended and the other began.

Grace set down her empty plate and leaned her head against his shoulder. Jim went still. Her body was warm against him, solid and real.

"Thank you," she said quietly. "For today. For this week. For all of it."

"You've already thanked me about six times."

"I know. But I mean it every time."

Jim turned his head slightly, pressing a kiss against her hair. "You're welcome. Every time."

They sat like that for a while, comfortable in the quiet. Boone's snoring provided a gentle backdrop. Through the window, Jim could see the last light fading from the sky, the purple-gray of twilight deepening toward true dark.

He was thinking about how natural this felt when Grace lifted her head from his shoulder. She was looking at him with an expression that was open and searching. Jim felt the weight of everything unspoken between them.

He held her gaze. She held his.

The moment suspended itself in the quiet room, and Jim was suddenly aware of his own breathing, of the pulse in his wrist, of the space between them that wasn't really space at all. He wanted to kiss her. He wanted to tell her things he hadn't found words for yet. He wanted to stay in this room with her until the sun came up and then stay longer still.

Grace looked away, and when she spoke, her voice was light. Easy. "What do you think we should tackle tomorrow? I was thinking maybe the cabinets for the kitchenette."

Jim blinked, adjusting to the shift. "Cabinets sound good. We should be able to get those hung in a few hours."

"Perfect. We can hit the ground running." Grace stretched her arms above her head, her shoulders rolling back in a way that spoke of tired muscles and a long day. "I don't know about you, but I'm exhausted. I can barely keep my eyes open."

"It's been a long day."

"It has." She smiled at him, warm and genuine, but something had changed. Some subtle thing Jim couldn't name. "We should probably call it a night so we can get an early start tomorrow. What do you think?"

Jim studied her face for a moment, looking for something he wasn't sure he'd recognize even if he found it. Grace had never been the one to suggest the evening end before. In all the time they'd spent together over the past weeks, she'd always seemed reluctant to see him go, always finding one more thing to talk about, one more reason to extend their time together.

"Early start sounds good," he said. "I'll be here by eight."

"Eight is perfect."

"Is everything okay, Grace? What just happened a few seconds ago? You—"

"Nothing. Nothing at all. I'm tired, and my mind was starting to think too deeply on things. Let's just call it a day."

She started gathering the takeout containers and paper plates. Jim collected the scattered napkins and fortune cookie wrappers, depositing them in the trash bag they'd been using throughout the day. The cleanup took only a few minutes.

"Boone," Jim called to his dog, who lifted his head and regarded him with an expression of profound reluctance. "Come on, boy. Time to go home."

Boone rose slowly, stretching each leg in turn before padding across the room to stand beside him. His tail wagged once, lazily, as if the effort of expressing enthusiasm was simply too much to ask at this hour.

"He had a hard day," Grace said, reaching down to scratch behind Boone's ears. "All that supervising. Very tiring work."

"He takes his responsibilities seriously."

Grace straightened, and Jim stepped closer to her. He cupped her face in his hands, his thumbs tracing the line of her cheekbones, and kissed her. The kiss was warm and tender and unhurried, the kind of kiss that said things words couldn't quite capture. Grace leaned into him, her hand coming up to rest against his chest, her fingers curling slightly into the fabric of his shirt.

When they pulled apart, she was smiling. "Thank you again. For everything."

"I'll see you in the morning."

"Bright and early."

Jim kissed her forehead softly and then stepped back. Boone was already nosing at the door, ready to be done with the day, and Jim opened it to let him through into the larger space of the inn.

"Goodnight, Grace."

"Goodnight."

He walked through the inn with Boone; their footsteps echoed slightly in the hollow spaces. The front door closed behind him with a soft click, and then he was standing on the porch in the cool April evening, the stars just beginning to show themselves against the darkening sky.

The drive home took fifteen minutes, the familiar roads of Serenity Crossing unspooling beneath his headlights. Boone was already asleep again, his nose tucked under his paw, his breathing slow and even. Jim drove in silence, not bothering with the radio, letting the quiet settle around him.

It had been a good day. A really good day. The kind of day that reminded him why he loved this town, these people, and this life he'd built for himself. Watching Grace's face as her living space transformed. Hearing his mother laugh with Jean McKenna over some shared memory from decades past. Seeing his father and Bruce working side by side, their conversation easy and unhurried. Feeling like part of something larger than himself, something rooted in community and family, and faith.

And Grace. Always Grace. The way she'd looked at him, her eyes bright and open and full of something he wanted to believe in.

But that moment... that quick moment of change, stayed with him as the truck wound through the quiet streets toward home. The way she'd looked away. The way she'd redirected the moment, asking about tomorrow's work. The way she'd been the one to suggest they call it a night.

It was nothing. He was making something out of nothing. They were both exhausted, running on the fumes of a long day and the lingering adrenaline of accomplishment. Of course, she was tired. Of course, she wanted to get some rest. There was no hidden meaning in a woman wanting to sleep after spending hours painting walls and hauling carpet and supervising a small army of helpers.

Jim pulled into his driveway and cut the engine. Boone stirred beside him, lifting his head and blinking at the windshield as if confirming they'd arrived at the correct destination.

"Come on, boy. Let's get you inside."

They walked together up the porch steps, Jim's keys jangling softly in the stillness. The door swung open, and he flipped on the light, illuminating the great room with its vaulted ceiling and stone fireplace. The house felt emptier than usual tonight. Quieter. Lonelier.

Jim filled Boone's water bowl and watched the dog drink deeply before settling onto his bed near the fireplace. Jim stood at the kitchen window, looking out at the darkness beyond the glass, and let the evening replay through his mind one more time.

Chapter 27

The rumble of a heavy engine and the sharp beeping of a truck backing up pulled Grace's attention away from the furniture catalog spread across the parlor's makeshift work table. The cabinets were here. The kitchen that existed only in her imagination and in carefully drawn sketches was about to become something she could touch with her own hands in a matter of time.

Grace followed Jim through the foyer and out onto the front porch. A large delivery truck had maneuvered into the parking area beside the inn, its white sides emblazoned with the Hartwell's Hardware logo. As she watched, the driver's door swung open, and Tuck Brennan dropped down from the cab with a grin splitting his face.

"Special delivery," he called out, spreading his arms wide as if presenting a prize. "Where do you want about two tons of kitchen cabinets?"

Grace laughed, the sound bubbling up from somewhere deep in her chest. "The kitchen would be the traditional choice."

"Traditional. Got it." Tuck was already moving toward the back of the truck, his long stride eating up the distance. "I brought reinforcements. Hope you've got coffee made."

Two more figures emerged from the truck's cab, men Grace recognized from the hardware store. They moved with the easy coordination of people who had done this kind of work before, lowering the truck's rear gate and revealing the treasures stacked inside. Boxes and boxes of white shaker-style cabinets. Behind them were larger boxes containing the appliances she'd ordered last week: a commercial-grade stove, a refrigerator sized for a working inn kitchen, and a dishwasher that promised to handle the demands of a bed-and-breakfast operation.

Boone had followed them onto the porch and now settled himself near Grace's feet, his tail giving a single lazy wag as he surveyed the activity. He seemed to understand that today was not a day for getting underfoot. Instead, he positioned himself where he could watch everything without being in the way, his chin resting on his front paws, his brown eyes tracking the movement of people and boxes with patient interest.

Tom Reeves arrived minutes later with two of his crew members, their truck pulling up behind the delivery vehicle. The contractor greeted Grace with a nod and immediately began conferring with Tuck about the logistics of unloading. Within moments, a system had emerged: Tuck's team removing boxes from the truck, Tom's crew receiving them and carrying them through the inn to the gutted kitchen space, everyone moving with purpose and efficiency.

Jim was in the middle of all of it, directing traffic with the ease of someone who had spent his life coordinating exactly these kinds of operations. He caught Grace's eye as he helped guide a particularly large box through the front door, and his expression made her smile.

He was enjoying this. Not just helping, but genuinely enjoying the work, the camaraderie, and the tangible progress of turning plans into reality.

Grace stayed on the porch for a while, watching the parade of boxes disappear into her inn.

Eventually, she made her way inside to watch the activity from the kitchen doorway. The room was a vision of cabinets, cardboard, and plastic wrap. Men maneuvering around each other in the limited space. Tom had already begun marking positions on the walls where the upper cabinets would hang, his pencil moving with precision. One of his crew members was assembling hardware, sorting screws and brackets into neat piles on a drop cloth spread across the floor in the corner of the room.

Jim appeared beside her, reaching down to scratch behind Boone's ears as the dog settled at Grace's feet once more. "Starting to look like a real kitchen in here."

"Starting to feel like one too." Grace watched Tom measure and mark, measure and mark, his movements methodical and sure. "I keep waiting for something to go wrong. For someone to tell me the cabinets are the wrong size, or the appliances won't fit, or the whole plan needs to change."

"That's not going to happen. Tom knows what he's doing. I know for a fact he measured everything three times before giving you the list of measurements." Jim's voice carried the same steady confidence it always did, the quiet certainty that had become one of Grace's favorite things about him. "This is going to work, Grace. All of it. Have a little faith."

She wanted to believe him. Most of her did believe him. But there was a small voice in the back of her mind that had learned, through painful experience, not to trust good things. That voice had been quiet lately, drowned out by the noise of progress and the warmth of Jim's presence, but it was still there. Waiting.

The morning stretched on, marked by the rhythm of work and the occasional burst of laughter from the crew. Grace made more coffee for everyone and ran to Sweet Surrender Bakery for pastries, earning grateful smiles from the men. She answered questions when they came up and watched her kitchen take shape, one piece at a time.

She was standing in the doorway again, watching Tom's crew remove the plastic wrap and packing materials from a set of cabinets, when a familiar voice cut through the noise.

"Gracie!"

Grace turned to see Faith walking toward her through the parlor, her sister's dark hair pulled back in a braid, her face lit with a smile. Faith was dressed casually in jeans and a light sweater, a shopping bag from one of the Main Street boutiques hanging from her arm.

"Faith." Grace met her halfway, pulling her into a hug. "What are you doing here?"

"I was in town picking up a few things and thought I'd stop by to see how everything was coming along." Faith pulled back, her eyes scanning the activity visible through the kitchen doorway. "I had no idea today was such a big day. I'm sorry if my timing is terrible."

"You're fine." Grace squeezed her sister's arm. "It's good to see you."

Jim appeared beside them, wiping his hands on his jeans. A smear of dust crossed his forehead, and there was a piece of packing tape stuck to his shirt that he didn't seem to have noticed yet. He smiled at Faith, warm and genuine.

"Hey, Faith. Good to see you."

"You too, Jim. Looks like you've got quite the operation going here."

"You can say that again." Jim turned to Grace. "You should take a break. Go get coffee with your sister. You've been going nonstop for days."

Grace hesitated, looking back at the kitchen. She wanted to be here for this. She wanted to watch every piece go in, to see her vision become reality in real time. But she was also tired in a way that went deeper than physical exhaustion. The thought of sitting down with her sister, of talking about something other than cabinet dimensions and tile grout, was appealing.

Faith looped her arm through Grace's. "Come on. I need some quality time with my favorite sister. You can spare an hour or two."

Jim gave Grace an encouraging nod. "Go. Enjoy yourself. I'll text you if anything catches fire."

"That's not reassuring."

"It wasn't meant to be," he said with a chuckle.

Grace grabbed her purse and let Faith lead her out the front door, down the porch steps, and onto Cedar Street. The fresh air and warmth of the sun felt good as she walked with her sister.

The Daily Grind appeared as they turned the corner onto Main Street, its windows bright with the mid-morning sun. The coffee shop had become one of Grace's favorite spots since she'd moved back to Serenity Crossing, a place where she could sit with a latte and her laptop and feel connected to the rhythm of small-town life.

The sisters entered the coffee shop. A few regulars occupied tables near the windows, but the counter was empty, and the barista greeted them with a friendly hello.

They ordered their drinks and settled into a corner table, away from the windows and the other patrons. Grace wrapped her hands around her latte and let the warmth seep into her fingers.

"So," Faith took a sip of her drink and set it down carefully. "Tell me everything. How's the inn? How's the renovation? How's life?"

Grace laughed; the question was so broad that she didn't know where to begin. "The inn is coming along faster than I expected. Tom's crew is incredible, and Sarah's team is almost finished installing the new windows. They'll start replacing the roof next week. The guest rooms are almost ready. The kitchen is finally happening, as you saw." She paused, considering. "Life is... good. Busy, but good. Better than I thought it would be when I drove into town weeks ago."

"You look happier. Lighter, somehow. Like you're finally breathing again."

"I feel like I'm finally breathing again." Grace traced the rim of her cup with one finger. "For so long, everything felt like I was swimming through mud. Getting through each day took everything I had. But now..." She shook her head slowly. "Now I wake up and I'm actually excited about what's ahead. I have purpose again. I have direction. I have something that's mine."

They talked for a while about the inn's progress, Grace sharing details about the kitchen design and the bedroom renovations, and other little details. Faith listened with genuine interest, asking questions that showed she understood how much this project meant. Faith shared stories about her students at the high school, about the end-of-year anticipation that always descended in May, and about a particularly memorable incident involving a failed science experiment and the fire alarm. Grace laughed until her sides ached, picturing the scene Faith described.

They talked about their parents, about the farm, and about Miranda's latest dramatic retelling of a customer interaction at The Book Nook. They talked about Josie's new project expanding the native plant section of the flower farm operation, about Graham's quiet progress on his cabin renovation, and about Cain's recent promotion at the police department. The conversation wound through their family the way it always did, touching on each sibling in turn, weaving a tapestry of shared history and present concerns.

Eventually, Faith's expression shifted. She set down her cup and leaned forward slightly, her dark eyes studying Grace's face.

"And how's Jim?"

"Jim is…" She paused, searching for words that would capture something she barely understood herself. "Jim is wonderful. He's been so patient with me. So steady. He took the whole week off to help with my personal living space, and then he organized a day when his parents and ours came to help paint and remove the carpet. He's been at the inn every day this week, helping with whatever needs doing." She smiled, the expression rising naturally to her face. "He's a good man, Faith. A really good man."

"He is." Faith nodded slowly. "I've always thought so. Even back in high school, when you two were together, I used to watch him and think that's what a man should be like. Reliable. Kind. Present."

"He makes me feel…" Grace trailed off, struggling to articulate what she was trying to portray. "He makes me feel like the world is in balance. Like everything is going to be okay. Like I can trust again."

Faith reached across the table and squeezed Grace's hand; her grip was warm and firm. "I'm happy for you. Really. You deserve this."

"But?"

Faith's eyes were gentle. "I know you, Grace. You're holding something back. There's a hesitation in your voice when you talk about him. Like you're waiting for the other shoe to drop."

Grace pulled her hand back and wrapped both palms around her latte again, needing something to hold on to.

"What if I'm wrong? What if I'm latching onto Jim because he's safe and familiar? What if this is just a rebound after Lee? What if I'm using him to fill a void in my life?"

Faith was quiet for a moment, absorbing the questions without rushing to answer them. When she spoke, her voice was measured. "Do you feel like you're using him?"

Grace shook her head, frustrated with her own inability to explain what she felt. "When I'm with him, everything feels right. Natural. Like, this is exactly where I'm supposed to be. But then I think about how fast everything has happened. I was signing divorce papers in February and driving away from a life that had crumbled around me in March. Now I'm in a relationship with my high school sweetheart, our families are encouraging us, and he's taking a week off work to help me renovate my inn, and..." She trailed off, the weight of it all pressing down on her. "It's a lot, Faith. It's a lot to trust when trusting got me so badly burned before."

"You're not wrong to question it." Faith's voice held no judgment, only understanding. "After what Lee did to you, after what you went through, it would be strange if you weren't questioning everything. That's not weakness. That's wisdom."

"But what if I question it so much that I push Jim away? What if my fear ruins something that could be real?"

"That's the risk, isn't it?" Faith leaned back in her chair, her expression thoughtful. "Trust is always a risk. Even when you've done everything right, even when you've been careful and thoughtful and wise, there's still a chance that things won't work out. That's just the nature of loving someone."

Grace felt the truth of those words settle into her chest. She had known it when she married Lee. She had known it when she let herself start falling for Jim again. But knowing something and feeling it were different things, and right now she felt the precariousness of her position with an acuteness that bordered on pain.

"How do you do it?" she asked. "How do you open yourself up again after someone has shown you exactly how badly it can go wrong?"

Faith was quiet for a long moment. When she spoke, her voice had dropped to something softer, more vulnerable. "I don't know if I can answer that. I haven't figured it out myself yet."

Grace looked at her sister, really looked at her, and saw for the first time the shadows that Faith carried. Her divorce had been finalized eighteen months ago, longer than Grace's, and she had seemed to recover more quickly, more gracefully. But sitting here in this quiet coffee shop, Grace could see the truth beneath the composure. Faith was still wounded, too. Still wary. Still trying to find her footing on ground that had shifted beneath her.

"You haven't started dating again," Grace said softly.

"No," Faith shook her head. "I'm not ready. I thought I might be a few months ago. There's a teacher at school who's asked me out twice now, and he's perfectly nice, and I keep finding reasons to say no." She smiled, but it didn't reach her eyes. "Maybe I'm the wrong person to ask about this. I'm still figuring out how to trust myself."

"But you think I should trust Jim?"

"I think..." Faith paused, choosing her words carefully. "I think Jim isn't Lee. I think what you have with Jim isn't what you had with Lee. And I think the fact that you're asking these questions, that you're being careful and thoughtful instead of rushing blindly forward, is actually a good sign. You're not the same person you were when you married Lee. You've learned things. Painful things, but real things. You see more clearly now. You notice what you missed before."

Grace thought about that. About the woman she had been when she walked down the aisle toward Lee Bennett, so certain she was making the right choice, so blind to the warnings she should have seen. She was different now. Scarred, yes. Cautious, certainly. But also wiser. More attuned to the subtle signals that indicated character and intent.

And when she turned that new awareness toward Jim, what did she see?

She saw a man who had waited four years after his own divorce before opening himself to love again. A man who had let her set the pace of their relationship, never pushing, never demanding more than she was ready to give. A man who showed up consistently, not with grand gestures but with steady presence. A man who had loved her enough to let her go fourteen years ago and who seemed prepared to love her enough now to let her find her own way back.

"He's different," Grace said finally. "Jim is different from Lee. I know that. I see that. But I'm different too, and I don't know if the woman I am now is capable of..." She stopped, unable to finish the sentence.

"Capable of what?"

"Capable of believing in something good without waiting for it to fall apart."

"Maybe that's not a capability, Grace. Maybe that's a choice. Every day, every moment, choosing to believe instead of choosing fear."

The words landed somewhere deep. She turned them over in her mind, examining them from different angles, testing their weight.

"When did you get so wise?" she asked, trying for lightness and not quite achieving it.

"I've always been wise. You just weren't paying attention." Faith smiled, and this time it reached her eyes. "Now. Finish your coffee.

You've got a kitchen to supervise, and I've got more errands to run before I head home."

They finished their drinks and walked back to the inn together, the May sunshine warm on their shoulders. Faith hugged Grace tightly while standing on the sidewalk in front of the inn, holding on for an extra moment before letting go.

"Call me," Faith said. "Whenever you need to talk. Day or night. I mean it."

"I will."

Grace watched her sister walk back toward Main Street. Then she turned and walked into the inn, Boone rising from his spot on the porch to greet her with a wagging tail before following her inside.

The kitchen had transformed in the time she'd been gone. Several of the upper cabinets were in place, their white surfaces gleaming against the freshly painted walls. Tom's crew was busy measuring, drilling, and lifting. The space that had been empty and full of potential was becoming something real, something tangible, something she could see and touch.

Jim stood near the far wall, helping one of Tom's crew position a cabinet above the spot where the stove would go. He was focused on the work, his hands steady as he held the heavy piece in place while his partner drove screws into the wall. But when Grace stepped through the doorway, he looked over, and the expression that crossed his face made the knot in her chest loosen.

He was happy. Happy to be here, in her kitchen, doing work that wasn't his responsibility. Happy to see her walking through the door.

Grace crossed the room to stand beside him, careful to stay out of the way of the installation work.

Jim stepped back from the wall as his partner finished securing the cabinet, wiping his hands on his jeans. He reached down and took Grace's hand.

"Have a good time with your sister?" he asked.

"I did." Grace looked at their interlaced fingers, at his hand holding hers. "I'm glad you suggested it."

He squeezed her hand gently. "Anytime."

The cabinet crew moved on to the next piece, and the work continued around them, but Grace stayed where she was, her hand in Jim's, watching her dream take shape one cabinet at a time.

Faith's words echoed in her mind. *Maybe believing wasn't a capability. Maybe it was a choice.*

Chapter 28

Grace made her way toward Hartwell's Hardware, a cardboard tray balanced in one hand with two steaming cups of coffee from The Daily Grind. A white paper bag from Sweet Surrender Bakery dangled from her fingers, the smell of fresh donuts escaping through the folded top and mixing with the spring air that drifted down from the mountains. She had no particular errand that required her presence at the hardware store today, no supply run or special order to check on, and no renovation emergency that demanded she hurry and gather supplies so the construction crews wouldn't be delayed. She simply wanted to see him.

The realization had struck her about an hour ago, sitting in her quarters at the inn with her laptop open and her notes scattered across the small table she'd been using as a desk. She had been working for most of the day, coordinating with contractors, reviewing invoices, and wrestling with the endless details that came with opening a business. And somewhere in the middle of all that productive work, she had found herself thinking about Jim. Wondering what he was doing. Wanting to hear his voice.

It was strange, this wanting. Grace turned the feeling over in her mind as she walked, examining it from different angles like she might examine an unfamiliar architectural detail. With Lee, she had never felt this particular pull. She had loved him, or thought she had, but she had also treasured her solitude.

This was different. Jim was different.

Being around him made everything feel more settled. Peaceful. More grounded. Like the world was operating at a frequency she could finally hear clearly.

Grace pushed through the front door of the hardware store and felt the cool rush of air conditioning wash over her, a welcome relief from the warmth of the sun. The store was busier than she'd expected for a Wednesday afternoon; customers browsing the aisles and the sound of conversation created a low hum beneath the music playing from speakers mounted near the ceiling.

Tuck stood at the register, helping an older man with what looked like a complicated return. He glanced up when the door opened, and his face split into a grin when he spotted Grace. He tilted his head toward the back of the store, a wordless direction that she understood immediately.

She found Jim in aisle seven, the one dedicated to cabinet hardware and drawer pulls, and specialty latches. He wasn't alone. A young woman stood beside him with a toddler balanced on each hip. Their small faces were nearly identical, their expressions suggesting they were about thirty seconds away from synchronized meltdowns. Grace recognized her from church, Mrs. Davis, though they had never spoken beyond the brief pleasantries exchanged during fellowship hour.

Jim had a package in his hands and was pointing to something on the back, his voice patient and unhurried as he explained the product to the harried mother.

"This one's magnetic," he said. "You install the latch inside the cabinet, and then there's a magnetic key that releases it. The kids can pull on the door all they want, but it won't open without the key."

"And they can't figure out how to use the key?" Mrs. Davis shifted one of the toddlers higher on her hip, and the child immediately grabbed a fistful of her hair.

"Not at this age. The mechanism requires a specific angle and pressure that's beyond most toddlers. My niece Lizzie couldn't crack it until she was almost four, and she's a determined child."

"I'll take six of them. No... make it eight. These two got into the pantry yesterday and dumped an entire bag of flour on the kitchen floor." Mrs. Davis's voice held the particular exhaustion of a mother who had cleaned up one too many messes. "I turned my back for thirty seconds. Thirty seconds, I tell ya."

"I know you have your hands full. I've heard stories from my brother about some of the things Lizzie got into when she was that age, and she was just one kid." Jim pulled several packages from the shelf and stacked them in Mrs. Davis's basket. "These should solve your problem. And if they don't, come back and we'll figure out something else."

Grace hung back, watching the exchange from the end of the aisle. Boone had been lying near Jim's feet, but his head lifted when he caught her scent, and his tail began to wag against the floor. He rose and padded toward her, his brown eyes warm with recognition, his whole body wiggling with pleasure.

Grace bent down to scratch behind his ears, keeping her voice low so as not to interrupt Jim's conversation. "Hey, boy. Keeping an eye on things?"

Boone's tail wagged harder.

This was who Jim was, Grace thought as she watched him finish with Mrs. Davis. Not just when he was with her, but all the time. Patient with frazzled mothers and curious customers and everyone else who walked through his doors. Generous with his knowledge and his time, made no one feel rushed or foolish for asking questions. He knew his products inside and out, but more than that, he knew his customers. He remembered their names, their projects, and their preferences. He treated each interaction like it mattered because to him; it did.

Jim pointed Mrs. Davis toward the register and promised that Tuck would check her out whenever she was ready. She thanked him profusely, wrestling her twins back toward the front of the store, and then he turned and saw Grace.

His face transformed. There was no other word for it. The professional friendliness he'd worn while helping his customer shifted into something warmer, something that seemed to begin in his eyes and spread outward until his whole expression had changed. A slow smile curved his lips, the kind that made Grace's stomach do a small flip even after all these weeks.

He walked toward her, his stride unhurried.

Grace held up the coffee tray and the bag of donuts. "I brought reinforcements."

"You're a lifesaver." He took the coffee she offered, his fingers brushing against hers in the exchange. The contact sent a small spark through her. "What brings you to my corner of the world?"

"I just wanted to see you."

Jim's smile deepened, reaching his eyes in a way that made them crinkle at the corners. "Now that's a reason I can get behind."

They walked together toward the back of the store, past the aisles of tools and building supplies and the section dedicated to plumbing that Grace had become far too familiar with over the past few weeks. Boone trotted ahead of them, leading the way as if he knew exactly where they were going. Through a door marked "Employees Only," down a short hallway lined with boxes of inventory waiting to be shelved, and into a small office that Grace had never seen before.

Jim's office was exactly what she would have expected if she'd thought about it. A wooden desk that looked like it had been there for decades, its surface worn smooth by years of use. A comfortable leather chair behind it and two simpler chairs facing it. Bookshelves lined one wall, filled not with decorative objects but with actual books, catalogs, and binders that suggested they were used regularly. A framed photograph of the Hartwell family sat on the desk beside a cup holding pens and pencils. The walls held a few pieces of art, landscapes of the Smoky Mountains that captured the rolling ridges and misty valleys Grace could see from almost anywhere in Serenity Crossing.

The space was masculine without being stark, functional without being cold. It felt like Jim. Solid and real and comfortable.

"I like this," Grace said, looking around. "It suits you."

"It was my grandfather's office before it was my dad's, and my dad's before it was mine. I haven't changed much." Jim gestured to one of the chairs facing the desk. "The furniture's older than I am."

Grace settled into the chair he indicated, and Boone immediately positioned himself at her feet, his chin resting on her shoe. Jim took the other chair rather than sitting behind the desk, turning it to face her.

They opened their coffees and pulled donuts from the bag; Grace chose a glazed and Jim went for the chocolate frosted. The office was quiet after the bustle of the store, a small haven of calm in the middle of a busy afternoon.

"How's your day been?" Grace asked between bites.

"Good. Busy. We had a shipment come in this morning that took longer to process than I expected, and then there was a situation with a special order that got sent to the wrong address." Jim shook his head, but there was no real frustration in the gesture. "The usual stuff. How about you?"

"Actually, I have news." Grace set down her donut and felt a small thrill of excitement move through her. "I hired someone. A virtual assistant."

Jim's eyebrows rose with interest. "Yeah? Tell me about it."

"Her name is Emily Sawyer. She's going to continue working on the website we started, create a social media presence for the inn, and develop an online booking system." Grace heard the relief in her own voice and didn't try to hide it. "I finally admitted to myself that I'm never going to finish the website that we started. Every time I sit down to work on it, I end up frustrated and annoyed and no further along than when I started."

Jim nodded slowly. "You were pretty determined to do it yourself."

"I was. But I've learned something about myself over the past few weeks." Grace wrapped her hands around her coffee cup, enjoying the warmth. "I'm good at a lot of things. I can design spaces and coordinate contractors and strip wallpaper until my arms feel like they're going to fall off. But website building and social media management? Those are not my strengths. And more importantly, they're not things I enjoy. Every hour I spent fighting with that website was an hour I could have spent on something that I actually understand, and I'm good at."

"Smart move."

Grace smiled. "Emily's even going to set up accounts on all the travel sites so people can find the inn when they're searching for places to stay in the area."

"Sounds like she knows what she's doing."

"She does. And honestly, just knowing that someone else is handling it has taken a huge weight off my shoulders. I can focus on the actual inn instead of spending hours trying to figure out why my navigation menu won't work properly."

They talked for a while longer; the conversation flowing easily between them. Jim shared more details about his day, the minor crises and small victories that made up life running a hardware store in a small town. Grace told him about her morning meeting with Tom, about the progress on the third floor of the inn, and about the timeline for the remaining work. They finished their donuts and their coffee, and Boone shifted occasionally at Grace's feet, sighing contentedly in his sleep.

Grace glanced at her watch and felt a small jolt of surprise at how much time had passed. "I need to go. I'm meeting my mom at Stone Creek Furnishings to look at furniture for the inn."

"Furniture shopping with Jean McKenna." Jim's voice held a note of amusement. "That sounds like an adventure."

"Mom has opinions. Strong opinions." Grace stood, brushing donut crumbs from her jeans. "But she also has excellent taste, and she knows what will hold up to guest use versus what just looks pretty in a showroom. I'm hoping to find at least some of what I need in stock and keeping my fingers crossed that whatever I end up having to order arrives sooner rather than later."

Jim stood as well. "Hey," he said, his voice taking on a different quality. Softer. More intentional. "What are you doing tomorrow?"

"Tomorrow?" Grace thought through her mental calendar. "Working at the inn, probably. Why?"

"I was thinking we could go out to the lake. Pack a picnic lunch and spend the day just enjoying ourselves. Toss the ball around with Boone, maybe hike one of the trails." He shrugged, but his eyes were hopeful. "It's supposed to be beautiful weather."

The idea settled into Grace like sunshine. A whole day with Jim, no renovation schedules or contractor meetings, no lists to check or decisions to make. Just the two of them and Boone, out by the water, doing nothing in particular.

"I'd like that," she said. "I'd like that a lot."

Jim's smile was immediate and genuine. "I'll pick you up around noon. We can grab food from the deli at Valley Grocery on the way."

"Perfect."

Grace stepped closer and rose up on her toes to press a quick kiss against his cheek. His skin was warm beneath her lips, and she caught the faint scent of his cologne and coffee and something that was simply Jim. When she pulled back, his eyes had gone soft in a way that made her want to stay right here in this quiet office for the rest of the afternoon.

But her mother was waiting on her by now; she was sure of it, and furniture wouldn't choose itself.

"I'll see you tomorrow," she said.

"Tomorrow."

Grace walked out of his office and back through the storage area, past the busy aisles and the customers and Tuck at the register, who gave her a knowing grin as she passed. The door swung open, and Main Street welcomed her back into the warmth of the May afternoon.

She was halfway to Stone Creek Furnishings before she realized she was still smiling.

Chapter 29

The blanket they had spread near the water's edge was warm from the afternoon sun. Jim leaned back on his elbows, watching the light play across the surface of Hawthorne Lake. Sliced turkey and fresh bread from Valley Grocery's deli counter had been reduced to crumbs and empty wrappers, and a bottle of sparkling cider sat half-finished beside the basket. Boone lay a few feet away, his coat damp from a swim in the lake, his tongue lolling sideways from his mouth.

It was a perfect Saturday. The kind of day that felt like a gift, where the sky stretched endlessly blue overhead and the mountains rose in soft ridges around the lake, and the world seemed to have paused long enough to let them breathe.

Jim turned his attention from the water to the woman beside him.

Grace lay on her back with her eyes closed, her face tilted toward the sun. Her hair fanned out across the blanket, dark against the faded blue fabric, and her hands rested loosely on her stomach in a pose of complete surrender. The tension she had carried in her shoulders when she first arrived in Serenity Crossing was gone. The anxious energy that had driven her through those early weeks of renovation and planning had quieted into something calmer, more settled. She looked peaceful in a way that seemed almost angelic, content to simply exist in this moment.

Jim watched her breathe. The slow rise and fall of her chest. The slight curve of her lips suggested pleasant thoughts. The way the sunlight caught the angles of her face and turned her skin golden.

And watching her now, something crystallized in his chest with an intensity that stole the breath from his lungs.

He loved her immensely.

He had known it for a while, though he had been careful not to examine the feeling too closely, not to hold it up to the light where it might evaporate or reveal itself as something less than what he hoped. Loving Grace McKenna when he was seventeen had been easy. Young love, uncomplicated by failure and divorce and all the wounds that came from learning how badly things could go wrong. That love had been instinct, had been certainty without experience, had been the kind of all-consuming feeling that teenagers believed would last forever because they didn't yet know that forever was something you had to fight for.

Loving Grace Bennett at thirty-two years old was different.

This love was deeper. More deliberate. He was choosing this with his eyes wide open, knowing exactly what he was risking, knowing exactly how much it would hurt if she didn't feel the same. He had already survived one marriage ending with words that had carved themselves into his bones. He knew what it cost to give someone your whole heart and have them hand it back broken.

But looking at her now, he couldn't imagine not choosing her. He couldn't imagine walking away from this blanket, this afternoon, this woman who had somehow become the center of everything. He had spent four years telling himself that contentment was enough, that a good life and meaningful work and family who loved him could fill the spaces that romantic love had left empty. And those things were good. They were enough, in their own way.

But Grace was more than enough. Grace was everything.

He had never felt this way about anyone. Not even Amanda. His marriage had been built on hope and compatibility and the belief that loving someone meant they would eventually love you back the same way. He had poured himself into being a good husband, had started to build a house and a life and a future, and none of it had been enough to make Amanda want to stay.

With Grace, he wasn't trying to earn anything. He wasn't performing or proving or hoping she would eventually see his worth. She already saw him. She had always seen him, even when they were teenagers who didn't understand what they had. And now, fourteen years later, she was here. On this blanket. In his life. Choosing to be with him not because she needed rescuing or because she had nowhere else to go, but because she wanted to be here.

That was the difference. That was everything.

Grace opened her eyes and caught him watching her. A smile spread across her face, soft and unhurried, the kind of smile that made Jim want to gather her in his arms and hold her until the sun went down and came back up again.

"What are you thinking about?"

You. Always you.

"Just enjoying the view," he said instead.

She laughed, the sound bright against the quiet lap of water against the shore. She sat up, brushing bits of grass from her hair where the wind had scattered them. "The lake is beautiful today."

"That's not the view I meant."

Her cheeks flushed slightly, a wash of pink beneath the golden warmth the sun had given her skin. Jim felt a surge of love for Grace so strong it startled him with its intensity. He sat up too, closing the distance between them.

"Grace."

Something in his tone made her turn again to look at him. Her green eyes searched his face, and Jim saw the moment she registered that this wasn't casual conversation. Her expression shifted, becoming open, attentive, and waiting. The world around them seemed to fade, the sounds of children playing somewhere in the distance, the call of birds over the water, the gentle rustle of wind through the trees—all of it receding until there was only her face and her eyes and the words that were demanding to be spoken.

Three words.

He had been carrying them for weeks. Longer than that, if he were honest. Years. Fourteen years of wondering what might have been, two months of discovering that some things couldn't be forgotten because they were too fundamentally true.

The moment was perfect. The sunshine was warm on his back. The water was sparkling in front of them. The privacy of this quiet stretch of shore, away from the families gathered near the playground and the couples walking the path. He opened his mouth, the words right there, ready to finally exist in the space between them.

Boone chose that exact moment to shake himself vigorously.

Lake water sprayed across both of them in an arc of cold droplets, soaking through Jim's shirt and hitting Grace square in the face. She shrieked and threw her hands up, laughing as she tried to shield herself from the assault. Jim sputtered, wiping water from his eyes, his shirt now plastered to his skin in several spots.

Boone stood there looking enormously pleased with himself. His tail wagged in broad sweeps, his head tilted to one side, and he let out a single bark as if to ask why they weren't praising his excellent timing.

"Boone!" Jim said, but he was laughing too, the moment dissolving around him like morning fog. "Your timing is impeccable, buddy."

The dog barked again, apparently agreeing with this assessment.

Grace was still laughing, reaching for the stack of napkins they had packed with the picnic supplies, dabbing at her face and neck while continuing to scold Boone in a voice that held no real reproach. "You are a menace," she told him affectionately. "An absolute menace. Yes, you are. Look at you, standing there all proud of yourself."

Boone's tail wagged harder.

The moment had passed. The intensity that had been building between them had shifted into something lighter, easier, the kind of comfortable humor that characterized so much of their time together. Jim told himself it was fine. The right moment would come. There was no rush.

But part of him wondered if he was stalling, letting the moment slip away on purpose. If some small, cautious part of his heart was still afraid to say the words out loud. Afraid that speaking them would somehow change things, would add weight to something that felt fragile despite all evidence that it was strong. Afraid that once he said, I love you, he would need to hear it back, and he wasn't entirely certain what he would do if she couldn't say it.

He pushed the thought away. Grace was here. Grace was happy. That was enough for now.

Boone, apparently deciding that his humans had been stationary for too long, began trotting toward one of the walking trails that wound around the lake. He paused after a few yards and looked back at them, his expression clearly communicating his opinion that they should follow.

Jim chuckled and pushed himself to his feet. He held out his hand to Grace. "I guess that's our cue. His majesty wants to go for a walk."

Grace took his hand and let him pull her up. "Far be it from us to disappoint him."

They left the blanket and basket where they were, trusting the quiet stretch of shore to remain undisturbed, and followed Boone toward the trail. The path was wide enough for them to walk side by side, packed dirt worn smooth by years of joggers and families and couples exactly like them. Grace slipped her hand into his as they walked, her fingers threading through his with an ease that felt like second nature.

The trail curved along the water's edge, offering views of the lake that shifted and changed as they walked. To the east, two resort properties were visible in the distance, their main buildings rising above the tree line, boats dotting the water near their private docks. To the west, luxury homes climbed the hillside in staggered rows, their windows catching the afternoon light, their manicured lawns stretching down toward the shore. Hawthorne Lake had been drawing visitors and residents for as long as Jim could remember, people who wanted the beauty of the mountains without giving up the comforts they were accustomed to.

Boone ranged ahead of them on the trail, his earlier exhaustion apparently forgotten. He darted from one side of the path to the other, investigating interesting smells and pausing to mark territory with the dedication of a dog who took such responsibilities seriously. At one point, a butterfly crossed his path, and he launched himself into the air in an attempt to catch it, landing in an undignified heap of legs and tail that made Grace laugh out loud.

"He's having the time of his life," she said.

"He's been cooped up too much lately. We both have."

They walked in comfortable quiet after that, no words needed, simply enjoying the scenery and each other's company and Boone's antics. He doubled back every few minutes to check on them before racing ahead again.

Jim found his thoughts drifting as they walked.

He thought about Amanda. About all the time he had spent pouring himself into a marriage that was never going to work, trying to build something permanent with someone who had been looking for an exit from the moment she arrived. He knew that now. Amanda had said she loved small-town life, but she had meant she loved the idea of it. The aesthetic. The romantic movie version where everything was charming and quaint and nothing ever got boring or repetitive. She hadn't loved the reality of Serenity Crossing: the same faces every day, the limited options, the way everyone knew your business before you'd finished doing it. She hadn't loved him either, not really. She had loved what she thought he could become, the potential she saw for something more ambitious, more successful, and more aligned with the life she actually wanted. And when it became clear that Jim was exactly who he appeared to be, a man content with his hardware store and his small town and his quiet existence, she had left.

Grace was different.

Grace had grown up here. She knew exactly what Serenity Crossing was: the good and the bad, the charm and the limitations, the way news traveled, and secrets didn't keep. She had left for fourteen years, had built a life in Atlanta, and had achieved the kind of professional success that could have kept her in the city forever. And she had chosen to come back. Because this was where she wanted to be. This town. This community. This life.

She was with him because...

Jim's thoughts stumbled. He had been about to complete the sentence automatically, to fill in the blank with the certainty he felt when he looked at her. But now, examining it more closely, he realized he didn't actually know why Grace was with him.

He sensed she liked being around him. He knew she felt comfortable with him, relaxed in a way she hadn't been when she first arrived. He knew she was happier now than she had been two months ago, that the shadows in her eyes had lightened, that she smiled more easily and laughed more freely. He knew she showed up for him, brought him coffee at work, and sought him out when she had no particular reason to. He knew she looked at him like he mattered.

But he had never heard her say the words that would tell him what he meant to her beyond that. She had never said she loved him. She had never said she was falling for him. She had never put language to whatever this was between them, had never named it or claimed it or made it explicitly her own.

The thought surfaced and then submerged again, pushed down by the force of his own certainty. He was being paranoid. Reading too much into silence. Grace was here, wasn't she? Walking beside him, holding his hand, choosing to spend her Saturday with him instead of working at the inn, or visiting her family, or doing any of the hundred other things she could be doing. That was enough. That had to be enough.

Actions spoke louder than words. Everyone said so.

Boone came racing back toward them, tongue lolling, ears flapping, looking like the happiest creature on earth. He circled them once, twice, then took off again toward whatever had caught his attention up ahead.

Grace laughed. "I think he's trying to tell us we're too slow."

"He's got four legs. He's got an unfair advantage."

The trail curved again, bringing them to a wooden overlook built out over the water. A family was gathered there, two adults and three children, tossing bread to a small fleet of ducks that had congregated below. The children squealed with delight every time a duck caught a piece mid-air, and the parents watched with the patient exhaustion of people who had learned to find joy in small moments.

Jim and Grace paused at the edge of the overlook, staying back to give the family space. The afternoon light had begun to turn golden, that particular quality of late-day sun that made everything look softer, warmer, and more beautiful than it had any right to be. The lake stretched out before them, vast and calm, reflecting the sky and the mountains, and the scattered clouds that drifted overhead.

"I needed this," Grace said quietly, her eyes on the water. "I'm so glad you suggested a day out. A day just to lounge and do nothing."

"You've been working too hard."

"I know. But it's worth it. Everything's coming together." She squeezed his hand, her grip firm and warm. "I couldn't have done it without you."

"You could have. You would have figured it out."

"Maybe." She turned to look at him, her expression soft in the golden light. "But I'm glad I didn't have to." She paused, and something in her face shifted, becoming more serious. "You've been so good to me, Jim. Through all of this. I don't know how to thank you for everything you've done."

Jim reached up and cupped her face in his hands, tilting it toward him so he could look directly into her eyes. Those green eyes that had haunted his memories for fourteen years. Those eyes that looked at him now with something he wanted desperately to name.

"You don't have to thank me," he said. "I wanted to be here. I want to be here. There's nowhere else I'd rather be."

He kissed her.

The kiss was soft at first, tender, full of everything he hadn't said earlier when Boone had interrupted. He felt Grace lean into him, her hands coming up to rest on his chest, her fingers curling slightly into the fabric of his shirt. The world around them faded: the family with their ducks, the trail behind them, the sound of water and wind and distant voices. There was only Grace and the warmth of her lips and the feeling of rightness that settled over him.

When they finally pulled apart, she was smiling.

"We should do this more often," he said. "In fact, both of us should take Saturdays off together. Remember, there's more to life than work."

"Deal."

They stood there a moment longer, the golden light washing over them, the lake spread out below. Boone had returned from his explorations and sat nearby, watching them with the patient expression of a dog who understood that humans sometimes needed time for their inexplicable human behaviors.

Jim looked at Grace, at her smile, at the way the setting sun caught the highlights in her hair. He thought about the words he hadn't said, the moment that had passed, and the questions that had surfaced in his mind during their walk and then submerged again.

She was here. She was smiling. She was holding his hand.

That had to be enough for now.

Chapter 30

The last verse of "How Great Thou Art" swelled through the sanctuary as the congregation's voices rose together in harmony. Jim held the hymnal open between himself and Grace, though neither of them needed it. The words had been written on his heart since childhood, sung in this same sanctuary with these same wooden pews worn smooth by generations of faithful attendance.

Grace sang beside him, her voice blending with the chorus, and Jim felt the rightness of this moment settle into his bones. Sunday morning. Church. The woman he loved standing next to him, her presence as natural as breathing.

The hymn concluded, and Pastor Davis stepped to the pulpit as the congregation settled back into their seats. The particular hush that preceded a sermon fell over the room, that collective quieting of rustling hymnals and shifting bodies as attention focused forward. Jim released Grace's hand so she could arrange her skirt as she sat, then reached for her again once they were settled. She gave his fingers a gentle squeeze without looking at him, her eyes already on Pastor Davis.

"If you've got your Bibles with you this morning, turn with me to the Gospel of Mark," Pastor Davis said, his voice carrying easily through the small sanctuary without the need for a microphone. "Chapter ten, starting at verse forty-six. And if you don't have a Bible with you, that's all right too. Just listen along."

Jim opened his bible to the passages, and Grace leaned slightly toward him as Pastor Davis began.

"Then they came to Jericho. As Jesus and his disciples, together with a large crowd, were leaving the city, a blind man, Bartimaeus, was sitting by the roadside begging. When he heard that it was Jesus of Nazareth, he began to shout, 'Jesus, Son of David, have mercy on me!'"

Pastor Davis continued through the passage, his voice taking on the cadence of a storyteller. He described the scene: the dusty road, the pressing crowd, and the blind man crying out despite being told to keep quiet. He read how Jesus stopped and called for Bartimaeus and how the man threw aside his cloak and came to Jesus. And then he reached the verse that would anchor the morning's message.

"'What do you want me to do for you?' Jesus asked him. The blind man said, 'Rabbi, I want to see.'"

Pastor Davis looked up from his Bible and surveyed the congregation with eyes that had seen them through births and deaths, weddings and funerals, seasons of plenty and seasons of struggle.

"Now, here's what strikes me about this passage every time I read it," he said, closing his Bible and setting it on the pulpit. "Jesus already knew. He could see Bartimaeus sitting there. He knew the man was blind. The crowd knew it. Everyone on that road knew it. And yet Jesus still asked the question."

He paused, letting the words settle.

"Jesus wasn't ignorant. He wasn't gathering information He didn't have. He was being intentional. And I think that tells us something important about how our Lord engages with His people."

Pastor Davis stepped out from behind the pulpit, moving closer to the congregation the way he often did when he was building toward his point.

"See, Jesus could have healed Bartimaeus without a word. He could have done it from across the road, never even stopping. He had that power. But instead, He stopped. He called the man to Him. He asked a question. He invited Bartimaeus into a conversation before He acted." Pastor Davis shook his head slowly, a look of wonder crossing his face. "That's not efficiency. That's relationship. And it tells us that God values the encounter as much as the outcome."

A baby fussed somewhere in the back of the sanctuary, and Pastor Davis waited with patient good humor while the mother slipped out with the child. When the door clicked shut behind her, he picked up where he'd left off.

"Now let's look at how Bartimaeus answered. Jesus asks him, 'What do you want me to do for you?' And Bartimaeus says, 'Rabbi, I want to see.' That's it. Four words. No explanation. No list of credentials. No argument for why he deserved healing more than somebody else."

Pastor Davis returned to the pulpit and rested his hands on either side of his Bible.

"Think about how risky that was. Bartimaeus names his deepest desire out loud, to the Son of God, with a crowd of people listening. He doesn't hedge his bet. He doesn't say, 'Well, if it's Your will, and if You have time, and if I'm worthy enough...' He just says what he wants. Plainly. Directly. And he trusts Jesus with what happens next."

The sanctuary was quiet now, that particular stillness that came when a sermon was landing where it needed to land.

"That's faith, friends. Real faith. Not just believing that Jesus can do something. Bartimaeus already believed that. He wouldn't have been shouting on the roadside if he didn't believe Jesus had power. No, this is something deeper. This is being willing to name what you want and trust God with whether or not you receive it."

Pastor Davis picked up his Bible and held it against his chest, his expression thoughtful.

"I wonder sometimes how many of us have stopped doing that. How many of us have learned to live with less rather than risk the disappointment of asking for more? How many of us pray around our desires instead of through them because naming what we really want feels too vulnerable, too dangerous, too likely to end in heartbreak if God says no?"

He was quiet for a moment, letting the weight of his words fill the space.

"But here's what I want you to see this morning. Jesus didn't ask Bartimaeus to prove himself worthy. He didn't require a testimony or a track record. He didn't ask the man to justify his request or explain his past. He simply invited him to speak honestly about what he wanted. And then He responded to that honesty with healing."

Pastor Davis smiled.

"God is not moved by how well we manage our lives or how carefully we package our prayers. He is moved by truth spoken without disguise. By hearts that trust Him enough to say, 'This is what I want, Lord. This is what I'm hoping for. And I'm placing that hope in Your hands, even though I don't know what You'll do with it.'"

He opened his Bible again, finding his place in the passage.

"'Go,' said Jesus. 'Your faith has healed you.' Immediately he received his sight and followed Jesus along the road." Pastor Davis looked up. "The healing came after the honest exchange. The transformation followed the encounter. Jesus could have done it differently. He chose not to. Because relationship matters to Him. Because He wants to know us and be known by us, not just fix our problems from a distance."

"So here's my invitation to you this morning," Pastor Davis said, his voice softening as he moved toward his conclusion. "Consider whether there's something you've stopped bringing to God. Some desire you've learned to manage on your own because asking felt too risky. Some hope you've buried because disappointment seemed inevitable." He paused. "Jesus is still asking the question. Every day, in a hundred different ways, He's asking: What do you want me to do for you? And He's waiting for an honest answer. Not a polished answer. Not a safe answer. Just an honest one."

The sermon ended, and the congregation stirred as Pastor Davis announced the closing hymn. Jim stood with everyone else, reaching for the hymnal, his mind quiet and receptive in the way it often was after a good sermon.

The closing hymn was "Blessed Assurance," and Jim sang the familiar words while Grace's voice blended with his own. Her hand found his again during the final verse, her fingers threading through his as naturally as if they had been doing this for years instead of weeks. When the music faded and Pastor Davis offered the benediction, Jim bowed his head and let the words wash over him.

The service ended with the usual bustle of Bibles being gathered and purses being retrieved, and conversations sparking to life throughout the sanctuary. Jim guided Grace into the aisle with a gentle hand at the small of her back, and they joined the slow procession toward the doors where Pastor Davis stood greeting his congregation.

"Jim, Grace." Pastor Davis clasped Jim's hand warmly and then Grace's. "Good to see you both this morning."

"Good sermon, Pastor," Jim said. "Gave me something to think about."

"That's all I can ask for." Pastor Davis's eyes crinkled with genuine pleasure. "You two have a blessed Sunday."

They moved past him into the small foyer, where clusters of church members had gathered in the way they always did after services, catching up on the week's news and making plans for the afternoon. Jim spotted his parents near the door, his mother already deep in conversation with Jean McKenna. His father stood beside her with the patient expression of a man who had learned long ago that post-church socializing was not a quick endeavor.

They made their way through the foyer, pausing briefly to greet a few people. Hank Morrison from the feed store. Mrs. Clark, who ran the alterations shop on Oak Street. Tom Reeves and his wife, who complimented Grace on how excited she is to hear the inn will be opening soon.

"Ready to head to fellowship for a bit?" Jim asked when they had finally reached a clear space near the door. "Grab some coffee, say hello to folks?"

"I'd like that." She said. "And then maybe we could head back to the inn for lunch?"

"Sounds perfect. We can swing by my place first and pick up Boone, if that's all right with you. He's been cooped up all morning."

Grace's expression softened the way it always did when Boone was mentioned. "Of course. He'd be so upset with us if we left him alone all afternoon."

They walked toward the fellowship hall together, Grace's hand warm in his. The hum of conversation and laughter spilled through the open doorway, familiar voices mingling with the smell of fresh coffee.

Jim glanced at her as they entered the hall and smiled. Sunday morning. Church. Lunch plans and an afternoon stretching out ahead of them with nothing to do but enjoy each other's company.

This was a good life. And she was the best part of it.

Chapter 31

Grace sliced tomatoes at the butcher block island while Jim assembled sandwiches beside her. The inn's new kitchen gleamed beneath the pendant lights that Tom's crew had installed just a few days ago. A few pieces of trim remained unfinished along the ceiling where the crown molding would eventually go. The built-in spice rack beside the range stood empty, waiting for bottles and jars that Grace hadn't yet purchased, but the space was functional now, beautiful in a way that made Grace smile every time she walked through the door. This kitchen had been her greatest challenge, and now it stood as proof that she could take something neglected and make it new again.

She glanced over at Jim as he spread mustard across a slice of bread. He had rolled his sleeves to his elbows after they'd gotten back from church, exposing forearms that flexed slightly as he worked. His tie was loosened at the collar now, the top button of his dress shirt undone, and there was something about the casual intimacy of the image that made warmth spread through her chest. In the corner near the doorway to the dining room, Boone lay sprawled across the floor, his breathing slow and even. His tail twitched occasionally in his sleep, chasing something only he could see.

"I still need to buy about a hundred things before this kitchen is ready for guests," Grace said, setting the sliced tomatoes on a small plate and reaching for the head of lettuce. "Mixing bowls, baking sheets, a decent set of knives. All the things you don't think about until you need them."

"Make a list," Jim said. "We can hit the restaurant supply store in Pigeon Forge next weekend if you want. They'll have everything you need at better prices than ordering online."

"That's a great idea."

Jim finished the sandwiches and cut them in half with a chef's knife. Grace gathered the plates of tomatoes and lettuce, and together they carried everything to the dining room.

The dining room looked nearly complete now, its walls painted a soft cream color that complemented the original oak wainscoting, and the built-in china cabinets gleaming with fresh polish. Grace had found a simple linen runner for the long table, and though the room still lacked the finishing touches that would make it feel truly ready for guests, it was a far cry from the dated, neglected space it had been just two months ago.

They settled into chairs across from each other, and Jim reached his hand across the table, palm up. Grace placed her hand in his without hesitation, feeling the warmth of his fingers closing around hers. This had become their rhythm, this moment of connection before meals, and she treasured it. She bowed her head as Jim spoke.

"Lord, we thank You for this food and for this day. We thank You for the work of our hands and the blessing of time spent together. Guide our paths and keep us in Your grace. Amen."

"Amen," Grace echoed softly.

Jim released her hand, and they began to eat. The sandwiches were simple but good: the turkey fresh from the deli counter at Valley Grocery, the bread still soft from that morning's baking. Grace added tomato and lettuce to her sandwich and took a bite, savoring the familiar flavors.

For a few minutes, they ate in companionable quiet, the only sounds the soft clink of plates and the distant call of birds through the open windows. A breeze stirred the air, carrying with it the green scent of late spring and the promise of summer waiting just beyond the calendar's edge. Grace thought about how different this was from the meals she had shared with Lee, where silence had always felt like a warning sign, a prelude to criticism or conflict. She had learned to dread those quiet moments, to fill them with chatter about work or plans or anything that might keep the tension at bay. She had become skilled at reading the set of Lee's shoulders, the tightness around his mouth, the way his fork moved against his plate—all the tiny signals that told her whether the evening would end in peace or in one of his cold, cutting assessments of her failures. With Jim, silence was simply silence. A space to breathe. A rest between conversations that needed no filling.

"What did you think of Pastor Davis's sermon today?" Grace asked, reaching for her glass of iced tea. She had noticed Jim sitting very still during the message, his expression thoughtful in a way that suggested the words were landing somewhere deep. "You seemed pretty engaged."

Jim set down his sandwich and was quiet for a moment. Something shifted in his posture, a subtle straightening of his shoulders, a stillness that settled over him like a change in weather. When he looked at her, his brown eyes held an intensity she hadn't seen before, something searching and serious that made her sit up a little straighter in her chair.

"It meant a lot to me," he said. "Made me think about some things."

Grace took another sip of tea, watching him over the rim of her glass. She waited for him to continue, curious about what had stirred such contemplation.

His jaw was set now, his expression serious in a way that told her this conversation was about to become something more than casual Sunday lunch chatter. He set his napkin beside his plate with deliberate care, as if buying himself a moment to gather his thoughts.

"Grace." His voice was steady, but there was weight beneath the words that made her pulse quicken. "I need to ask you something, and I need you to be honest with me."

Her stomach tightened. She set down her glass and nodded.

"Where are we headed?" he asked. "You and me. What is this to you?"

She took a breath, wanting to choose her words carefully. This moment deserved her honesty, her full attention, and her best attempt at articulating what had been growing between them. She reached her hand across the table, and he took it, his fingers closing around hers with a gentleness that made her throat tight.

"I didn't come back to Serenity Crossing looking for this," she said. "For you. I came back because my life had fallen apart and I needed somewhere to land. I came back to fix up an old inn and prove to myself that I could build something on my own." She squeezed his hand gently. "But that's what makes this different. I wasn't looking for you. I wasn't trying to replace what I'd lost or fill some void in my life. You just... happened. And I'm so grateful that you did."

Jim was watching her intently, his thumb tracing small circles against the back of her hand. He didn't speak, didn't interrupt. He just listened with focused attention.

"I used to think love was supposed to feel a certain way," Grace continued, her voice growing more thoughtful as she searched for the right words. "Intense. Complicated. Exhilarating. Fireworks. Subtle. Fierce. Steadiness. Accountability." She shook her head slowly, remembering the constant anxiety that had defined her marriage.

She looked at their joined hands, at the way his fingers curled protectively around hers.

"Being with you is calming. Natural," she said, and she meant it as the highest compliment she knew how to give. "When I'm with you, I feel peaceful. Settled. Like I can finally breathe again after holding my breath for so long. You're steady, Jim. You're consistent. I always know where I stand with you. I don't have to wonder what mood you'll be in or walk on eggshells or brace myself for whatever's coming next. I don't have to worry about where you are or who you're with." She met his eyes, willing him to understand what she was trying to say, to see how much these words cost her and how much she meant every one. "After everything I've been through, that's exactly what I need. I don't need the fireworks. I don't need my heart to race every time I see you. I need steadiness. I need peace. You give me that."

Jim's expression hadn't changed, but something flickered in his eyes that Grace couldn't quite read. A shadow passing. A door closing somewhere deep inside.

"I don't need drama," she said, pressing forward, wanting him to understand. "I don't need uncertainty or intensity or any of the things I used to think meant love. I need someone I can count on. Someone who shows up. Someone who's the opposite of everything that hurt me." She squeezed his hand again, tighter this time, her grip almost fierce with the need to make him see. "You're everything Lee wasn't. You're kind and patient and present. You don't play games or keep me guessing. You're just... you. And that matters more to me than I know how to say."

She finished and looked at him, her heart full of everything she had just laid bare. She had tried to be honest, tried to tell him what he meant to her, and tried to explain how much she valued what they had built together. She waited for his response, expecting... she wasn't sure what. Gratitude, maybe. Relief.

Jim was quiet for a long moment. Long enough that the silence began to press against Grace's skin. Long enough that she began to wonder if she had said something wrong.

When he finally spoke, his voice was calm, but there was something beneath the surface that sent an alarm zipping through her mind, a wrongness she couldn't quite name.

"I hear what you're saying," he said.

Grace watched his jaw tighten almost imperceptibly, a small movement that might have gone unnoticed if she hadn't been watching him so closely, if she hadn't spent these past weeks learning the landscape of his face.

"But Grace..." He exhaled slowly, and the sound carried a sadness she hadn't expected. "You just told me everything you don't need anymore. You told me what I'm not. You told me what I give you." His eyes held hers, and the warmth that usually lived there had shifted into something more guarded, more careful. "You didn't tell me you wanted me."

Grace blinked. "What?"

"You said you need steadiness. You said you could count on me. You said I'm everything Lee wasn't." Jim's voice remained even, measured, but something had changed in his expression. A wall going up that hadn't been there before. A withdrawal so subtle she might have missed it if she hadn't been paying such close attention. "But you didn't say you wanted me. You said you don't need your heart to race anymore. You didn't say it races when you see me. You said you don't need fireworks. You didn't say you feel them, anyway." He released her hand gently, carefully, as if setting down something fragile, and sat back in his chair. "You described what I provide, Grace. You didn't describe what you feel."

Grace opened her mouth to respond, to explain, to correct whatever misunderstanding had crept into this conversation, but Jim continued before she could find words.

"I was married to a woman who told me I was safe." His voice had dropped lower, quieter, and there was an edge to it now that Grace had never heard before. Not anger. Something older than that. Something that had been waiting a long time to be spoken. "Dependable. Steady. Amanda told me all of those things. She told me I was exactly what she needed after the chaos of her childhood and college years. She told me I was her soft place to land." His hands rested flat on the table, perfectly still, but Grace could see the tension in his shoulders, the way he was holding himself together through sheer force of will, and the cost of speaking these words aloud after years of keeping them locked away. "And then one day she looked me in the eye and told me that I wasn't enough. That she needed more than what I could give her. More excitement. More money. More... everything." He shook his head slowly, and there was a bitterness in the gesture, a glimpse of old wounds that had never fully healed. "She chose me because I was safe. And then she left because safe wasn't enough."

Grace felt something cold settle in her chest, spreading outward like ice water through her veins.

"Jim, I didn't mean..."

"Didn't you?" His voice was kind, and somehow that made it worse. The gentleness in his tone when he was clearly hurting. The grace he extended even as she had unknowingly torn open his deepest wound. "I don't think you're trying to hurt me. I don't think you even realize fully what you said. But I heard it, Grace. I heard everything you didn't say."

He stood, the chair scraping softly against the floor, and looked down at her with an expression that made her heart physically ache. There was no anger on his face. No accusation. Just a quiet devastation that was somehow worse than any harsh words could have been.

"I can't do that again," he said, and his voice carried the pain of four years of rebuilding himself after Amanda had left. "I won't be someone's soft place to land because they're tired of being hurt. I won't be chosen because I'm the opposite of a mistake. I need to be wanted, Grace. I need to know you see me—really see me—and you still reach for me anyway."

Grace stared at him, her mind racing, trying to understand how this conversation had gone so terribly wrong. She had been honest. She had told him the truth. She had laid her heart bare and explained what he meant to her, and somehow, in trying to show him how much she valued what they had, she had made him feel like he wasn't enough. Like he was a remedy instead of a choice. Like he was the absence of bad things rather than the presence of good ones.

"Jim, please..." She pushed back from the table and stood, wanting to go to him, to take his hands, to make him understand, but he held up a hand gently, a gesture that asked for space without demanding it.

"I'm not angry," he said. Grace watched his throat move with the effort, watched him fight to keep his composure. "But I need more. I need to be chosen for who I am."

He moved toward the doorway, and Grace stood frozen, her legs unsteady beneath her, her voice trapped somewhere in her chest where the cold had settled.

"I think we both need some time," he said, pausing at the threshold. His hand rested on the doorframe, and she noticed the way his fingers gripped the wood, the only outward sign of how much this moment was costing him. "To think about what we really want. What this relationship really is between us."

He turned back to look at her, and the pain in his eyes was something she would carry with her for a long time. He wasn't trying to hide it; he wasn't trying to pretend he was fine. He was letting her see exactly what her words had cost him, and the vulnerability of that nearly broke her. This was Jim at his most honest, stripped of the easy smiles and the patient steadiness that she had come to rely on. This was the wound beneath the surface, the one Amanda had left when she'd told him he would never be enough, and Grace had just torn it open again without even knowing she held the knife.

"I deserve to be chosen for who I am. Not for who I'm not," he said quietly, his voice rough around the edges.

He called Boone's name softly, and the dog rose from his spot by the doorway, confused, his brown eyes moving between Jim and Grace as if trying to understand what had shifted in the air around them. Boone's tail hung low, uncertain, and after a moment's hesitation, he padded after Jim toward the front door.

Grace heard the soft click of the latch, and then they were gone.

She stood in the dining room, staring at the empty space where Jim had been just moments ago. The silence that filled the inn was nothing like the comfortable quiet they had shared during lunch. This silence had teeth. This silence pressed against her chest until she could barely breathe. Even the birds outside had gone quiet, as if the whole world had paused to witness the wreckage of a conversation she still didn't fully understand.

She replayed the conversation in her mind, searching for where it had all gone wrong. She had told him the truth. She had told him how much he meant to her. She had told him he was everything she needed.

But his words echoed through the empty room, settling into her bones like a chill she couldn't shake.

You didn't tell me you want me.

She slowly sank into her chair, staring at the half-eaten sandwiches, the glasses of tea sweating onto the linen runner, the evidence of a meal that had been interrupted by something she still didn't fully understand. Jim's napkin lay where he had placed it, folded beside his plate. His chair sat pushed back at an angle, empty now in a way that felt permanent.

She examined what she had actually said, turning each word over in her mind like stones in her palm.

Peace. Steadiness. How different he was from Lee. What she didn't need. What he gave her. What he provided.

She had described him as a remedy for everything that had broken her. A balm for wounds that Lee had inflicted. The opposite of a mistake she had made. She had painted a picture of a man who filled gaps, who provided stability, who served a purpose in her healing. She had talked about him the way someone might talk about a warm blanket on a cold night. Necessary. Comforting. Useful.

She hadn't said she loved him.

She hadn't said she wanted him.

She hadn't said that her breath caught when he walked into a room, that something in her chest lifted every time she heard his truck pull into the parking area.

She'd never told him that she thought about him when she woke in the morning and again before she fell asleep at night.

She'd never told him that watching him with his family made her imagine futures she had been afraid to name—pictures of holidays and Sunday dinners and ordinary Tuesday evenings.

She'd never told him that his laugh was one of her favorite sounds, that his voice on the phone could turn an ordinary day into something worth remembering, or that the way he said her name made her feel like she was someone worth knowing.

She'd never told him that when he held her hand, she felt more herself than she had in years.

She had described what he could do for her. She had listed the ways he made her feel safe. She had cataloged his usefulness in healing her wounds.

And he had heard every word she didn't say.

The afternoon light slanted through the windows at a lower angle now, casting long shadows across the dining room floor. Time had passed while she sat here, though she couldn't have said how much. The tea in her glass had grown warm. The ice had melted to nothing.

She had been trying to tell him what he meant to her.

And somehow, in trying to describe what they had, she had made him feel like he wasn't enough.

Grace pressed her palms flat against the table, trying to ground herself in something solid. The wood was smooth beneath her hands, real and present when everything else felt like it was dissolving around her.

She had spent months building walls to protect herself. She had learned to describe her feelings in terms of what she needed, what she lacked, and what she was escaping. She had become so accustomed to framing love as the absence of pain that she had forgotten how to name it as its own thing entirely. She had forgotten—or maybe she had never learned—how to speak of joy without referencing the sorrow that had come before it.

The chair across from her sat vacant, pushed back from the table at the angle Jim had left it. His plate still held half a sandwich, a few bites of lettuce, and the tomato slices she had cut for him just an hour ago when everything had been simple and good and right.

She had no idea what to do next.

Chapter 32

Grace pulled her SUV into the gravel driveway of the McKenna family home and sat for a moment, staring at the farmhouse where she had grown up. The flower fields stretched out to her left, rows of color that should have lifted her spirits the way they always had in the past. She could see figures moving among the plants in the distance; her father probably, maybe Josie or Graham, tending to the blooms that kept this place running. She should go out there. She should wave and smile and pretend that everything was fine. Instead, she turned off the engine and walked toward the house, climbing the porch steps and pulling open the screen door with a hand that trembled slightly despite her best efforts to steady it.

"Momma?" Her voice came out rougher than she intended, scraped raw from three days of tears and sleepless nights. "Are you home?"

"In the kitchen, sweetheart."

Grace followed the familiar path through the house, past the living room with its worn furniture and family photographs covering every available surface, past the dining room where she had shared a thousand meals with her parents and siblings, until she reached the kitchen doorway and stopped.

Jean stood at the counter, her hands busy with something Grace couldn't see. She turned, and her welcoming smile transformed into something else entirely the moment her eyes landed on her daughter's face.

"Grace?" Jean wiped her hands on her apron and crossed the kitchen in three quick strides. "What's wrong? What happened?"

Grace understood her mother's alarm. She looked exactly as wrecked as she felt. Her jeans were the same ones she had worn yesterday and possibly the day before. The oversized t-shirt hung loose on her frame, chosen for comfort rather than appearance. Her hair was piled on top of her head in a messy knot that she had secured with whatever elastic band she could find this morning. The circles under her eyes told the story of seventy-two hours spent replaying the same conversation over and over until the words had worn grooves into her mind.

"Momma," Grace's voice cracked on the word. "I really messed up. I hurt Jim. I hurt him badly, and I didn't mean to."

Jean's expression shifted from alarm to something deeper. She took Grace's elbow and guided her toward the kitchen table, pulling out a chair and pressing gently on her daughter's shoulders until Grace sank into it.

"Sit down. Let me get you something to drink."

Grace watched her mother move around the kitchen. The coffee pot was already half full from this morning, and Jean poured a cup, adding a splash of cream before setting it on the table in front of her. Then she pulled out the chair across from Grace and lowered herself into it, folding her hands on the worn wooden surface, and waited.

That patience undid something in Grace that had been held together by sheer force of will.

"I've been going over it in my head for three days," Grace said, wrapping her hands around the warm ceramic mug but not lifting it to drink. "Over and over. Every word I said. Every word I should have said instead. I can't sleep. I can't think about anything else. I just keep hearing his voice and seeing his face when he..." She stopped, swallowing against the tightness in her throat.

Jean remained quiet, her eyes steady on Grace's face. She didn't rush to fill the silence with comfort or questions. She simply waited, present and patient, giving Grace the space to find her own way into the telling.

"I'm not making any sense. Let me back up. Jim asked me where we were headed," Grace continued, her voice flat with exhaustion. "What this thing... this... relationship between him and me meant to me. What he meant to me. And I tried to answer honestly, Momma. I really did. I thought I was telling him how much he matters."

"What did you say?"

The question was gentle, free of accusation, but Grace flinched anyway.

"I told him I feel peaceful with him. That he's steady. That I don't need drama anymore, that I don't need my heart to race." She heard the words coming out of her mouth, and they sounded even worse now than they had three days ago. "I told him he's everything Lee wasn't."

Jean's expression flickered, just slightly, but she said nothing.

"And then he told me what I didn't say." Grace lifted her eyes to meet her mother's gaze.

"Grace... honey. Take a deep breath and start over. You're talking in fragments, and I'm unable to fill in the spaces. Start over from the beginning and tell me what happened."

Grace sat back and shook her head as if she were trying to clear her mind. She took a deep breath and proceeded to tell her mother everything from the beginning.

"He's right." Grace's voice dropped to something barely above a whisper as she finished relaying what had happened on Sunday. "I went over it a hundred times, Momma. A hundred times. And he's right. I described him as a medicine. Like a band-aid for everything Lee broke in me. I talked about what he provides and what he represents. I never said what I actually feel. I never said that I want him."

Jean reached across the table and took Grace's hand in both of her own. Her fingers were warm and work-roughened, familiar in a way that made Grace's eyes sting with fresh tears.

"Oh, honey."

A long pause settled between them. Grace watched her mother's face, watched her think, and watched her choose her words with care.

"I can see why that hurt him," Jean said finally.

Grace nodded, miserable. "I know. I understand now. I just didn't hear it when I was saying it. I thought I was being honest. I thought I was telling him how much he matters to me."

"You were being honest, Grace." Jean's voice was gentle but clear. "That's the hard part. Everything you said was true. But truth isn't always the whole truth. And sometimes what we leave out says more than what we put in."

Jean was quiet for another moment, her thumb stroking across the back of Grace's hand in a rhythm that was soothing and ancient, the same motion she had used when Grace was small and frightened of thunderstorms.

"Can I ask you something?"

Grace nodded.

"When you were with Lee..." Jean paused, as if weighing whether to continue. "Did you ever tell him how you felt? Really felt?"

The question opened something Grace had kept locked away for longer than she wanted to admit. Not just since the divorce. Since before. Since the marriage itself, maybe. Since she first started to realize that the man she had married was not the man she thought she knew.

"In the beginning, I tried." Her voice went flat, distant, the tone of someone recounting something painful. "Before we got married, he made me feel like I was the center of his world. He pursued me as if I were something precious. Something worth cherishing."

"But after the wedding, everything changed. Almost immediately. He was never home. Always a meeting, always a client dinner, always somewhere else. I told myself it was just the demands of running a firm. I told myself it would settle down."

Jean waited, her face carefully neutral, though Grace could see the tension gathering in her mother's shoulders.

"When I tried to talk to him about it." Grace's jaw tightened at the memory. "About feeling lonely, about wanting more time together. He made me feel foolish. Dramatic. Needy." The words tasted bitter on her tongue, carrying the residue of a hundred small dismissals that had accumulated into something crushing. "He had this way of looking at me like I was being unreasonable for wanting my own husband to come home at night. Like my feelings were an inconvenience he didn't have time for."

"Grace..."

"So I stopped." Grace met her mother's eyes, and the rawness there made Jean draw a sharp breath. "I learned to keep everything inside because there was no point in saying it out loud. He didn't care what I felt. He never asked. He never wanted to know."

Jean's eyes glistened, but she didn't interrupt.

"I was a prop, Momma." The words came out harsh, bitter, carrying two years of accumulated understanding. "A pretty wife to bring to firm events. Someone to make him look good. Make him look stable and successful. He didn't love me. He never did. I was just useful." Grace heard her own voice catch and forced herself to continue. "And when I found out about the affairs, that he'd been cheating the entire time, that everyone at the firm knew except me, I realized I'd spent two years married to a man who saw me as nothing more than an accessory. A decoration. Something to display when it served his purposes and ignore when it didn't."

The silence that followed was heavy with everything Grace had never told anyone. Not her sisters. Not her brothers. Not even Faith, who understood divorce in her own way, knew the complete truth of what Grace had lived through during her two years of marriage.

"That man," Jean said quietly, and there was steel beneath the softness, a maternal fury that Grace had rarely heard in her mother's voice, "didn't deserve a single day of your life."

"I know that now." Grace's voice wavered, threatening to break. "But Momma, the damage is done. I learned to keep my heart hidden because the one person who should have treasured it treated it like it was nothing. Like I was nothing. And now..." She took a shaky breath. "Now I finally have someone who actually wants to see it. Who's asking me to show him what I feel. Tell him how I feel... and I don't know how anymore. I gave Jim the protected version because that's all I know how to give. Lee took everything else."

Jean was quiet for a long moment, absorbing everything Grace had laid bare. When she finally spoke, her voice was measured but fierce with love.

"Lee didn't just hurt you, Grace. He taught you that your heart wasn't safe to share. That your feelings were a burden. That loving someone would only get you dismissed or ignored." She paused, letting the words settle. "That's a hard lesson to unlearn. And it makes sense that when Jim asked you to be vulnerable, you gave him the version of yourself that Lee trained you to be. The version you forced yourself to be when you were married to Lee."

Grace felt the truth of it move through her, recognition and grief tangled together.

"But Jim isn't Lee." Jean's voice firmed with conviction. "Jim is asking to see your heart because he wants to treasure it, not dismiss it. And I know that's terrifying after what you've been through. But Grace, if you want Jim to know you love him, you're going to have to risk being vulnerable in a way that Lee made it feel dangerous. You're going to have to show him the parts you've been protecting. Not because it's safe, but because he's worth the risk."

Jean was quiet for another moment, studying her face. "Grace. Do you love him?"

"Yes. I love him."

"Do you want him?" Jean pressed, her eyes steady on Grace. "Not just what he gives you. Him?"

"Yes." Her voice broke on the word, shattered open by its truth. "I want him. I want his laugh and his steadiness and the way he looks at me like I'm the only person in his world. I want Sunday dinners and ordinary days and his hand reaching for mine when we say grace before a meal. I want to know what his face looks like first thing in the morning. I want to be the one he calls when something good happens or something bad happens or nothing happens at all." The tears were flowing freely now, and she didn't try to stop them. "I want him. Not just what he provides. Him. All of him. For the rest of my life."

Jean squeezed her daughter's hand, her own eyes bright with moisture.

"Then why didn't you tell him that?"

"Because I didn't know how." The admission tore out of Grace like something that had been trapped too long. "Because I've forgotten how to talk about love without talking about pain first. Because Lee taught me that wanting someone that much was dangerous. That showing that much of yourself just gave someone the power to dismiss you. And I've been so busy protecting myself that I forgot how to just love someone out loud."

She drew a shaky breath, her chest aching from everything she was finally saying.

"Lee taught me to hide. Jim makes me want to be seen. But I've been hiding so long I don't remember how to step into the light."

Jean was quiet for a long moment. When she spoke, her voice was gentle but honest, offering no false comfort, no easy answers.

"I wish I could tell you there's a simple way to fix this. But there isn't."

Grace looked up, something desperate flickering in her eyes.

"Words matter, Grace. And the words you didn't say, Jim heard those loud and clear. He heard echoes of someone else. Someone who chose him because he was safe and then left because safe wasn't enough." Jean paused, letting the weight of that settle. "You can't unsay what you said. You can't unhurt him. What's done is done."

"So what do I do?"

Jean shook her head slowly. "I don't have a perfect answer for you, honey. I wish I did. But I think you need some time. Just you and God. To work through why you speak about love the way you do. To find the words that are true. Not just the safe ones, but the real ones. The ones that scare you. You need to set your fear aside and speak the truth. Take it to God, child."

"And then, if you're certain, really certain, that Jim is what you want, not just what you need, you're going to have to find a way to tell him that. Really tell him. In words he can't misunderstand. In words that leave no room for doubt."

"What if he won't listen?" Grace's voice was small, frightened in a way she rarely let herself be. "What if I already broke it beyond repair?"

"That's possible. I won't pretend it isn't. Some hurts go deep, and Jim's already been through this once with Amanda. He might not be willing to risk it again."

Grace's face crumpled, and Jean reached across to cup her daughter's cheek, her palm warm and steady against Grace's skin.

"Jim is not the kind of man who walks away from something real without a fight. He stepped back because he needed to protect himself. That's not the same as giving up. That's not the same as closing the door forever." She held Grace's gaze with the fierce certainty of a mother who believed in her daughter even when her daughter couldn't believe in herself. "If you come to him with your whole heart, not the protected version but the real one, the vulnerable one, the one that Lee taught you to hide, I have to believe he'll hear you. I have to believe love is stronger than fear."

Something in Jean's expression shifted then, softer, remembering.

"Your father makes me feel safe too, Grace. He's steady and reliable, and I always know where I stand with him. After all these years together, I could tell you exactly what kind of man your daddy is."

Grace looked up, listening.

"But that's not why I married him."

Jean's eyes were soft with memory, with decades of love that had weathered every storm and come out stronger on the other side.

"I married your father because I couldn't imagine my life without him in it. Because when he walked into a room, something in me settled into place. Not because he was safe, but because he was home to me. I knew it in my bones the same way I knew my own name. I wanted him. Not just what he could give me, but him. His laugh and his stubbornness, and the way he hums when he doesn't think anyone's listening. The way he looks at me like I'm still the girl he fell in love with, even when I've got dirt under my fingernails and I haven't brushed my hair. He still chooses me."

She smiled, and it transformed her whole face, made her look younger somehow, and made visible the woman who had fallen in love with Bruce McKenna all those years ago.

"There's a difference between being grateful for someone and being in love with them. Between needing what they provide and wanting who they are. Jim needs to know which one you mean. He needs to hear you say it. Not in terms of what you escaped, but in terms of what you feel. What you want. What you choose. You need to tell him... and even showing him probably wouldn't hurt."

Grace sat with this for a moment. The kitchen was quiet around them, filled with the ordinary sounds she had grown up with: the tick of the clock on the wall, the distant hum of a tractor in the flower fields, and the creak of the old house settling into itself. The rhythms of the McKenna home that had anchored her whole life.

"I don't know how to fix this," Grace said finally, her voice steadier now but still heavy with uncertainty. "I know what I feel. I know what I should have said. But I don't know how to make him hear it. I don't know if he'll even let me try."

Jean stood and wrapped her arms around her daughter. Grace leaned into her mother's embrace, breathing in the familiar scent of her.

"Then that's what you need to figure out," Jean said, her voice soft against Grace's hair. "Take some time. Pray about it. Let God show you the path." She pulled back and met Grace's eyes with fierce maternal love. "But Grace, don't wait too long. And when you go to Jim, don't protect yourself. Give him everything. The real words. The vulnerable ones. The ones that scare you to say out loud. The ones Lee taught you to hide. They're in there... inside you... you just need to let them out."

She cupped Grace's face in her hands, her palms warm and steady.

"Show him your heart. All of it. And trust that he's the kind of man who will hold it gently."

Grace nodded slowly.

She left her parents' house with more clarity than she had arrived with. She loved Jim. She wanted Jim. She understood why she had failed to say it and what had taught her to hide. But the path forward remained unclear, shrouded in uncertainty and fear and the terrible possibility that she had already lost him.

The gravel crunched under her tires as she pulled out of the driveway, and the mountains rose around her as she drove back toward town, their peaks sharp against the May sky. The depth of what she needed to do settled over her, not lighter but clearer. She knew what she felt. She knew what she wanted.

Now she had to find the courage to say it in a way he could hear.

The road curved ahead of her, winding through the valley toward Serenity Crossing, toward the inn, toward a future that felt less certain than it had a week ago. Grace gripped the steering wheel and let out a long breath.

Three days of silence.

Three days of distance.

Three days of Jim believing that he wasn't wanted, only needed.

She had to fix this.

She had to find the words.

But first, she had to figure out how to stop being afraid of them.

Chapter 33

Jim sat on his front porch with a glass of sweet tea sweating on the arm of his chair, the condensation pooling against the weathered wood. The afternoon light fell warm across his property, painting the neat yard in shades of green and gold. The treeline stood sentinel beyond the fence posts; the mountains rising blue and hazy in the distance where the Smokies met the sky. It was the kind of May afternoon that usually filled him with quiet contentment, the kind of day when he would sit here with Boone and count his blessings and feel the rightness of the life he had built. Today he barely saw any of it.

Boone lay at his feet with his chin resting on his paws; those soulful brown eyes lifted every few minutes to study Jim's face with an intensity that bordered on uncomfortable. The dog seemed to understand that something had shifted in the landscape of their world. His tail gave a half-hearted thump against the porch boards now and then.

Jim had taken the day off work. He'd called Tuck that morning and said he needed a personal day, and Tuck hadn't asked questions. "Got it covered, boss," he'd said in that easy way of his, leaving room for

Jim to explain if he wanted and not pushing when he didn't. That was Tuck. Always had been. The kind of friend who knew when to talk and when not to ask questions.

A few weeks ago, Jim had taken an entire week off to help Grace with her quarters at the inn. That had felt different. Purposeful. There had been joy in stripping wallpaper and pulling up carpet and watching her face light up as the space transformed into something that felt like hers. He had wanted to be there. Had counted the hours until he could see her again each morning, had lingered each evening until the last possible moment before heading home. Taking that time off had been easy because it was for her.

This day off felt nothing like that. This was avoidance, pure and simple. This was sitting on his porch because he couldn't face the store and couldn't face the customers who would want to make small talk and expect him to smile. He would rather not face the possibility of Grace walking through that door and having to pretend he hadn't spent five days hoping she would. He didn't want to face the other possibility: that she wouldn't walk through that door at all.

Five days of silence.

Five days of replaying the conversation in his mind until every word was worn smooth from handling.

Five days of knowing he had done the right thing by naming what was missing and still feeling like something inside him was breaking apart.

The sound of a truck coming up the driveway pulled Jim from his thoughts. He recognized the sound of the vehicle before it rounded the final curve and came to a stop near the porch, the familiar blue Ford that his father had been driving for longer than Jim could remember. The engine cut off, and Bill climbed out with the deliberate movements of a man who had learned to take his time and wasn't in a hurry for anything. Boone's tail thumped harder against the porch boards, and he rose to greet Bill with a nudge of his head against the older man's weathered hand.

Bill scratched behind Boone's ears, his eyes on Jim. Watching. Reading. Seeing more than Jim would have liked.

"Stopped by the store," Bill said as he climbed the porch steps, his boots heavy on the wood. He lowered himself into the chair beside Jim with a soft grunt of effort. "Tuck said you took the day off."

Jim didn't respond. He kept his gaze fixed on the tree line, on the way the leaves shifted in the breeze that came down from the mountains.

"That's not like you, son. You okay?"

Jim could've brushed the question off. He could have said he was fine or that he needed a break. His father would accept that answer if Jim offered it, would let the subject drop, and sit with him in silence until one of them found something else to talk about. Bill Hartwell had never been the kind of man to push where he wasn't wanted.

But he had also never been fooled by deflection.

"Grace and I had a conversation on Sunday," Jim said finally. The words felt strange in his mouth, too small to contain everything they represented. "About where we're headed. What we are to each other."

Bill waited. He'd always been good at waiting.

"I asked her to be honest with me. And she was." Jim's jaw tightened as he remembered the earnestness in Grace's green eyes. "She told me I make her feel peaceful. Settled. That she doesn't need drama or intensity anymore. That I'm steady and consistent." He paused, the next words catching somewhere in his chest. "Everything Lee wasn't."

Bill remained silent, his attention focused entirely on his son.

"She told me what I provide, Dad. What I give her. What she doesn't need anymore." Jim's voice roughened despite his efforts to keep it even. "But she never said she wants me. She never said she loved me. She described me like... a safe harbor after a storm. Something useful. Something that serves a purpose in her healing."

The breeze stirred the leaves again, carrying with it the scent of cut grass and warm earth and the faint sweetness of the honeysuckle that grew wild along the fence line. Somewhere in the distance, a mockingbird ran through its repertoire of songs.

"So I told her," Jim turned to look at his father, needing to see his reaction. "I told her I can't do that again. It can't be someone's soft place to land because they're tired of being hurt. I need to be wanted for who I am, not for who I'm not."

Bill nodded slowly, his expression thoughtful. "You were right to say that."

Jim blinked, surprised by the directness of the response. He had expected... he wasn't sure what. Sympathy, maybe. Gentle suggestions that he might have overreacted.

"I mean it," Bill continued. "That took courage. A lot of men wouldn't have had the words for it. They would've felt wrong and not known why, would've swallowed it down and let it fester until it poisoned everything. You spoke your truth."

The knot in Jim's chest began to ease, not disappearing entirely but shifting into something more manageable. Having it acknowledged. Having his father say that he hadn't been unreasonable or demanding or unfair. That mattered.

"But I walked away, Dad."

"You created space." Bill's eyes were steady on Jim's face. "That's self-respect."

They sat in silence for a moment. Boone had settled back down at Jim's feet, his breathing slow and even, though his ears twitched at every sound as if he too was waiting for something.

"What are you afraid of, son?"

The question cut deep. Jim stared out at the tree line, at the way the shadows were beginning to lengthen as the sun tracked westward across the sky. His father had always had a way of finding the heart of things, of asking the questions that no one else thought to ask or dared to voice.

"That I was right," Jim said finally. "That I heard her correctly. That she really does see me as... useful. Comfortable. The opposite of a mistake." His voice dropped lower, quieter. "That Amanda was right about me all along."

"Amanda told you that you weren't enough," Bill said, his voice low and measured. "And you heard echoes of that in what Grace said."

"Yeah. I did."

"Makes sense. Anyone would hear echoes after what Amanda did to you." Bill paused, his weathered hands folding together in his lap. "But Jim..."

Jim turned to look at his father, waiting.

"Do you believe Grace is the same kind of person as Amanda?"

Jim frowned, turning it over in his mind like a stone in his palm. "What do you mean?"

"Amanda knew exactly what she was doing when she married you." Bill's gaze was steady, unflinching. "She chose you because you could give her the life she thought she wanted. And when she decided she wanted something different, she told you the truth. That you weren't enough. That she needed more than what you could give her." He shook his head slowly. "She meant every word of it, Jim. Amanda's problem wasn't that she couldn't express her feelings. It was that she expressed them perfectly. She didn't want you. She wanted what you provided. And when she didn't want that anymore, she left."

Jim felt the old wound pulse beneath his ribs, familiar and sharp. Four years had dulled the edges but hadn't erased the scar.

"Grace..." Bill paused, selecting his words with the care of a man who understood their importance. "Grace was betrayed. Her husband cheated on her, and that kind of wound goes deep. It changes a person." He shook his head slowly. "I don't know everything that happened in that marriage of hers, but I know what betrayal does. It makes you guard yourself. Makes you afraid to trust. Makes you hold back the most vulnerable parts of yourself because the last time you offered them, someone crushed them."

Jim thought about Grace in those first weeks after she'd returned to Serenity Crossing. The wariness in her eyes. The way she held herself at a distance, ever so slightly. The walls she'd built to protect herself from ever being hurt like that again.

"When someone's been hurt like that, they don't always know how to say what they feel. They describe what's safe to describe." He looked at his son with an expression that held both compassion and challenge. "That doesn't mean she doesn't feel more. It might mean she's afraid to say it."

"That doesn't excuse what she said," Bill added, his voice firm. "You deserve more than being someone's remedy. You deserve to be wanted. You were right to name that."

"Then what are you saying?"

Bill was quiet for a moment, his gaze drifting out toward the mountains that rose blue and eternal against the afternoon sky. When he spoke again, his voice carried the distinction of hard-won wisdom.

"There's a difference between someone who won't give you what you need and someone who doesn't know how yet. Amanda knew how to express desire and what she wanted from you." Bill turned to look at his son. "She didn't want you, Jim. She wanted what you provided. She used you. And when she didn't want that anymore, she was honest about it."

The old wound throbbed, but Jim held his father's gaze.

"Grace..." Bill's voice softened. "Grace may feel everything you're hoping she feels. She may love you in all the ways you need to be loved. But after what she went through, after being betrayed by someone she trusted, she might be afraid to say it. Might not trust herself to reach for it. Might not believe she gets to have it."

"How do I know which one she is?"

"You don't. Not yet." Bill's voice was gentle but firm. "But you won't find out by deciding for her. You told her what you need. You gave her your truth. You gave her space. Now she needs to respond. You either wait for her to come to you or you go to her. The choice is up to you, son."

Jim was quiet for a long moment, turning over his father's words. Boone shifted at his feet, pressing closer, the warm weight of him a comfort that required no words.

"I've been checking my phone," Jim admitted quietly. "Hoping she'd call. Even though I was the one who walked away."

Bill nodded, unsurprised. "That tells you something."

"What?"

"That you're not done hoping. And that's not weakness, son. That's your heart telling you she might be worth the risk."

Jim stared at his hands, at the calluses on his palms from years of honest work. These hands had helped to build his own home. Had stocked shelves and helped customers and held Boone when he was nothing but a scared, skinny pup who'd shown up at the store one day and never left. These hands had held Grace's face when he kissed her for the first time in fourteen years. Had traced the curve of her cheek and felt her lean into his touch.

"What if she can't say it? What if she never learns how?"

"Then you'll have your answer. And you'll have honored yourself by asking for what you deserve." Bill paused, letting the words land. "But don't close the door so tight she can't come back through it. Not yet. Give her time."

The afternoon was beginning its slow fade toward evening; the shadows growing longer across the yard; the light taking on that rich amber quality that came in the hour before sunset.

"Your momma would tell you to pray about it," Bill said, leaning back in his chair. "And I agree with that. Give it to God and trust His timing. Love is patient, son. Real love. The kind worth having. It makes room for people to grow. To heal."

He met Jim's eyes with the steady gaze of a man who had loved the same woman for forty years.

"Grace stumbled. She used the wrong words, or she couldn't find the right ones. That doesn't mean she doesn't love you. It might mean she's still learning how to trust again after someone broke that trust so badly."

Bill stayed a while longer. They didn't talk much after that, letting the evening settle around them in layers of deepening blue and purple. Father and son, sitting together on the porch the way they had done a thousand times before, watching the day give way to night while Boone dozed at Jim's feet.

Before he left, Bill put a hand on Jim's shoulder. The grip was firm, grounding, the touch of a man who had raised six children and held his wife's hand through the good times and the bad times.

"You're a good man, Jim. You deserve to be chosen for who you are, not for who you're not. Don't settle for less than that." He squeezed once, then released. "But give Grace her time, son. I suspect she needs it."

Jim watched his father's truck disappear down the driveway, the taillights winking through the trees before vanishing around the bend. The evening had settled in fully now, the first stars beginning to emerge in the darkening sky, and the ache in his chest hadn't disappeared.

His father's words echoed through him as he sat there in the gathering dark: There's a difference between someone who won't give you what you need and someone who doesn't know how yet.

Chapter 34

Grace sat on Jim's front porch with her back pressed against one of the rough cedar posts that held up the roof, her phone clutched in her hand like a lifeline. The afternoon sun fell across the empty space where his truck should have been parked, and it mocked her with its silence. She didn't know when he would come home. She only knew that she would be here when he did.

She had arrived an hour ago. Maybe longer. Time had become something slippery and unreliable over the past six days, the hours bleeding into one another in a blur of sleepless nights and cold coffee and the endless, relentless replaying of the conversation that had shattered something precious between them. She knew she looked terrible. She had caught her reflection in the rearview mirror before climbing out of her SUV and had barely recognized the woman staring back at her. Shadows carved deep beneath her eyes. Hair scraped back into a messy ponytail because she couldn't summon the energy to do anything more. Clothes pulled on without thought or care: a faded sweater over yesterday's shirt, jeans she had worn twice this week already.

None of that mattered now. What mattered was being here. What mattered was finding the words she had failed to find before.

The porch boards were warm beneath her, heated by hours of spring sunshine, and she shifted her weight slightly to ease the ache in her lower back. She had been sitting in this same spot for so long that her muscles had begun to protest, but she refused to move to one of the chairs arranged near the front door. The chairs felt too casual, too comfortable, like she belonged here. She didn't know yet if she still belonged anywhere in Jim Hartwell's life.

A cardinal landed on the porch railing a few feet away, its red feathers bright against the weathered wood, and regarded her with a tilted head and gleaming eyes. Grace watched it without really seeing it. Her mind was elsewhere, caught in the endless loop of last Sunday's conversation.

You didn't tell me you want me.

Those words had been echoing through her mind for six days. She heard them when she woke in the gray hours before dawn. She heard them when she stood in the inn's kitchen staring at renovation plans she couldn't focus on. She heard them in the silence that had replaced the easy conversations and shared laughter that had filled her days for weeks.

Grace pulled her knees up and wrapped her arms around them, making herself smaller on the wide porch. The cardinal flew away, startled by her movement, and she was alone again.

She thought about leaving. The impulse rose up three separate times, a panicked voice in the back of her mind insisting that this was foolish, that she should go home and call him instead, that showing up unannounced at his house was too much, too desperate, too vulnerable. The first time she ignored it. The second time, she argued with it. The third time, she had actually considered following through.

She thought about what her mother had said to her.

Don't protect yourself. Give him everything. The real words. The vulnerable ones. The ones that scare you to say out loud. The ones Lee taught you to hide. They're in there... inside you... you just need to let them out.

The sound reached her before she saw anything. The low rumble of an engine, distant at first, then growing closer. Grace's heart lurched against her ribs, and she pushed herself to her feet, her legs unsteady beneath her after so long sitting in one position. She wiped her palms on her jeans, a nervous gesture, and moved to stand near the top of the porch steps.

Jim's truck appeared around the bend in the long driveway, sunlight glinting off the windshield. He pulled into his usual spot and cut the engine.

For a long moment, Jim sat in the truck, watching her through the windshield. Grace stood on the porch, watching him back. The distance between them felt infinite, an ocean of unspoken words and wounded silences, and at the same time it felt impossibly small, like she could close it with three steps if only her feet would move.

She could see Boone scrambling in the passenger seat, his whole body wiggling with the desperate energy of a creature who had spotted someone he loved. Jim pushed the door open. Boone didn't wait for an invitation. He launched himself over Jim's lap and out of the truck, hitting the ground at a run, his long ears flapping and his tail a blur of motion as he made a beeline for the porch. Straight for Grace.

Grace dropped to her knees as Boone reached her, her hands finding the familiar softness of his fur, her fingers scratching behind his ears the way he liked. His whole body wiggled against her, his tail sweeping wide arcs through the air, and he licked her face once, twice, three times before settling at her feet with a contented sigh. He pressed his shoulder against her leg and looked up at her after she stood back up with those soulful brown eyes, and something in Grace's chest cracked open at the simple, uncomplicated welcome in his gaze.

She looked across the yard to where Jim had climbed out of his truck. He had closed the door behind him and now stood with his hands in his pockets, his posture guarded, his expression unreadable.

Grace walked to the porch railing and leaned against it, her eyes finding Jim's across the distance. Her hands shook as she unlocked her phone and navigated to her music, looking for the song. Their song. The one Jim used to play for her on his guitar when they were seventeen. The one he had sung to her in her living room while they stripped wallpaper and the world outside had ceased to exist. The one that said everything she had been too afraid to say.

She hit play and turned the volume all the way up.

The opening notes of ***"Wanted"*** drifted across the yard, familiar and achingly beautiful, and Grace saw Jim's whole body go still. She saw recognition flash across his face, saw his hands come out of his pockets, and saw the shift in his expression.

She walked down the porch steps, phone still in her hand. Boone stayed on the porch, watching her go, as if he understood that this was something she had to do alone.

Each step felt monumental. Each step brought her closer to the moment she had been building toward for six days, for eight weeks, for fourteen years.

Jim didn't move. He stood by his truck, hands at his sides now, watching her come toward him. His brown eyes were fixed on her face, and even from twenty feet away she could see the tension in his jaw, the way he was holding himself so carefully still, and the guarded hope that flickered beneath the surface of his expression.

She stopped in front of him. Close enough to see the shadows under his eyes that told her he hadn't been sleeping either. Close enough to see the muscle that jumped in his cheek when their eyes met. Close enough to touch if she dared.

The song continued to play from the phone in her hand, but Grace barely heard it anymore. Everything had narrowed to this moment. To the man in front of her. To the words she needed to say.

"I want you."

Three words. The exact words she had failed to say six days ago. The answer to the question he had asked her at her dining room table. The truth she should have spoken when she had the chance.

Jim's expression shifted. Something flickered in his eyes—surprise, hope, and pain all tangled together—and Grace watched him swallow hard.

She took a breath that shuddered through her whole body.

"I said all the wrong things. I told you what you give me. What I need. What you're not. I described you like a prescription. A remedy. Something I needed because I'm broken and you were the cure."

She shook her head, feeling tears gather at the corners of her eyes, hot and unwelcome and impossible to stop.

"But that's not what you are to me, Jim. That's not what you've ever been."

He stood there, silent and still, and the weight of his attention was almost more than she could bear. But she had come here to say these words, and she was going to say them even if her voice cracked and her tears fell and she made a complete fool of herself on his front lawn.

"My heart races every time I hear your truck pull into the inn's parking lot. It has since the first week I came back to Serenity Crossing." She pressed her free hand against her chest, against the wild hammering beneath her ribs. "I think about you when I wake up in the morning. You're the last thing on my mind before I fall asleep at night. I dream about you, Jim. I dream about your laugh and the way you look at me like I'm something precious."

A tear slipped down her cheek. She didn't wipe it away.

"When you walked out of my dining room on Sunday, I couldn't breathe. I sat at that table for hours thinking about what I had said and how I had managed to hurt you when all I wanted was to make you understand how much you mean to me. I'm not choosing you because you're safe. I'm not choosing you because you're steady or reliable or the opposite of Lee."

She stepped closer to him, close enough that she could see the shine in his eyes that might have been tears.

"I'm choosing you because you're Jim. Because when you laugh, something in my chest gets lighter. Because the sound of your voice makes ordinary days feel like gifts. Because watching you with your family makes me imagine futures I was afraid to hope for again." She reached up and touched his face, her fingers trembling against the rough stubble along his jaw. "Because when you look at me, my world stops, and I know I've found my home."

Jim reached out and took her phone from her hand. His fingers brushed against hers, warm and steady, and she watched as he looked at the screen and pressed pause. The music stopped.

Silence fell over the yard. Just the birds calling to each other in the trees. Just the creek murmuring somewhere in the woods behind the house. Just Grace standing in front of the man she loved with her heart cracked open and everything she felt laid bare between them.

"Keep going," he said quietly.

Grace took another breath.

"I love you."

The words hung in the air between them, three syllables that changed everything.

"I love you, Jim." She let her hand slide down from his jaw to rest against his chest, against the strong and steady beat of his heart beneath her palm. "I love the man who talks to his dog in full sentences and waits for answers. I love the man who remembers every customer's name and knows exactly what they need before they ask. I love the man who designed his house and helped build it... with extra bedrooms for the family he was hoping for."

Jim's hand came up to cover hers where it rested against his chest. His fingers curled around hers, holding on.

"I love the man who let me go fourteen years ago because he thought that's what I needed, even though it broke his heart." Grace's voice cracked, but she pushed through because he deserved to hear all of it, every word she had been hoarding behind her fear. "I love you, and I was so afraid to say it. So afraid to want something this much."

The tears were falling freely now, tracking down her cheeks and dripping off her chin, but she didn't care. She didn't care about anything except the man standing in front of her and the words she still needed to say.

"You deserve to be wanted, and you deserve to be chosen." She stepped even closer, until there was barely any space left between them, until she could feel the warmth radiating from his body. "I choose you, Jim Hartwell. I'm choosing you because I cannot imagine my life without you in it. Because when I think about the future, you're in every version of it. Because I want to be the one who makes you laugh. I want to be the one you come home to. I want to spend the rest of my life making sure you never doubt, not for one single second, how much you are wanted."

Jim had been silent through all of it. Listening. Really listening, the way he always did, with his whole attention and his whole heart. His eyes never left her face, and she could see the emotion swimming in them: the tears he was fighting to hold back, the years of doubt and pain and loneliness that her words were slowly washing away.

His hands came up to cup her face, his palms warm against her cheeks, his thumbs brushing away the tears that wouldn't stop falling. He held her as if she were something fragile and precious, like he was afraid she might disappear if he let go.

"Say it again," he said, his voice barely above a whisper.

"I want you."

"Again."

"I want you, Jim. I love you."

His expression broke open, a dam giving way, and when he spoke again, his voice was thick with everything he had been holding back.

"I love you, Grace. I've loved you since we were teenagers pretending we knew what love meant. I never stopped. Not when you left for college. Not when I married someone else trying to forget you. Not when you came back to town with walls so high I wasn't sure I'd ever find a way through." His thumbs traced gentle paths across her cheekbones, and she leaned into his touch like a flower turning toward the sun.

He kissed her.

Not gentle, not tentative. This was a kiss that said finally and yes and don't ever leave again. His hands slid from her face into her hair, pulling her closer, and Grace wrapped her arms around his neck and held on like he was the only solid thing in a world that had been spinning out of control. She could taste salt on his lips, couldn't tell if the tears were hers or his, and didn't care because nothing mattered except this moment, this man, this love she had almost been too afraid to claim.

When they broke apart, Jim rested his forehead against hers, his hands still tangled in her hair and his eyes closed.

"You came to my house," he said, and there was wonder in his voice, amazement that she was here, that she had done this, that she had chosen him.

"I came to your house."

"You played our song."

"I played our song."

"You told me you want me."

Grace pulled back just enough to look into his eyes, to see the love shining there, unguarded and overwhelming. "I want you, Jim Hartwell. Today. Tomorrow. For as long as you'll have me."

Boone had made his way down from the porch at some point, and now he circled them with his tail wagging, pressing against their legs like he was trying to join the embrace. Jim laughed, the sound startled out of him, and the joy in it made Grace's heart squeeze with something too big to name.

He took her hand and led her toward the porch, toward the house, toward whatever came next. But before they reached the steps, he stopped.

"Wait here," he said, and disappeared through the front door.

Grace stood on the bottom step, Boone pressing warm against her leg, and wondered what he was doing.

Jim came back through the door, carrying his guitar.

Grace's breath caught in her throat as he settled into one of the porch chairs and gestured for her to take the one beside him. She climbed the steps on legs that still felt unsteady and sank into the chair, turning to face him. Boone flopped down at their feet with a contented sigh.

Jim positioned the guitar in his lap, his fingers finding the familiar positions on the strings. He looked at her with an expression that held everything: the seventeen-year-old boy who had loved her before either of them knew what love cost, the man who had rebuilt himself after his world fell apart, and the hopeful heart that had never stopped believing she might come back to him.

He began to strum, and the opening notes of "Wanted" floated out into the evening air, softer now, more intimate than the recording that had played from her phone. And then Jim began to sing, his voice low and rich and meant only for her, and Grace let the music wash over her like a benediction.

She had come here afraid she might lose him. She would leave knowing she had found something worth holding onto for the rest of her life.

When the last note faded into silence, Jim set the guitar aside and reached for her hand. His fingers interlaced with hers, strong and certain, and he lifted her hand to his lips and pressed a kiss against her knuckles.

"Stay for dinner," he said. "Stay and let me cook for you. Stay and watch the sunset from the back porch with me."

Grace smiled and felt something settle into place inside her chest.

"There's nowhere else I'd rather be."

"Good," he said, rising from his chair and pulling her up with him, keeping her hand clasped firmly in his. "Because I have a lot of time to make up for, Grace Bennett. Fourteen years of time. And I intend to start right now."

He led her through the front door and into the house, Boone trotting happily behind them, and Grace crossed the threshold into a future she had finally found the courage to choose.

Leave A Review

If you enjoyed this book, please consider leaving an honest review on Amazon

Visit Our Website:

www.tarabaisden.com

Visit Our Amazon Author Page HERE

Find Us On Social Media:

Facebook

Facebook Author Page

Instagram

Scan the QR code above to sign up for our newsletter!

Also by Tara Baisden

<u>Serenity Crossing: The Hartwell's Series</u>

#1 Hometown Sweethearts

#2 Hearts Restored – coming March 6, 2026

#3 The Art of Starting Over – coming April 3, 2026

#4 Love in God's Timing – coming May 1, 2026

#5 Wildflower Heart – coming June 5, 2026

#6 Brave Enough to Love – coming July 3, 2026

<u>Laurel Ridge Series</u>

#1. Season of Hope

#2. Finding Grace

#3. His Perfect Plan

#4. Love Redeemed

#5 Snowbound Blessings

#6 Sheltered Hearts

#7 Restoring Faith

#8 Love Rekindled

#9 Where She Belongs

#10 Shelter in His Arms

#11 Where Love Stands

#12 The Pieces We Mend

#13 Where Love Grows

#14 Where Hearts Heal

#15 Harvest of the Heart

#16 Heart of the Season

#17 Season of Forgiveness

#18 Threads of Grace

<u>Riverbend Valley Series</u>

#1 A Cowboy's Second Chance

#2 Wanderlust & Wild Horses

#3 Heartstrings on the Horizon

#4 Runaway in Riverbend Valley

#5 Mended Hearts

#6 Healing Hearts

#7 Home to Lost Creek

<u>Mistletoe Falls Series</u>

#1 Whisk Me Under the Mistletoe

#2 Once Upon a Christmas

#3 The Mistletoe Express

#4 Candy Canes & Sweet Dreams

#5 Wrapped Up in Christmas

#6 Jingle All the Way Home

About The Author

Tara Baisden is a Contemporary Christian Inspirational Romance author who proudly calls the beautiful state of West Virginia her home. Nestled on a sprawling mountainous property, she is surrounded by the peace and serenity of nature. Her days are happily spent in the quiet of country life, writing heartwarming stories of love, faith, and second chances. Tara also enjoys quilting, working in her garden, tending to her beloved pets, and soaking in the beauty of her surroundings.

With deep roots in West Virginia, family is everything to Tara. One of her favorite pastimes is gathering on the front porch with loved ones, sharing stories, laughter, and enjoying the simple, meaningful moments that life offers. When she's not crafting her novels, Tara can often be found exploring the rich history of her home state, visiting local historical sites, and, of course, stopping by every bookstore she passes! Her passion for reading and discovery always fuels her next adventure.

Tara is the author of the Laurel Ridges series of novels, as well as the Riverbend Valley series of novels, of which have been beloved by fans of inspirational romance. Her novels reflect her love for faith, family, and the timeless beauty of the world we live in.

Known for her sweet and clean romances, she creates characters that feel like family and settings that make readers want to visit again and again.

You can find out more about Tara and her latest releases at www.tarabaisden.com or follow her on social media for updates and behind-the-scenes glimpses of her writing process. Stay connected—you won't want to miss the heartfelt stories of love and family she has in store!

About Serenity Crossing

Nestled in a valley of the Great Smoky Mountains, Serenity Crossing, Tennessee, is the kind of small town that makes everyday life feel a little softer around the edges. Around 8,200 neighbors call it home—enough to keep things lively, but small enough that a wave from a porch swing still counts as a proper greeting. Downtown curves around a historic square with a beloved gazebo at its heart, framed by timeworn brick storefronts and wide sidewalks where it's easy to linger. The coffee is always brewing at The Daily Grind. Minnie's Diner always seems to have a seat, and shop owners tend to learn a newcomer's name by the second visit.

Life here is stitched together by simple pleasures and steady rhythms: morning mist settling in the valley and lifting by mid-morning, church bells chiming at eight, and quiet kindness that shows up in casseroles, carpools, and prayers offered without fanfare. News travels fast—often faster than anyone means it to—but so does help when it's needed. Serenity Crossing has a way of rallying that feels less like a decision and more like instinct.

Nature isn't "nearby" in Serenity Crossing—it's part of the daily scenery. Hawthorne Lake sparkles just beyond town with walking paths, fishing piers, and secluded coves made for unhurried conversations. The Rolling and Flint Rivers curl along the valley's edges beneath old stone bridges, while the ridgeline offers overlooks locals swear are best at sunrise. And tucked away on a moderate two-mile hike, Serenity Falls has earned a reputation as the town's favorite spot for big questions and brave promises.

Serenity Crossing knows how to celebrate, too. Thursday evenings typically bring music to the gazebo, and Saturday mornings (April through October) fill the square with a farmers market and familiar faces. Come the last weekend of September, the Harvest Festival turns the town into pure cozy delight—pie contests, craft booths, live music, and an apple butter competition taken very seriously, right down to the crowning of the Apple Queen. Winter brings its own magic with the Christmas Stroll, hot cider and cookies, carolers in the square, a tree lighting, and Santa arriving by antique fire truck.

In Serenity Crossing, faith runs deep, community runs strong, and love has room to grow—slowly, sincerely, and surrounded by the kind of belonging that makes visitors want to stay awhile.

www.ingramcontent.com/pod-product-compliance
Lightning Source LLC
Chambersburg PA
CBHW011848300726
48970CB00009B/2699